PRAISE FOR *Up from the Blue*
BY SUSAN HENDERSON

"Susan Henderson's *Up from the Blue* deftly portrays a family with contradictions we can all relate to—it's beautiful and maddening, hopeful and condemning, simple, yet like a knot that takes a lifetime to untangle. This is a book that you will love completely, even as it hurts you. It is a heartbreaking, rewarding story that still haunts me."

—Jamie Ford, author of *Hotel on the Corner of Bitter and Sweet*

"A haunting tale of the terrible ways in which we fail each other; of the whys, the what-ifs, and the what nows. This is not a book you'll soon forget."

—Sara Gruen, author of *Water for Elephants*

"A rare literary page-turner full of shocking discoveries and twists. Susan Henderson has created a remarkable narrator—as memorable for her feistiness as for her tenderness. *Up From the Blue* is going to be one of this year's major debuts."

— Josh Kilmer-Purcell, author of *The Bucolic Plague*
and *I Am Not Myself These Days*

"*Up From the Blue* is a heart-wrenching, tender story with a mystery that kept my pulse racing. What a joy to discover Tillie Harris, the most memorable, charming, and plucky narrator in fiction since Scout Finch."

—Jessica Anya Blau, author of *The Summer of Naked Swim Parties*

"In *Up from the Blue*, Susan Henderson delivers a compelling, deeply felt tale about the complexities of family life. You'll fall in love with young Tillie Harris, whose attempts to navigate her parents' unruly world are portrayed with genuine warmth and tenderness."

—Michelle Richmond, author of *The Year of Fog*

"Through her gorgeous, perceptive debut, Susan Henderson reveals the truth—a family's effort to hide its secrets and shame will break a child's heart. *Up from the Blue* is an unflinching, emotionally honest novel, one of the most insightful stories I've ever read."

—Ronlyn Domingue, author of *The Mercy of Thin Air*

ABOUT THE AUTHOR

SUSAN HENDERSON is a two-time Pushcart Prize nominee and the founder of the literary blog LitPark: Where Writers Come to Play (www.litpark.com). She is the recipient of an Academy of American Poets award and a grant from the Ludwig Vogelstein Foundation. Her work has appeared in *Zoetrope*, the *Pittsburgh Quarterly*, *North Atlantic Review*, *Opium*, *Other Voices*, *Amazon Shorts*, *The Future Dictionary of America* (McSweeney's, 2004), *The Best American Nonrequired Reading* (Houghton Mifflin, 2007), and *Not Quite What I Was Planning* (Harper Paperbacks, 2008). Henderson lives in New York and *Up from the Blue* is her first novel.

Up

FROM THE

Blue

Up
FROM THE
Blue

A NOVEL

Susan Henderson

HARPER

NEW YORK · LONDON · TORONTO · SYDNEY

HarperCollins books may be purchased for educational, business, or sales
promotional use. For information, please write: Special Markets Department, HarperCollins Publishers, 10 East 53rd Street, New York, NY 10022.

Designed by Cassandra J. Pappas

Library of Congress Cataloging-in-Publication data is available upon
request.

ISBN 978-0-06-198403-7

10 11 12 13 14   OV/RRD   10 9 8 7 6 5 4 3 2 1

To David, who knows everything about me,

and he's still here

Up

FROM THE

Blue

MAY 29, 1991, 8:47 AM

I T STARTS LIKE A *tingling at the top of my abdomen. And then, as if I'm wearing control top pantyhose——which I'm not, I've never been that girlie——it begins to shrink in around me, tighter and tighter, until my belly feels rock hard. Nervous, I pace our new apartment, hoping to simply walk it off. It's not a contraction. I won't allow it——not now. The baby isn't due for six more weeks.*

When my belly relaxes again, the tingle fading, I dig through the moving boxes trying to find my address book and a telephone to plug in. I'm not even sure if we hooked up the service or not. I try to breathe slowly. The boxes are packed randomly, my husband's idea to keep it simple and take the stress out of moving. "It's all going to the same place," he had said. He knows I have issues with too many orders and too many rules. Unfortunately, I also have issues with chaos.

I peel the tape off one box and find oven mitts, books, and shoes. Another has cups, a tape dispenser, and a notebook of unfinished poems that were better in my head than they are on paper. My hair, far past my waist, drips into the next carton filled with a lampshade and stuffed animals from the baby shower. No phone. No address book. My breath comes faster as I scan the stacks of boxes lining this room I've only known for two days, and when I consider the time and the amount of lifting it would require to go through them all, I realize I could be in trouble.

I can't reach Simon because he's still midflight to Paris, where he's helping to choose art pieces and oversee their shipment for the modern art museum that just hired him. He didn't want to travel this late in the pregnancy, but he's lucky to have this job. Majoring in art history is a lot like acquiring an expensive degree in unemployment, and now more than ever he wants to bring stability to our family.

I slam the cardboard flap closed on another box. And now I'm scared. I shouldn't have been going up and down the stairs so much. If something hurts this baby, it's all my fault.

Next door is a row house that looks like ours, Queen Anne style, brick—though ours is red with a round bay window and the other is white with a square bay window. I see glimpses of my neighbor moving from room to room, tidying up, sipping her coffee or tea. She looks about my age, and is the perfect image of how I planned to spend my day— slowly unpacking and cleaning, and later scoping out local restaurants to find a way to reclaim this town I thought I'd never live in again.

There's another tightening in my belly. Out of options, I open the door to the bustle of traffic and fast-walking men and women with brief-cases. I hold the rail and walk quickly down our steps and up the neighbor's, knocking normally at first and then more frantically.

As I listen to her footsteps approaching, I'm stunned by my reflection in the glass on either side of her door. I was wrong to think I resembled this woman I'd seen through the window in any way.

"Can I help you?" she asks. She looks as if she dressed from an L.L.Bean catalog, professionally relaxed, makeup and hair done, but lightly. We may both be in our midtwenties, but with my wet, stringy hair, gray maternity jumper, and untied, red high-tops, once again, I look like the kid without a mother.

"I just moved in next door, and . . . I think I need a doctor. Can I use your phone?"

"Of course. Of course."

We move quickly through her immaculate house, past knickknacks and tapestries from Africa, Russia, China. This neighborhood is filled with young diplomats. The only reason we could afford something here is because we got a fixer-upper we have no immediate plans to fix up. I follow the woman into the kitchen, where she points to the telephone hanging on the wall.

"I'll be in the next room if you need me," she says. I wonder if she's told me her name. I simply nod, take the receiver in my hand, and freeze. I don't have anyone to call. I don't know the name of the local hospital. I haven't memorized my former doctor's number and haven't yet found a new one. I was going to get to all of that.

I'm aware that the woman who owns this house is listening for me to do something, and because I'm afraid, I dial the number of my childhood home, wishing I could talk to my mother, but of course she doesn't answer.

"Hello? General Harris speaking."

I haven't heard my father's voice in two or three years, maybe a call a few Christmases ago, and at first I say nothing. Then, because my belly is tightening again and I'm standing in a stranger's house I say, "I'm scared."

"Tillie?"

I never officially cut him off. There was no big falling out. Life just got busy, and the less we were in touch, the more peaceful I felt. I didn't even tell him I got married.

"Tillie, is that you? Talk to me."

"I'm in Dupont Circle. And I need a doctor."

"You're in D.C.? What's wrong?"

"I'll tell the doctor what's wrong. I just need to get to a hospital, and I don't know which one or how to get there."

This is what he's good at, ignoring the emotions of the moment and solving a problem. After four or five minutes of him trying to give me directions I'm too panicked to follow, he decides to call me a cab that will take me to G.W. Hospital.

"Where are you?" he asks.

And I don't remember that either. I haven't memorized the new address yet, and when I ask the woman of this house where I am, I'm keenly aware that I'm giving her a very bad, though fairly accurate, first impression.

As I hang up the telephone, the neat, closed box that held my past is smashed open and oozing into the present. I had felt it coming though. This whole year it seemed that the world was conspiring to bring us together: First, it was the television coverage of Desert Storm this winter that flaunted my father's satellite-guided bombs dropping on targets with the accuracy of a video game. Then it was Simon finding the rare opening for an assistant curator at an art museum here in D.C. Now this.

Still holding the phone to my ear I stand motionless, hoping to feel that little upside down foot kick my rib cage. I press in different spots to see if the baby will push back. Nothing.

I don't want to have a full-on panic attack in a stranger's house, but I'm definitely on my way. When I spot a pan of brownies on the stove top, I take just a pinch, hoping the sugar will get the baby moving. I turn to the wall, pretending I'm still on the phone, and say, "M-hmm," eating one bite at first, and then going ahead and eating the entire brownie.

"Okay. And thank you," I say to no one, then hang up. I only nod my thanks to my neighbor, afraid there might be brownie on my teeth.

Waiting on her front steps, I work my fingers through my wet hair, letting the loose strands float away in the breeze. I don't dare turn around to see if she's watching me from her doorway. Instead, I think how good the sidewalk will be for hopscotch, what a nice climbing tree we have in the front yard, what a normal childhood we can offer this baby, if he or she will just hold on.

There's the pain again—at first a wave of bad cramps, not just in my belly but in my back this time. And now the tightening.

My neighbor opens the screen door and asks, "Can I help? Want me to wait with you?"

I shake my head and raise my hand as if to say, I'm fine, everything's cool, grateful to see the Red Top Cab pulling into view.

"G.W. emergency room," I say, just as Dad told me to. As we drive away, I realize I have no wallet, no ID, and no cash. Head in my hands, I spend the rest of the trip with a view of the never-vacuumed floor.

When the cab pulls up to the hospital, I pat the seat beside me as if I've only now realized I've forgotten my purse. I figure he'll be sympathetic to a distressed pregnant woman, but he drives off fast and pissed. I walk through the sliding glass doors and into the chaos of sick people. I have to pee, but I get in the registration line first, as people in front of me cough and complain and one applies pressure to a bloody wound. I'm terrified of another pain, of what waiting too long might mean for the baby, and wander up to the front of the line.

"Wait your turn," a patient says.

"It's not about me," I tell him. "Me, I'd stay at the end of the line, but my baby needs to be seen right away."

"You're no more important than anyone else," another patient says. "Get in back."

I feel a hand on my arm. Instinctively I shrug it off, whipping my head around with a kind of growl, and there's my father. His hair's been gray since I was born, but now his skin seems to match it. He stands there facing me, the only one in the ER wearing a suit, his shoulders rounded from all the years hunched over his weapons research. I back up, folding my arms over my chest so he can't do anything weird and uncharacteristic like hugging me.

He stares first at my belly, then at my wet hair—something familiar—and finally at my wedding ring. I register his look of surprise, possibly because I never sent him an invitation, but my gut says it's surprise that someone would have me.

"You didn't have to come," I tell him, trying to discover what looks so odd about his face.

"What's the matter?" he asks, maneuvering me to the back of the line, his hand stiff against my shoulder.

"Dad, just leave me alone."

"But you called me."

"I needed a ride. I didn't ask you to be here."

And now, of course, I realize what looks odd about him is that he shaved his mustache, leaving this pale, swollen patch above his lip and exposing facial expressions I've never seen in him: uncertainty, nervousness, grief. When I find myself at the front of the line again, I shoo Dad away while the woman behind the desk takes down my information.

"Name?"

"Tillie Harris." I spell it.

"ID"

"I don't have it with me," I say, combing my hair with my fingers.

"Address."

"Um. I need to skip that one, sorry."

"Insurance card."

"That, too."

"It'll be fee for service, then."

"I'm good for it. You don't have to worry about me not paying."

No change in her expression, she continues down the sheet of questions. "Date of birth. Social security."

Finally, numbers I know.

"Next of kin."

"My husband. Simon Williams. I kept my last name."

She could care less. "His work phone?"

"I should know it."

"Medical complaint?"

"I'm having pains across my abdomen, like something's gripping me."

"Pregnant?"

"Thirty-four weeks."

She looks at me for the first time, and I start to tear up. "Something's wrong," I say quietly, my voice cracking. "I'm scared."

"Name and number of your regular obstetrician?"

Another number I don't know, but I give the name and city.

I see the triage nurse next, who looks over the paper full of non-answers. I tell her about my pain and when it started and how long it lasted. She takes my vitals, tells me my blood pressure's elevated.

"Empty your bladder first," she says. "And then I'd like you to take this paper cup and fill it up at the water fountain. Try to drink the whole thing while you wait for your name to be called."

I'm slow to stand up, afraid to move toward the bathroom, where I may discover I'm bleeding, or find a blue arm slipping out between my legs.

When my father reaches out to help me up, I hurry to do it on my own. My wet hair has soaked the back of my dress, and I know this bothers him. Worries him. He takes out his handkerchief, and the slightest touch of it against my back makes me stomp my foot. A child having a tantrum. And this, more than anything else, is why I've stayed away from my father. Because when I'm around him, I am eight again, trapped in that year that scarred us all.

I find a seat in the waiting room, where patients cough and argue, and a TV hanging from the ceiling plays a soap opera at too high a volume.

Dad takes the only other chair that's free—too far away to offer his unsolicited advice, but close enough to show his irritation at the way I've shredded the rim of my paper cup.

When I close my eyes, I see our old house on the air force base in Albuquerque, New Mexico—planes constantly overhead, their vibrations strong enough to start cracks in the sidewalk. I can practically taste the red dust that was always in the air, staining our walkway and our shoes. It was the spring of 1975, near the end of the school year. I'd just had a birthday, always the last one in my class, but that year, every single child I invited had an excuse for why they couldn't come. Peeking from behind the curtain of our old house, I see Momma, just her shadow.

Our neighbors didn't know exactly what the trouble was inside our home. I don't think any of us understood, either. We were still of the belief that it would pass, that my dad could solve everything, that all of us would survive.

1

❧

The House with the Blue Door

I WAS BARRED FROM SCHOOL for the day because I'd been biting again. Whenever I pressed my teeth into one of my classmates, my teacher stopped the lesson and called, "Tillie, Tillie." There was always a struggle as she tried to wrestle the hand or arm from my mouth, but I held on—fighting until the last string of spit released—because I liked to leave a mark.

Although I had nowhere to go, I got up early and sat on the front steps in my nightgown, knees together, bare feet arched to keep my legs off the cold concrete. American flags rose up the poles and flapped against the Sandia Mountains, pale gray in the distance, as lights popped on inside the little square houses of our neighborhood, each the same size with their well-mowed lawns and rectangular flower beds under the front windows.

Soon, the men from each home walked tall and purposefully out their doors, one after another, in their crisp blue uniforms or camouflage jumpsuits, all with the same haircuts, the same pair of glasses. Some, like my father, had more decorations on their uniforms. But from this distance I noticed the sameness.

There was a sense of music to the slamming car doors and starting engines, a distinct sense of order as each man backed out of his driveway. Looking from one open garage to the next, I could see that we all had bikes, silver metal trash cans, reel mowers, and rakes. Our home was like all of the others on our street. The only difference was our front door. My mother had painted it turquoise blue.

The children were the next to leave with their lunch boxes and textbooks—girls in plaid and flowered dresses that fell just above the knee, boys in jeans and short-sleeved, checkered button-ups. When I recognized another second grader, her pigtails tied in yarn, I waited for her to see me there with my face decorated in yellow smiley stickers.

At first, she seemed to pass without noticing me, but at the last moment she turned her head over her shoulder and shrieked, "You have rabies!"

I smirked until the stickers pinched my skin. "I get to stay home," I said.

And then came Mary Beth, wearing a huge Band-Aid with my teeth marks underneath it. During yesterday's class, while she cried and held her arm, I had to stand in the corner of our classroom with my nose to the wall. I found the exact smudge where I'd put my nose the other times, and I listened to Mary Beth's whimpering, the whispers of her friends, and the stern voices of teachers. But there were giggles, too, because even with my nose to the wall, I could still turn my feet inward like pigeons' toes or shake my behind.

"My dad says you should keep your teeth to yourself," she said, suddenly gripping the hand of the girl in pigtails.

"So what?" I said, standing as they ran together toward the school. "*My* dad's the boss of *your* dad."

Finally, my brother rushed out of the garage door, trying to close his Scooby Doo lunch box without dropping his textbooks. He stopped beside me to see why it wouldn't latch, opening the lid and shifting the jar of green olives and the two hot dog buns inside.

"You have to slam it," I said.

He did, and it bent the lid but closed shut.

"Did you check on Momma?" I asked.

Phil shook his head.

Our mother had not left her bedroom in four days. The last time she'd come out was suppertime the night Dad left for his business trip. She said she felt too tired to cook and handed us a box of chocolate donuts before shutting her door. She was so tired these days, I wasn't surprised when we didn't see her the next morning. Phil made sure we left for school on time. And when we still hadn't seen her leave the bedroom by suppertime the next evening, we opened the door just a crack. The room smelled strong and sweet, like rotting flowers, and Phil shut the door again, saying we should wait for Dad.

My brother gripped the handle of his lunch box, sitting too straight, the way Dad taught him, as students continued to stream past our house on their way to school.

I pulled a piece of hair from underneath one of the smiley stickers. "Do you think we should tell someone?"

His head shook slowly back and forth. "Dad will be home tonight," he said. "We should just wait." He kept his eye on the passing students, and when he spotted a fifth grader from his class, he jogged to catch up, the jar of olives banging back and forth inside his lunch box.

· · ·

My father's business trip came up suddenly, just after the local newspaper did a feature on him. Copies of the paper, with photos of the men who'd flown from Washington to meet him, were posted at the PX and in the lobby where he worked. I understood almost nothing of what he did, only that he designed missiles. When I visited his office at the weapons lab, with its long blackboard full of formulas and diagrams, he always saved an area for me in the right-hand corner, where I was allowed to draw with chalk.

The children had all passed our house and started down the hill to school, my brother walking in a perfect line on the right side of the sidewalk, eyes down in case he found something to put in his pocket. Our side of the street was the last to get sun, and even this close to summer vacation the steps froze the backs of my legs right through my nightgown. When I could no longer see the back of Phil's perfectly combed hair, I went inside, entering the house through the garage. I stepped over dirty dishes, crumpled napkins, empty bread bags, t-shirts, apple cores, and pieces of board games, stopping outside my mother's bedroom.

Some days she sang and twirled through the house in sleeves like angel wings, wearing frosted eye shadow and matching nail polish. I remembered the day I sat on the kitchen floor as she poured a can of mushroom soup over chicken. It was the only meal she cooked. She fried it up, shouting at the oil that popped out of the pan. I laughed and began singing military songs real loud:

> *Off we go into the wild blue yonder,*
> *Climbing high into the sun;*

Here they come zooming to meet our thunder
At 'em boys, give 'er the gun!

I swung my head back and forth, letting my braids hit the lower cupboards so my ponytail holders went *click click*. Momma banged her spoon against the frying pan, and I thought we sounded like a marching band. Then, just like that, it stopped. I'd seen it happen before, how she could change moods so quickly, how anything could cause it—a plane flying overhead, an oven mitt that was missing right when she needed it, me asking one too many questions. That day, she closed her eyes and squeezed the handle on the pan. "I can't do this anymore," she said. "I can't. I just can't." And she left the grease-spattered room, left the chicken soaking in oil and soup.

I pressed my nose and lips against her door, felt the wood dampen with my breath while I gradually turned the handle. The blinds were drawn, the smell overpowering, as I felt my way through the sticky air to her bed. She lay there pale and beautiful, as if drowned and washed back ashore, her face blank. She'd covered the bed in books, five of them spread out across Dad's side. She once told me she liked to read the first chapters and then dream the rest. Perhaps she was dreaming right then.

In the quiet, I heard the gurgle of steam moving through the pipes, and the *swoosh swoosh* of blood in my ears. My fingers touched the sheet, and I considered saying her name, but suddenly feared she'd open her eyes, blue as robins' eggs, the fat black pupil tracking me. And which mother would she be?

Backing out of the room, I slowly pulled the handle until there was a near-silent click, and then continued going back-

ward all the way to the kitchen, where my shoulder slammed
into the doorframe.

We'd eaten most of the snack food. Phil tried to cook spaghetti one day, but didn't realize he was supposed to boil the
water before he added the spaghetti to the pot. It came out stuck
in one large clump, like a tube—too crunchy to eat, and even
worse when he tried to recook it. Scouring the counters, refrigerator, and the very backs of the cupboards I could reach,
I found Chiclets gum, pickles, and crumbs at the bottom of a
Charles Chips tin. I left a trail of crumbs showing the path I
took to the living room, and, later, I would pretend this was not
on purpose.

I made a game of trying to touch everything in the living
room without waking her: fabrics from her sewing kit, pine
cones from a basket, every record in the hi-fi.

The front window rattled as a plane roared overhead, and I
stopped to listen, remembering how Momma had once thrown
a plate against the kitchen cabinet, angry that the noise had interrupted her. Once it passed, I waited to hear if she was awake,
but there was only quiet. And bored of touching everything, I
climbed onto the sofa and bounced up and down, surprised to
see a woman approaching our blue door. Her blond hair stayed
perfectly stiff as she walked closer, and behind her a child
pushed a baby carriage filled with dolls and carried a shiny red
pocketbook.

We rarely had visitors. Usually when the doorbell rang
Momma would instruct us to hide in another room, telling us
she didn't want to play with the other mommies and she didn't
want to buy their products, either.

When the doorbell rang, I stopped jumping and pressed my
forehead against the glass, enjoying our staring contest. She

rang the bell again, and I sang "ding-dong" right back at her. When I remembered my face full of stickers, I smiled until I broke into a laugh. "Ding-dong," I sang again, and she held her daughter close like she knew I was a biter.

I was never able to explain to my teachers how I could be sorry for biting but come right back to school and do it again. The feel of my teeth sinking into something so soft was only part of it. There was something comforting about that first yelp when I went deep, something about the crying, and the teacher shouting my name as she pulled us apart, asking, *Why, Tillie? Why did you do it?* I liked how everything happened the same way each time, right up to me walking home with a note pinned to my shirt that proved the things I thought had happened were the very same things my teacher thought had happened. Everything made sense.

The woman rang the bell again, and after a long wait, she led her daughter and the carriage full of dolls back toward the sidewalk, looking over her shoulder all the way. She didn't know that I couldn't have opened our blue door even if I'd wanted to. Momma had painted it shut.

When my brother returned from school, he entered the house through the garage. "What's with the crowd?"

"What crowd?" I was organizing Momma's record albums by the ones I liked best, but now I joined him at the window, where nearly a dozen women dressed in Popsicle colors huddled on our lawn, pointing to the blue door.

"Let's go see what's happening," I said.

"You should get dressed. You can't wear pajamas all day."

"Momma does."

He jingled coins together in his pocket. "You should get dressed."

I grabbed a t-shirt and shorts off the living room floor, and put them on while Phil, in the kitchen, climbed the cluttered counters in search of food. He grabbed two packages of Kool-Aid, while I found the cleanest cups in the sink. We mixed both flavors together and added water but no sugar because I'd eaten what was left of it the night before. Our drinks came out brown and impossibly sour, but we giggled, daring each other to gulp them down.

It was rare to see him laugh like that anymore, and as soon as he noticed, he quickly shut his mouth. Over the winter, he'd crashed on his sled. His front tooth had chipped so badly the dentist covered it with a silver cap. Ever since, he tried to keep it hidden.

We left the house through the garage and took a seat on the front steps. Phil brought his homework and began to study despite the commotion—so serious except for his mouth stained blue brown. I enjoyed the audience—how their eyes followed when I jumped off the steps and spun in the grass. I couldn't stop smiling as I walked over to the bush that was always filled with ladybugs and reached my hand inside. Once Momma had told me to count them and tell her when I knew the exact number. Plucking them from the branches, I set the bugs along my arm—not one of them completely round or completely red.

"Little girl?" A woman wearing an orange minidress crossed the yard as the others looked on. "Is your mother home?"

"Yes. My mother's home," I said. I touched the hem of her dress because I couldn't help myself.

"And where is she?"

Dad had told me that he would answer all questions regarding my mother, and Phil reminded me with a forceful stare to follow the rules.

"That little girl's Matilda Harris," said the blonde who'd rung our doorbell.

"Matilda?" the woman in orange continued, and now she knelt down, holding me by the shoulders. I liked the way she smelled of Life Savers. "Can you ask your mother to come out and talk with us?"

I stayed mum, gently tapping the red back of a ladybug, hoping to see its outer case open and the wings unfold.

"See, I told you," the blonde said mysteriously.

The woman in orange approached Phil next. "How about you, young soldier? Will you help us?"

Phil didn't say anything, either. He watched the bugs crawl across my arm without expression as I made believe my mother was beside me, saying what the colors reminded her of: pepperoni, cinnamon gum, strawberry jelly.

The curious women had gone to their homes to cook dinner, occasionally peeking at us from their steamed kitchen windows. I was pleased to notice how much Phil and I looked like the other kids in our neighborhood. Sitting on the front porch with our Kool-Aid-stained mouths, we were all hungry for dinner and waiting for our fathers.

"I opened her door today," I finally said.

"Did she wake up?"

"Uh-uh."

Phil rubbed his finger over the silver tooth, and didn't ask any more, just kept his eye out for Dad. When his station wagon pulled onto our street, I saw his gray hair was swept to the side, and with his chin up, his mustache caught the sunlight. I stood and saluted.

As he turned into the driveway, the women in Popsicle colors came out of their homes again, some wearing aprons now. When he got out and fetched his briefcase and hanging bag from the backseat, they came so close he seemed to sense them there.

"Is there a problem?" he asked before turning to face them.

The blonde stepped forward, then hesitated, staring at the bars and stripes on his uniform, and then his nametag, which read ROY HARRIS. Finally she said, "Your daughter's been home all day."

"That's because I bit Mary Beth," I said, helpfully, running from the front steps to greet him.

"She says her mother is inside," the woman continued. "But I've been ringing the bell for hours."

My favorite thing about my father's mustache was how it hid his expression. I could look right at him and pretend he wasn't mad. "I appreciate your concern," he told the woman. "I'll handle this."

I nodded to her because I was convinced he could handle all of this, but he placed his hand on the top of my head to stop it from moving. "Tillie, clean that mess off your face," he said, and quickly disappeared through the garage door.

As Phil and I followed him, I pulled off the stickers, my eyes watering when invisible hairs came with them. We stopped short of going into the house, staying there beside the trash cans.

"What on earth is going on here?" he yelled from inside.

"I think he's in the kitchen," I said.

Phil leaned his head through the doorway, concentrating—and when we heard the bedroom door open we held our breath. For a while it was silent, and then Dad said something too quiet to hear.

I grabbed a piece of Phil's shirt. "Do you think—"

"Sh."

Dad's voice got louder, and finally words we could make out: "What's wrong with you?"

I inhaled the smell of oil stains from the cement floor.

"Tell me," Dad shouted, still in the bedroom. "Did you even know she stayed home from school today? Did you think to feed her? Because nothing's making sense to me right now."

"She's alive," Phil said in practically a whisper.

I tipped my head backward to stretch out the cramp in my throat, staring a long while at the pink insulation on the ceiling, then down the wooden walls to Phil's sled, hanging midway, and the mower propped in the corner. What a relief, all the yelling and stomping through the house.

"Why is there food in the living room? What's the heat doing on?" When he headed our way again, his keys rattling, we hurried closer to the trash cans as if we hadn't been eavesdropping. "In the car," he told us. "We're not going to eat frozen meat for dinner."

As we walked down the driveway together, our neighbors all appeared to be busy—checking an empty mailbox, coiling a garden hose, buffing the car with a sleeve.

"Nothing to see," Dad told the blonde, who stood at her front door as if waiting for a report. He opened the back door of the car for me.

When we pulled off our street, Phil, who had taken Momma's seat up front, rolled the window all the way down and turned around to see how it messed up my hair.

I rolled down my window, hoping for the same effect, but the wind didn't touch him. Kneeling into the breeze, I slid my mouth along the bristly strip of the window frame, tasting metal and dust. My teeth hurt whenever we drove over bumps in the road.

If I concentrated, I could smell a hint of Momma's gardenia

lotion, even though it had been a long while since she'd ridden in the car. She'd swing her orange hair back and forth to the music—she knew every song on the radio—and when the 5th Dimension or Peter Paul & Mary came on, she'd turn up the volume and I'd sing with her. The only sound when we drove with Dad was the air rushing through the open windows. Sometimes as we drove, Momma's orange hairs still blew through the car.

We had to park two blocks away from the commissary because the marching band had taken over the parking lot to practice for the weekend parade. "Can we go?" I asked Dad, feeling the band play the notes on my ribs. There would be flyovers and songs I knew and miniature flags for all the kids to wave. "Can we?"

"We'll see," he said. A phrase I learned a long time ago meant no.

When Dad marched down the sidewalk, one soldier after another stopped to salute him. "Evening, Colonel Harris, sir." And he returned the salutes with such a sudden whipping motion I thought his wrist would snap.

"Keep up, Tillie," he'd shout now and then. "You've got to hustle."

I tried, but the trombones kept sliding my head in the direction of all those blue uniforms and white gloves.

Phil stayed by Dad's side as if he were on an invisible leash. He had a knack for finding pennies on the sidewalk whenever we went out, but he picked them up so quickly, he hardly lost a step.

"Come on, Tillie." Dad's voice was farther away now.

The parade music jiggled my insides, and lifted the hair up on my arms. I wanted to be the girl with the pompons tied to her shoes, jabbing a baton at the sky. I danced along behind my father, danced to the *womp womping* of the tuba, the wild drumming. I trotted with fancy steps, keeping my eyes on my father's hand, held out to the side with his fingers spread apart. If I could only catch up, I knew he'd take hold.

We drove home to the sound of Phil flipping the lid of the ash-tray open and closed. Sitting in the backseat with me were paper bags filled with hamburger meat, buns, a carton of milk, and an assortment of cleaners—liquid Lysol, Brillo soap pads, and pow-dered Ajax with bleach. I was beginning to enjoy the tiny pain of hunger and how I could make it hurt more or less with my mind. Curled just below my window, I felt the car turn left and slow, stop and slow—the rhythm that meant we were near home. But when I raised my body to see our ladybug bush and our blue door, I saw the neighbors watching us pull into the drive.

Dad stiffened his shoulders, stepping out of the car with the kind of posture that reminded you he was used to being in charge. He carried a grocery bag in one arm and turned my head forward with his other hand, so I would face our house. When he let go, my head swiveled right back to the neighbors, heading to their own homes now. I wondered if the little girl pushing her baby carriage thought of me—jumping at the window—even as she disappeared around the corner.

"Go inside," Phil said. "Go on!"

Dad walked right over the trail of crushed potato chips on his way to the kitchen and began to bang the pots and dishes around and mop the floor, lecturing the empty room until, fi-nally, hamburgers hissed in the frying pan.

I waited in the living room with the dolls Momma had made—long-nosed elves, brown- and pink-skinned Raggedy Anns, their big button eyes watching the closed bedroom door to see if she would come out. How many days had it been since she bathed and dressed and left her room smelling of gardenia lotion? How many days since I sat beside her on the couch, our legs touching, as she sewed? I remembered those times as if they were rolled into one overstuffed day: the hi-fi turned all the way up, Rod Stewart then Dusty Springfield singing. Momma would make up her own words—"Isn't this more fun than cleaning?"—and sing them right over top of the ones playing on the albums.

When Dad called us to the table for dinner, my eyes and throat burned from the intense cleaning he'd just given the kitchen. As he served the food, he lectured about how we ought to pick up after ourselves, how we ought to behave at school, and how I should not choke down my food, but I couldn't make myself eat any slower.

After we cleared the table, Dad brought a hamburger and a pile of wrinkled peas to Momma. I followed him like a shadow into the humid room, where he raised the blinds and set dinner on the bed beside her face.

"Please," he said. That was all.

Without raising her head, she reached her thin hand from the sheet to take nothing but the top bun. She barely opened her mouth, straining to take a single bite, and soon she and the bun slid beneath the covers so that only her orange hair showed.

Dad swatted me on the bottom so I'd leave the room, and when I was in the hallway he asked, "What am I supposed to do?"

My brother stayed out of all of it, hunched over the rug in his room, where he took apart his rubber band ball, band by band. It went from a sphere the size of a cantaloupe to a hundred loose ends covering the floor.

. . .

There was so much the neighbors couldn't have understood about our family by staring at our blue door from the lawn that day. They could not have known the relief I felt in hearing grown-ups in the house—even the sound of Momma crying facedown on the bed and Dad cursing as he scrubbed the different rooms, putting everything right. They couldn't have known the comfort of sinking into bathwater for the first time in days and washing the fine clay dust from my skin, or of hearing clothes tumble in the dryer along with the scrapes of pennies that had fallen out of Phil's pocket. Most of all, they could not have appreciated the small miracle of Momma coming to my room that night to tuck me in.

She came in her pink terry cloth robe, carrying the beautiful cup we'd made together. It had started out as just an ordinary white mug from our cupboard, but we had glued plastic rubies to it.

"There you go, Bear," she whispered, handing me the steaming cup. She settled at the edge of my mattress, her face still creased from her long sleep. I chattered about baby carriages, ladybugs, and sour Kool-Aid until she closed my hands around the cup and insisted, "Taste it."

I sipped the warm, bitter drink, feeling the rubies with my tongue in between swallows.

"I'm trying," she said. "I'm trying for you, okay?" And she reached for *Alice in Wonderland*, turning to the page where we last stopped. I was captivated with her singsong voice, how quiet it was that night. Sometimes she read the same sentence twice, and sometimes she had to pause until she'd wiped the tears from her eyes.

I was fading, blinking, trying to will myself to stay awake, to have this time with her a little longer, but every part of me felt heavy. The cup began to slip from my hands, and when I squeezed my fingers closed to catch it, one of the rubies fell into my lap.

Momma took the cup from me, and I picked up the ruby, saving it in my pillowcase, where I liked to tuck my hands. What the neighbors couldn't see as I lay my head down was how Momma adored me, how she didn't leave until I was asleep. I tasted the bitter drink in the back of my throat, and the room began to spin.

2

❧❦❧

Bear

A SMALL, BARELY LEGAL TRAVELING circus had pulled into our town in the middle of the night and set up in the parking lot of Ace Hardware. Dad and Momma took three-year-old Phil to this circus, where they sat on the shaky bleachers with the store to their backs and the mountains creating a backdrop for the performers.

Sometimes when Momma told the story she left out the fight. Other times it was the focus—how Dad had seen other officers with their families sitting higher up in the bleachers, and how forcefully he'd insisted that our family join them. Despite his wishes, Momma chose a seat in the front row, where she and Phil shared a box of Cracker Jack, eating the caramel corn and throwing out the peanuts. Dad paced there in front of them, shoulders hunched, believing my mother would change her mind. His gray hair and the ten-year age difference between them was only one reason my parents were regularly mistaken for father and daughter. The other was the way he scolded her, and the way she fought his control.

Eventually, Dad sat down beside Phil because he was blocking someone's view. My brother spent most of that hour and a half shrieking and flinging himself off of the bench, mad that he no longer fit on Momma's lap because I was there, still in the womb, but already invading his space and stealing attention from him.

Even with all of this distraction, Momma was completely absorbed in the show, which featured animals in ankle chains, standing on one leg, waving and roaring on command. Throughout the performance, Momma heard complaints from the officers' wives that the tricks were pitiful, a waste of their money and an afternoon when they might have otherwise grilled hotdogs with neighbors. But Momma found the circus perfectly marvelous: the musky smell of animals, the taste of Cracker Jack stuck to her back teeth, the oohs and ahs of children holding pinwheels that spun in the wind. And there was the woman wearing a gold sequined gown who presented each act with her arms raised to the sky.

When the bear came on, or rather, when the sheet over its cage was pulled away, Momma said I began to kick wildly.

"Our baby loves this bear," she had told Dad.

It was a young bear and meant to dance when given the command. Instead it stood on its hind legs and roared. When the sheet was dropped back over the cage, it continued to roar and I continued to kick.

Dad wanted to leave right away to avoid traffic, but Momma insisted on staying after the performance to ask the name of the bear. Taking hold of Phil's hand, she climbed onto the wooden platform, where the woman in gold knelt beside the bear's cage, still covered in that white sheet, counting a stack of dollar bills.

"Excuse me," Momma said to her back. "Excuse me, please. Can you tell me the name of the bear?"

The woman turned to Momma with eyes thickly lined in black, and in a Russian accent she said, "You mean this naughty little girl?"

She banged on the bars with the palm of her hand, the cage rocking back and forth, and the bear sniffing the fabric into its nostrils. Phil pulled free of Momma's hand, sprinting to Dad.

"You want to know her name?" The woman drew the sheet to the side, her arm shining with sweat, and the bear tottered closer, shaking its head, reaching its paw, like a giant fuzzy slipper, through the bars. The woman did not speak the name, but sang it: "Ma-teelda!"

They walked back through the parking lot of the hardware store—carpenters wheeling lumber in rattling metal carts and children with cotton candy stuck to their faces pulling against their parents' hands—when Momma announced, "If our baby is a girl, her name will be Matilda."

Dad's only response was to grumble about the line of cars all trying to exit at once. But Momma wouldn't let him ruin her mood, saying, "Imagine just deciding one day that you'd like to buy a bear and travel from town to town, and you go and do it. And then you say, 'I'd like to wear a sequined gown in a parking lot in the middle of the day,' and you do that, too."

Momma had recounted this story so often. Sometimes details were left in or out, but there was always the gold sequined dress, and always the officers' wives passing judgment from their higher seats.

Back when she still picked me up after school, Momma had always been different from the others with her long orange hair and Indian-print skirts that went to her ankles. I remember, once, finding her with another mom as I worked my way to her through the crowded schoolyard.

"It's never done," I heard her say. "Every day I spend hours cleaning, cooking, doing these things I hate, and it's never ever done."

The other mom nodded, but also took a step backward as if to make clear they were not friends. "What if you relaxed in a bubble bath?" she suggested.

By this time, I was near enough to reach Momma's skirt, and as I scrunched the fabric in my fist, she pet the top of my head and pulled me close into her hip.

"If I take a bubble bath, I'll be even more behind!" she said. And laughing, she added, "What if I sink under the water to rinse my hair and just decide to stay there?"

When the other woman's child rushed to her arms, they left abruptly. Even though we were all headed in the same direction, she dragged her child up the hill so fast we couldn't catch up.

Momma had always been different from the others, and perhaps that was the reason we were slow to notice she wasn't well. She began to do things only partway. She'd start a sewing project, then become bored of the color thread she'd chosen. She'd quit the Game of Life and Uncle Wiggily right in the middle, would just wander away and not come back. Dirty clothes went into the washer, but by the time she remembered to put them in the dryer, they needed to be washed again. Often I went to school in clothes I'd already worn, and once I had to borrow a pair of my brother's clean underwear with an old stain in the seat and a weird pocket in front.

But if anything pointed to her decline, it was the wicker

laundry basket she kept on her side of the bedroom closet. When the mail came, she dumped it there. Our school work went in, too—drawings we'd made, permission slips, stray socks, even a few dirty dishes. Momma kept a dress draped over the top of it.

My parents shared the bedroom closet—Momma on the left, Dad on the right. Momma's side didn't close all the way because there were jeans, pantyhose, and slips hung over the rod. Dad's side was tidy: five work shirts buttoned to the top, slacks carefully folded along the crease, shoes filled with shoe trees and lined in pairs. When the dress that covered Momma's laundry basket crossed the line over to his side and he bent down to pick it off the floor, he discovered a problem larger than the unpaid bills and notes from my teacher.

After he was done shouting and balling his fists, he took her to the local clinic. Maybe a blood test or an X-ray would explain this change in Momma. Maybe her trouble getting dressed in the morning or doing the simplest things was caused by cancer or some other medical problem. That he would have understood. But after a thorough exam and a series of blood tests, the doctor concluded that she was absolutely fine.

This news from the doctor sent Dad into a rage. "Enough of this! You don't have cancer!" he shouted at her the next time she said she couldn't get out of bed. Momma's problem, he decided, was one of stubbornness. She was sloppy, helpless, emotional. Unforgivable things.

I didn't like when he shouted at her, and it was not because I was afraid of shouting. I liked the way an angry voice brought out goose bumps on my arms and legs, like I'd been plugged in and something suddenly buzzed through me. But every time he shouted or criticized her, she was less likely to get out of bed.

I tried to help her clean so he wouldn't yell. When dishes disappeared into a sink filled with brown water that never drained, I pointed to a switch on the wall and told her, "Flip that up and it'll clean the sink."

"Oh, but the garbage disposal is so loud," she said. Then she bent down and whispered a secret just between us. "Besides, I always get the strangest urge to stick my arm down the drain and let it gobble me up."

"No, *I'm* going to gobble you up!" I told her, giggling.

She reached down to tickle me and I danced out of the way. When she finally caught me, she curled me in her arms, planting loud kisses on my cheeks. Then she tickled under my chin, and always, when someone tickled me, I bit.

"I'm sorry. I'm sorry, Momma."

The single joke in our family, when we still joked, was to be careful naming children after wild animals. "You can't be wild now," Dad would say. "You have to be a tame bear."

And Momma famously answered, "You can't tell a bear not to be a bear."

❧

WHEN DAD RETURNED FROM his trip to Washington, the sight of our neighbors gathered on our lawn and the state of our house when he came inside convinced him to get control of Momma. Each morning he physically dragged her out of bed. As she would slump to the floor, he shouted, "Stand up, and pull yourself together." He tucked his arms under her armpits and pulled. "Stand up, damn it!"

Most days she would stay where he left her, collapsed on the floor, looking almost purposefully uncomfortable. I stayed with her until I had to leave for school, braiding her hair or decorating her wrist with bracelets. "Momma, get up. Don't cry."

Once Phil tried to lift her off the floor, as Dad did. He had always wanted to be the little man—hammering scrap wood when Dad built bookshelves, handing him tools when he changed a bike tire, shaving beside him, but with a comb in place of a razor. He wrestled his arms under Momma's and tried to stand her up.

"Leave me alone," she snapped, and he removed his hands from her as if he'd received a shock, Momma crumbling back to the carpet in tears.

My brother was not the type who had to be told anything more than once. From that day on, he left her alone—walking around her in the mornings, going straight to his room after school to do his homework or build his model airplanes. When the weather was good, he left the house. He liked to play at the very edge of the yard, digging roads for his Matchbox cars around the roots of our piñon tree, or near the fence, poking things through to the other side. When Dad allowed it, he hopped on his bike and rode to the opposite side of the base where the planes took off, and tried to outrace them.

My father's plan for getting control of Momma was clearly failing—she just wasn't cooperating, he said—and it interfered with his work. He didn't have time to wake her up or lift her off the floor or check on her throughout the day. He understood that leaving us with her was the same as leaving us on our own, and so he began coming home when we returned from school, but with no patience for stories about what we'd learned in class or what we'd played at recess. There were dishes and clothes to wash and dinner to cook, and in every spare moment he sat in the armchair with papers in his lap and a ballpoint pen in the corner of his mouth.

If we needed him, we stood near his chair until he looked up and asked, "What is it?" And when we told him that we were bored or hungry or had had a disagreement, he gave a frustrated sigh, and we knew we'd interrupted him with something unimportant.

After a while, I could predict his answers: "I suppose, if you're hungry, you'll eat all your vegetables at dinner" or "You two will have to figure out how to resolve it, then." Phil stopped going to him at all. But I kept trying.

"Yes? What is it, Tillie?"

"A scrape," I said, showing him my elbow and trying not to let him see my tears.

"And you don't know where the Band-Aids are?" he asked.

"The hall closet," I said, my shoulders dropping. I had not even taken a step away when he was scribbling notes again.

I walked right past the hall closet and into my room because it wasn't the Band-Aid that stopped the tears; it was someone pressing it where it hurt and saying, "There, there."

❧

DAD WORKED DURING EVERY bit of free time, reading stacks of papers and filling up yellow legal pads with formulas, until one evening he set us on the couch. The government wanted him to work in a new office, he said, on something called DNSS. He used a ruler to draw a picture of a five-sided shape with a hole in the center of it, and tapping on the drawing with his pencil he said, "My new job will be right here."

Later, I asked Phil, "Did you understand anything he said?"

My brother sat at the back table in his room, where he painstakingly glued model airplanes together. His room was hot and stuffy, but he wouldn't open the windows and risk letting the red dust ruin his work.

"He's designing guided missiles," he explained. "They say his inventions will make our country mightier than we've ever been."

He opened his drawer and took out a notebook filled with newspaper clippings. Again and again, there were articles with my father's name underlined, and pictures of him with important-looking people, receiving awards. In one picture, I recognized the faces of men who'd flown in from Washington, D.C. to meet with him.

"But why did he draw a donut?"

"Not a donut, Tillie. The Pentagon. It's a building. He was trying to tell us we have to move."

"Oh," I said. "I didn't know."

"That's where he went on his business trip. They told him right away that they wanted him. He spent most of the trip finding our new house."

"We have a new house?"

Phil nodded, as if these were things I would know if I paid better attention. My brother worked so hard to listen and to do what he was told, but while he *knew* more of what was happening than I did, he was never *a part of* what was happening. He was so quick to understand and cooperate that he faded into the background. You could see this even when we were in public together. The four of us could stand in line at a restaurant, and the waiter would ask, "Table for three?"

At bedtime I lay awake, wondering what our new house looked like and how far it was from here when I heard Momma's bedroom door open and her soft footsteps down the hallway. This was the sound I'd been waiting for. Since Dad returned from his trip, she'd been leaving her bedroom each night to tuck us in, though it seemed to take all of her strength to do it.

She went to Phil's room first, where her good night was brief. "Time for bed," she said.

Phil, who always did as he was told, immediately turned off the lights and closed his eyes. Sometimes she stood there a little longer in the dark. "Do you need anything?" she asked in a quiet voice. "Can I bring you a glass of water or read to you?" But Phil always gave the answer that made Dad proud: He didn't need anything.

When it was my turn, I got so excited that I kicked my feet against the mattress. Now, the warm drink had become part of our nightly routine, and I had to wait a little longer. But finally she came to my room, carefully handing me the ruby cup. I took slow sips as she sat beside me, her hair tangled, her pajamas damp with sweat.

"Why do you tuck me in every night if you're so tired?" I asked.

"So every night you'll go to sleep remembering that your mother loves you," she said, opening our book. "I want that to be your last thought of the day."

When she neared the end of the chapter, I felt so drowsy, the cup slipped out of my hands and crashed to the floor.

"It's all right," she said, setting the book aside. "It's still good."

I leaned over the edge of the bed, the floor blurring, as she picked up the cup.

"See?" she said, calming me. "Only the handle broke. I think I like it better this way, don't you?"

She opened my hand and set two rubies in it. I tried to smile, but I needed to lay my head down.

"Thatta girl," she said, stroking my hair.

I closed my eyes, thinking of rubies and the fantastic five-sided donut. It seemed everything was about to get much better.

3

❧❧

The Sooner the Day Ends

WE DISMANTLED THE HOUSE, little by little, emptying the bookshelves, cupboards, and closets, trusting all would reappear, unharmed, on the other side. Phil was allowed to wrap breakables, rolling them in newspaper. I was in charge of clothes, sofa pillows, blankets, stuffed animals. We packed when we were finished with our homework and while we waited for dinner. Dad packed whenever he took a break from his work and then again after we went to bed.

Momma was rarely up during the day anymore. Sometimes she'd wander down the hall to use the bathroom or walk through the room and drop something into a box. After, she might sit at the very edge of the cushion on the couch, staring forward, her eyes glazed like she'd cry if she weren't so tired. Dad no longer tried to involve her, and we didn't either. She would sit there and eventually get up and return to her room. I no longer pleaded with her to stay because I knew we'd have our tuck-in time. And somehow we put all of our hope into the move—that things would be better once we were in the new house. The new house was where we'd begin again.

Steadily, the music and decorations disappeared. Dad used the end of the hammer to pull nails out of the wall, though the holes remained. And last of all, the day before we moved, he unstuck our blue front door, using a putty knife to break the seal. He was touching up the paint along the edges when his secretary pulled up.

Phil and I peeked from the open doorway.

"Go on and say hello," Dad said, pushing us down the walkway to greet her. "You remember Anne."

I did. Anne kept a candy dish on her desk at the weapons lab, and she wore sweaters and jewelry that matched the holidays. She'd once worn a little Santa pin with a small red light bulb for a nose. If you pulled the string, it lit up, but Dad told me not to pull it.

Anne stood by the curb in her very ironed skirt, her hair just above the collar of her blouse, so groomed she reminded me of a store mannequin. She shook Phil's hand; then she turned to me.

"You're getting so big," she said. "You must be almost seven by now."

"I'm eight."

"Oh, don't wrinkle your nose at me," she said. "Some day you'll be glad to look so young for your age."

She reached for me with both arms and before I knew it, my cheek was pressed against the belt of her skirt. I held my breath and tried to stay calm. Dad told me I had to get used to being hugged, but it made me feel cornered. I kept my eyes open wide and my shoulders hiked up to my ears as her belt dug into my cheek. And when it seemed I might smother to death, I pushed back from her, gulping air and rubbing the side of my face.

Anne laughed a weird, high laugh, and my father chuckled once but at the same time gave me the look that meant, *Be nice.*

"I'll get those papers for you," he said, and headed back down the walkway toward the house. When she followed, he told her, "The house is full of boxes. It's a real mess."

What he meant was that she should wait outside, but she went right in and began sniffing the air. "Is everything okay in here?"

It was a smell I noticed when I returned from school, but it gradually disappeared the longer I was home, especially when Dad shut Momma's door.

"I'll open some windows," he said, weaving between the cardboard boxes to reach the nearest one. "I'd hoped to be further along. I'm scheduled to pick up the U-Haul tomorrow morning and plan to be on the road before dinner."

"Can I help with anything?"

"Some neighbors are going to help with the furniture. I don't anticipate needing anything else."

"Well, if you do, just ask."

"Dad, I'm hungry," I said.

"Tillie, just hold on. I need to find where I put my briefcase."

"Would you like me to find something for you to eat?" Anne asked me and walked toward the kitchen.

"No, no, please," Dad said. "Tillie needs to learn to be patient."

"It's no trouble," she said. "Really, I don't mind."

She found a loaf of bread on the counter and took out a slice, but after opening several empty cupboards, she found nothing to spread on it. Phil had been standing stiff like a wooden soldier as Dad and Anne scurried around him, but he suddenly turned toward the hallway, his cheeks growing pink.

Momma was out of the bedroom. It was so rare to see her during the day, and as she came around the corner, it was clear she'd dressed in a hurry—lipstick freshly applied but her hair uncombed. Her dress, while pretty, was pulled from the bottom of the hamper. She was barefoot and marching straight for the kitchen.

"Want me to do a load of dishes, Roy?" Anne asked, unaware that Momma had walked up right behind her. "I can—"

"May I help you with something?" my mother asked.

Anne startled at the sound of Momma's voice, and Dad looked up from the box he'd been searching in and rushed to the kitchen, a slight panic in his eyes.

"Anne is here to pick up some documents," he said.

"From our kitchen?" Momma asked.

"No, of course not. It's just that Tillie was hungry." He turned to Anne. "She's been under the weather," he said in an attempt to explain Momma's appearance.

"I'm so sorry to hear that, Mrs. Harris."

"I'm certainly well enough to ask you to stay for dinner," Momma said, and my brother and I exchanged looks of surprise. We knew very well that she didn't like company, and it had been weeks since she sat at the table with us.

"Really. I couldn't impose."

"She just came for some documents," Dad said. "I'm sure she has other plans. The moment I find my briefcase—"

He tried to catch Momma's eye as if to relay some secret message, but she turned away from him and toward Anne with an odd sort of smile on her face. "I absolutely insist we have dinner together," she said. "I just need a little time to get ready. Maybe everyone could go for a walk around the neighborhood to give me a few moments."

"If we're going for a walk," Phil said, "we could bring my pennies to the bank."

He kept an old Goober's jelly jar on his desk where he saved the pennies he found, as well as those Dad emptied into it at the end of each day. Whenever the jar was full, we walked to the bank so he could trade them in for silver dollars.

"Well," Anne said, putting her hand on Phil's shoulder. "Who could say no to an invitation like this? A trip to the bank and dinner with such fine company? I'm going to have to say yes."

And suddenly everyone had agreed to something I wasn't sure any of us thought was a good idea.

I walked on my heels through our yard while we waited for Phil to come out of the house with his jar.

"Won't you be chilly without a jacket?" Anne called.

I shook my head, and later, during the stroll through base, I kept to the patches of sun so she wouldn't catch me shivering. Phil's jar of pennies clanged each time he took a step. He kept perfect beat.

"Come on, Tillie. Keep up," Dad said.

I zigzagged behind them. Unless I watched my feet, I couldn't walk a straight line.

We passed the movie house, the bomb-proof buildings you couldn't enter without ID, the enormous hangars, and runways that reflected so much sun you had to shield your eyes.

I had always felt pleased with how well I knew my way around, and I liked the smiles and laughter I received from strangers when I went by—though I was never sure what was so funny.

We passed the playground where the kids on summer vaca-tion chased each other up the monkey bars, pumped high on the swings, and pushed the merry-go-round so fast they could barely jump on. I longed for Momma to take me there, and she had said, *Maybe one day.*

When we got to the bank, we stayed just inside the entrance as my brother got in line between the velvet ropes, never once touching them, as I would have. I tried to catch his attention so I could remind him to get me a lollipop, but he kept his eye on his favorite teller. Even if all the other tellers were free, he'd wait in line to see the one person on base who still treated him like a kid.

"Should I be concerned about you, Roy?"

I turned my head toward Anne, who put her hand on Dad's wrist and then promptly removed it.

"There are some problems right now," he told her. "But things will get better once we move."

"I'm sorry. It's not my business," she said. "Only if you want it to be."

I heard the sound of pennies being poured from a jar, and knew Phil was now at the window. He stood with his chin against the counter. The teller held up one pointer finger as if he were about to sneeze, and after a dramatic lead up, he did sneeze, and a silver dollar fell out of his nose. He did this again and again until Phil's shoulders jiggled because this stranger would keep it up until he made my brother laugh.

"That's awfully thrifty of you to save all those coins," Anne said when Phil had joined us again with his roll of silver dollars and his nearly empty jar. Then, laughing, she added, "But you might want to rinse them in some hot, soapy water when you get home."

I pushed between them, trying to see if he was holding anything besides coins. "Did you get me a lollipop?" I asked.

He moved the roll of silver dollars to his other hand and dug in his pocket. "Here. You can have mine."

It was green, the flavor neither of us liked, but with no other flavors to choose from, it would do. I took it and tore the wrapper off with my teeth.

"You're a real gentleman," Anne told him, a compliment I was certain she meant as a scolding for me. I thrust the lollipop into my mouth and danced out the door and along the curb of the sidewalk.

"Be careful, Tillie," she said. "You'll choke."

"No I won't. Watch." I hopped on one foot to prove my point, but Dad swatted me on the behind, and we headed for home.

We walked past the perfect rectangle houses, stopped at driveways if cars pulled in, and saluted the men who stepped out of them. Soon, our blue door came into view and I wondered, as I often did when I approached my house, what I'd find inside.

I half expected to smell mushroom chicken cooking, but when we opened the door, there was only the same odor that seemed to bother Anne so much, although this time, rather than scrunching up her nose, she had the most unusual grin on her face, as if she had just won a game of some sort.

Momma had spruced up. Her hair was combed and she'd finished putting on her makeup. She wore a pretty pair of heels and had squirted herself with perfume, though it was clear she hadn't had time for a bath.

"Welcome back," she said. Her voice sounded put on, as if she were pretending to be one of the officers' wives she disliked so much. She tucked her hair behind one ear, and once we were all inside she said, "I'll go start dinner."

"Would you like me to help you put something together, Mrs. Harris?" Anne asked.

Momma shook her head, shooing us with her hand, but Dad followed her into the kitchen.

"Here," he said, and pulled a pan from the lower cupboard. "Let me cook some spaghetti."

"I can *do* it," Momma said, then whispered, "I can make spaghetti. Please."

"Let me help you," he said.

"Just sit down in the living room." She stared directly into his eyes as she took the pan from him. Then suddenly smiling at the rest of us she added, "Everyone relax in the other room. I'll call you when dinner's ready."

Phil went first and sat tall and stiff on the couch. I slouched beside him, swinging my legs, staring at the room, stripped of its life—all but the dolls Momma had made, which peeked their heads out of the cardboard boxes.

"I'm happy to give you a hand," Anne shouted occasionally toward Momma, but there was no answer—only the sound of her lighting the gas burner and filling the pan with water.

"I'm sorry for causing such trouble," she said to Dad.

"It's no trouble," he said, but when I listened closely I could hear Momma sniffling in the other room.

Dad searched again for his briefcase, making more noise than necessary to drown out the sounds coming from the kitchen. When he finally found it right beside the chair he'd been sitting in, Anne smiled, trying not to laugh.

I kicked my feet to pass the time. Usually when Momma made dinner, we just found something at our placemats—a bowl of cereal, a sandwich and chips, an avocado sliced in half with dressing where the seed had been. This would be something if she cooked a hot meal and sat down to eat with us.

Phil sat expressionless while Dad wound his watch, and

Anne studied something on her blouse. "I have to learn not to wear light colors," she said, dusting her hand across her bosom. "The red clay gets on everything."

It seemed for a moment that my father and his secretary were the only two in the room. Their smiles were long and strange, my father's face an embarrassing pink.

"Dinner." Momma's voice broke as she spoke this single word, standing in the center of the room with oven mitts over her hands and her shoulders trembling.

We sat at the table as Momma brought out the pan of spaghetti, then a jar of sauce, which she opened and poured in without stirring. We served ourselves, and Anne asked, "Would you like me to make a side of vegetables or some garlic bread for—? Mrs. Harris, are you all right?"

Momma sat quivering and staring at her empty plate. This was no longer something that alarmed our family—Momma not eating or speaking. Sometimes she tapped her nail over and over on the edge of the table, no sign of life in her eyes, and you knew the reason she didn't answer you was because she wasn't there.

Dad stared at Phil and me and mouthed, *Eat.*

We tried to hurry the spaghetti into our mouths, but it was slippery, falling off my fork, slapping Phil's cheeks. Anne, with a worried expression on her face, did the same. We didn't bother with drinks, and no one asked for seconds.

When we had finished eating—in fact, at the very moment when Phil, always the slowest eater, put the last forkful in his mouth—Anne rose cautiously.

"Well," she said, straightening her skirt. "I know you have a busy day tomorrow. I should take those papers I came for and get on my way."

Momma stood too, collecting the dishes and bringing them to the sink, while Dad, red-faced, walked with Anne into the other room. He unlocked his briefcase and passed her documents with the word CONFIDENTIAL stamped in big red letters.

I ran to be with Momma, tugging on her dress and telling her, "I'm ready for bed."

"Bed? But it's still light outside."

"Please, Momma. We'll read."

She gave me a tired smile. "If I tuck you in now, you'll wake up in the middle of the night."

"I won't. I'll sleep the whole way through."

"I don't know, Bear."

"Please. I want to know what will happen in the book. Then I'll go right to sleep and I'll stay asleep."

"Okay. If you promise. The sooner this day ends, the better."

"I promise. I'll wait in my room for our story."

"All right," she said, putting the kettle on. Her voice was tired. "I'll be in as soon as I can." And she reached into the cupboard for my ruby cup.

Before I got to my room, I could hear all three grown-ups in the living room—the hard-to-believe thank yous for dinner, talk about the busy day ahead, hopes that Momma would soon feel better, and finally, the latch closing on our front door. As I waited for Momma, I skated in sock feet over the shiny wood floor, brushing my hand against the walls. In the kitchen, there was the sound of plates clanking into the dish rack and my parents arguing in low voices. My father said, "Pull it together," and I moved to the far end of my room until their voices disappeared. There, I opened the lid to my music box so the plastic ballerina would turn in circles with me.

When I heard the whistle of the kettle, I hurried into

my nightgown and under the covers. Momma took slow steps into my room and handed me my drink carefully so it wouldn't spill. Then she sat, slumped, on the edge of the bed, her hands shaking. "I'll just sit here tonight," she said. "We'll read tomorrow."

Alice in Wonderland was turned upside down on the nightstand. We had one chapter to go. I chattered about Alice and ballerinas and a new hole in my sock. She placed her hand on me. "Sh. Enough talking now." She was crying, and when her tears fell on me, she gently rubbed them into my skin. "It's been a long day, Bear," she said.

She handed me the cup filled with bright orange liquid, an ice cube melting inside of it. I felt the rough edge where the handle had broken off, listened to the ice squeak and crack as I took tiny sips. My eyes never left her.

She sat there, trembling, trying to keep it in, but soon covered her face with her hands and sobbed. Mascara and the ivory base she used to coat her skin melted down her face and between her fingers.

"Don't cry," I said out of habit, though I loved how she was so full of emotion. She was like the beautiful women who cried on the movie screen, the scenes you remembered even after you forgot what the rest of the movie was about.

The drink had cooled enough to finish it in one last swallow. "There you go," Momma said, taking the cup and resting her hand on me.

"This is my favorite part of the day," I said, not sure if I had spoken aloud or not.

I could feel the numbness I knew as sleep moving through my limbs. Momma cradled my head in her hand and lowered me to the pillow. I closed my eyes and felt her tears again. I pretended we were at the playground together, lying on our backs on the merry-go-round, turning and turning in the rain.

I woke to the sound of stomping and banging. My head felt heavy on my pillow, but I pulled myself up and stumbled to the bedroom door. Phil was listening from the hallway.

"What's happening?" I asked. My tongue felt swollen and my words were slurred.

"I'm not sure. The doorbell rang while we were eating breakfast, and Dad jumped up and started rushing around the house."

"It's morning?" I felt woozy and held on to the wall.

Before he could answer, Dad barreled down the hallway, carrying a suitcase, which bumped against the wall every few steps. I moved out of the way as he turned into my room.

Another wave of dizziness caused me to bend over and place my hands on my knees, but he didn't stop to check on me. Instead, he began taking clothes out of my dresser drawers.

"Dad?"

He handed me my sneakers. "Here, put your shoes on."

I was too tired to grip them and they fell to the floor. "What's happening?" I asked.

"Anne is here to pick you up. She's going to take you back to her place for a bit."

I rubbed my face, trying to wake up. "I don't understand."

"You'll stay with her for a few days while we pack up the U-Haul and drive it to the new house."

"You're moving without me?"

"It's a very long drive, Tillie. You'll join us as soon as we have the new house set up."

I held to the side of my costume box, overstuffed with tutus and cowboy vests and dress-up shoes. I leaned over it like I might get sick. "Dad, I don't want to go with her."

"Don't argue with me." He rolled the clothes the way he rolled socks so he could pack tight without anything wrinkling. "Hurry up, now. Anne is waiting out front."

"But Dad."

"Put your shoes on."

I reached for the closest pair from inside the costume box, slammed them to the floor, and stomped my feet inside. "I won't go!" I shouted, then turned to Phil and said, "Tell him we won't go!"

Phil, who never raised his voice or questioned what he was told, looked stunned and said, "Dad? I'd rather stay here, too."

"She's only taking Tillie," Dad told him. "I can use your help."

I felt the same sort of shock as if waking from a bad dream where nothing made sense. All I knew was I needed Momma and bolted out of the room, tripping most of the way until I'd pushed open her bedroom door, letting the light shine in from the hallway.

There were serving trays, pill bottles, half-empty glasses on the end table. On the far side of the bed, the covers rose and fell. I stepped into the room and slowly closed the door so Dad wouldn't hear it latch.

I tiptoed closer and leaned against the bedspread. "Momma? Tell him I won't go. I want to stay with you." I crawled under the warm, sour-smelling covers and pressed my back against her belly. "I want to stay with you, Momma," I said, tucking my hands under my chin.

She did not move. Outside, I heard Anne's car start up, as Dad stomped through the house. I pressed closer and slid my legs under the covers, wincing when I heard the blast of a horn.

"That's her honking. Please don't let her take me. I don't want to go, Momma. Momma?"

All of the muscles from my throat down to my stomach tightened as I waited there, staring at the serving tray with the fold-down legs. My eyes followed the tray's gold edge back and forth until it became two blurry lines. Then, very slowly, Momma's arm, blue white and freckled, rose from the covers and she closed her fingers around my hands and warmed them. "I don't deserve you, Bear," she said.

As she wrapped her arm around me tight, I started to cry. It came in waves and it came with no sound. Nothing, not my father or even my long-gone mother who used to twirl in circles and smell of gardenia lotion, could have comforted me more. I wanted to fall asleep there. Her arm was heavy, but until it hurt, I wasn't going to move.

There was a moment of peace, a slippery sense of calm in which I believed that Dad's secretary would leave and our family would load the U-Haul and drive away together. I wanted to believe in this, though I heard Dad calling for me. I could hear him in the hallway, and I braced myself for the sound of his hand on the doorknob. There it was.

The door opened and he entered the room. His shadow approached the bed, and I quickly closed my eyes, believing he would not want to wake me. I tried my best not to move, sure he could hear every swallow. And when I felt his hand on my shoulder, I flinched.

"Come on, Tillie. It's time."

I kept my eyes closed, my heart wild and thumping.

"Please don't be difficult now," Dad said and started to pull me away from her.

"Bear," Momma whispered into my ear with dark and powerful breath. "My little Bear." Her arm stayed limp around me.

I grabbed hold of the mattress, kicking my legs and arching backward when he tried to lift me, but his grip was strong. He carried me, thrashing, down the hallway past my silent brother and out the front door. Anne's white hatchback, stained by the red dust, was waiting at the end of our walkway with the engine running and the passenger door open. Dad wrestled me in beside his secretary.

"I won't go!" I screamed.

He tried to buckle me in, but I flailed around so much he couldn't get close. I didn't realize he'd shut the door until I tried to launch myself back out of the car and hit my head against the window. But it was when he held his hand up to say good-bye that the panic started. My teeth chattered and my legs began to tremble as if I was only then awake enough to understand what was happening.

"Tillie, you have to settle down," Anne said, as if I could.

"I want my mother!" I yelled, but my voice sounded far away, drowned out by the sound of blood pumping in my ears. I felt the thud of my suitcase landing in the trunk, and lunged for the handle. She slapped my hand away, and we began to drive.

Sobbing and dazed, I turned around in my seat and stared out the back window at the house I'd never see again. It got smaller and smaller, and then Momma rushed across the lawn in yesterday's clothes, waving her arms desperately over her head.

"Let me out!" I shrieked. I couldn't catch my breath.

Anne kept her eyes on the road, accelerating as Momma called my name again and again before she fell to her knees in the grass.

4

❧

Teacups and Violins

I OPENED MY EYES TO see flat, beige land speeding by, and sat up suddenly, feeling the seatbelt across my lap.

"Awake already?" Anne asked.

Seeing her behind the steering wheel, I remembered that I was in her car, remembered how she slapped my hand when I tried to run back to Momma.

"You were out so quickly. I thought you might sleep the whole way."

Everything ached—my back and neck from leaning away from her, my head and throat from screaming. My feet, which didn't touch the floor, felt tingly from hanging still for so long.

"I'm only about thirty minutes off base," she said. "But it feels like we're way out in the country, doesn't it?"

I kept my face against the glass, watching the heat rise and blur the red earth and purple mountains. Closing my eyes again, I thought of Momma—how she'd held me till the very moment Dad yanked me from her arms and shoved me into the car. I thought of her running after me with her hands in the air, and wondered if Dad had brought her back inside or if she was still there on the lawn. I cried again, but softly this time, so my head wouldn't pound.

Finally we pulled into the parking lot of a grocery store. "Hungry?" she asked, tapping my leg. I wasn't in the mood to be touched.

I hadn't had breakfast and just the mention of food made my stomach rumble. Still, I didn't speak as she pulled the key from the ignition. I simply got out of the car and stood beside it. Anne slammed the door with surprising force, and I followed her inside, keeping several paces behind her.

"Who've you got there, Anne?" a woman wearing a store apron asked.

"Long story," she answered. "I've got her for the week while her father relocates."

"Her dad's that big shot you work for?"

She nodded, then turning toward me, noticed for the first time that I was still in my nightgown. I fixed the strap on one of the high-heeled sandals I'd taken from my costume box. The shoes were a good deal larger than my feet, making my steps unsteady.

"Oh, dear," Anne said. "We'll have to make this quick. This is not exactly proper dress for grocery shopping."

I stood still, hands hanging loose at my sides.

"Look at those red eyes," she said. "They must sting." She sighed and tried to put her hand on the side of my face but I ducked.

"Okay. I get it," she said. "We'll just get on with the shopping." She began to push the cart down the aisle. "I suppose you should know I don't believe in junk food."

This was the dumbest thing I'd ever heard. How could she not *believe* in junk food? It was right there on both sides of us, real as could be: cheese that sprayed out of aerosol cans, cereals that turned the milk pink, and chocolate donuts like Momma bought us.

Thinking of her right then gave me a sharp pain in the chest.

"Will you eat fruit leather?" Anne asked.

"No."

Her shoulders hunched and she took a deep breath. "Well, you can try it, at least," she said and dropped a package into the cart.

A man with a handlebar mustache wheeled beside us, and said, "I heard about your new addition."

"Very funny, Walter."

"Can't wait to hear how *this* happened," he said.

"Well, Tillie's father is very busy working on a space-based navigation system for the Department of Defense, and she's going to stay with me while he unpacks and gets settled in at the Pentagon."

"Oh, so this is the colonel's kid," he said. "But why isn't she with her mother?"

"Her mother is . . ." and suddenly whispering, she said, "troubled."

He made a not-too-subtle cuckoo sign by his temple, and Anne nodded, putting her finger to her lips.

"You don't even know her," I said in the same quiet voice they'd been using, and then I swept my arm across a shelf, causing two cans of tuna to hit the floor.

"Careful now," the man said, staring at me with one eyebrow raised. I stared back at him and did not, would not, make a move to pick up the cans.

Anne was bent over a bin of cheap sneakers, oblivious to our staring match. "What size shoes do you wear?" she asked.

"I won't wear those," I said.

"She's spitting mad," Walter said.

"Like a cat," Anne said.

"A bear," I said.

"What?"

"My mother calls me Bear."

"Yes, but you're not one," Anne said. "You are not a bear. You are a young lady."

"Not yet, she's not," Walter laughed. He rolled his cart ahead of ours, and still laughing, said, "Good luck to you, Anne."

"We'll manage just fine," she called over her shoulder.

When we got back in the car, the windows were so coated in red dust it felt dark and cramped inside. Anne promised the ride to her house would be short, so I sat ready to get out, not even touching my back to the seat as we passed cactus, sage brush, more of the mountain I knew, and the colorful houses of her neighborhood. The driveway led to a yellow cottage, and when she got out of the car, she once again slammed the door with surprising force, locking the seatbelt on the outside of it. We walked into what looked like a hotel room—carpet striped by the vacuum cleaner, artwork that matched both the sofa fabric and the wallpaper. Then there were the violins, barely notice-able at first, like music in a waiting room, but soon it was what you noticed above all else.

I walked over to the couch. "Just a minute," she said abruptly.

A moment later she returned with a towel and laid it down, indicating where I was now allowed to sit. I decided to stand.

"I'm sorry," she said, finally, as if only just noticing what a weird idea it was. "It's expensive fabric. My house isn't very well equipped for children." She walked to the kitchen, her floral dress blending with the wallpaper as she reached to a shelf of fruit-themed teacups and saucers. "I want you to be happy here, Tillie. Juice?"

Though I hadn't answered, she poured something brown into a teacup painted with tiny strawberries and set it at the kitchen table. I stayed where I was.

"Would you like to play backgammon?" she asked.

I shook my head.

"I'm afraid there aren't any girls your age nearby," she said.

"Doesn't matter."

I opened the sliding glass doors to the backyard.

"Maybe get dressed first?" she suggested, but I was already outside.

There was nothing in the backyard but a wilted garden and some chairs stacked in a corner of the patio. Most of the yard was grass—dry as straw—that poked my ankles. There was no reason to stay outside except for it was not *inside*, where Anne sprayed Windex on the glass to wipe away my fingerprints.

My brother would have thought up a good way to spend the time. Before he got so serious, before everyone became so fond of calling him the young soldier, he was a kid with a lucky rabbit's foot attached to his belt and was the best at inventing games just when you thought there was nothing to play. We made our own ink by pounding flowers with rocks, adding water, and stirring with our fingers. We danced to the cardboard records we cut off the backs of cereal boxes. And sometimes we pretended to steal Dad's briefcase full of top secret work. We'd blow things up, then run back to invent bigger weapons as we needed them.

Without my brother, I only thought of things like how hot I

was and how much I didn't like to be tickled, even by grass. I stood on that blazing patio for as long as I could stand it until, defeated, I went back through the sliding glass doors and sat on the towel.

I stared forward at the TV set, though it was not on. We didn't have a TV at home—not one that worked anyway. Dad once bought a kit, and successfully built the heavy wooden frame, but the electronics proved more difficult. The picture was snowy, and stripes moved up the screen, then started again from the bottom. After several attempts at taking the tubes and coils out and putting them back in again, he declared the kit "defective" and the frame became just another place to set things on in the living room. Some of the fathers in our neighborhood liked to tease him for this, saying, "How are you supposed to shoot a missile into space if you can't put a television kit together?"

Anne, for the longest time, tidied the already-clean room, humming along to the violins and arranging a collection of painted thimbles into a circle. When the last thimble was in place, she said, "I'm trying to do your father a favor. I wish you wouldn't take it out on me."

I don't think she expected me to answer. It seemed that she just needed to say it out loud. She turned on the TV, and even before an image appeared on the screen, I heard a couple having a painfully slow conversation with an organ playing in the background. The picture of the fancy living room that emerged was neither black-and-white nor color, but a mix of various grays with occasional pink and green bands running through it. Even so, I was glad to pretend I was in that living room instead of Anne's. But what I enjoyed the most were the commercials that showed familiar scenes from the air force base—the hangars, the uniforms, and close-ups of the American flag.

Later that night, she remembered my suitcase in the trunk of her car and brought my things to the bedroom where I'd stay for the week. Though I was already dressed for bed, she insisted I change into clean pajamas.

When she left me alone in the room, I opened my suitcase to find Dad had packed two butterscotch candies and the *World Book Encyclopedia* for the letter D with photos of every breed of dog. Beneath the book were clothes that smelled like home. I simply tipped my face into them, holding my stomach tight as I bent over, though it did nothing for the ache.

By the time Anne came back to check on me, I was under the covers with an armful of clothes, and when she leaned down to say good night, I pretended to be asleep.

My mind was full of images that had piled up through the day: miles of cactus; painted thimbles, perfectly spaced; the man making a cuckoo sign in the grocery store; the gray American flag with green and pink horizontal stripes. One week. One long week, but then I would be back with my family.

I tried to imagine Momma beside me, opening *Alice in Wonderland* to the last chapter while I touched the remaining rubies and the spots of glue where the jewels had once been attached to the cup. I tried to feel the warm, bitter drink moving down into my limbs, tried to feel her right there, staying at the edge of the bed until I fell asleep. But when I shut my eyes, I saw us screaming each other's names, and getting farther and farther apart.

⚘

IT WAS THE SUDDENNESS of leaving Momma that had upset me the most—the shock of being warm and sleepy one moment and then confused and hurried the next. When I woke up in the strange bed, I had that same feeling of disorientation, of being wrenched from all that was familiar and known.

My neck was sore and there were creases on my arms and legs from the clothes I'd tucked under the covers. I opened the door and headed into the violins.

"You're not an easy sleeper," she said over her teacup, taking a different vitamin with every sip.

"Momma usually tucks me in."

"Well, *I* can certainly tuck you in."

I shook my head so violently I could feel the beginning of another headache.

"Okay. It's okay. Here, sit down for breakfast."

She set a steaming bowl in front of me, something lumpy like tapioca but without the sweet smell. When she went to the sink to wash her hands, I unwrapped both butterscotch candies my dad had given me and put them in my mouth.

"Do you want something hot to drink?" she asked, picking up her teacup and taking another sip.

"Muh-uh," I said, trying to keep the candy in my mouth without clicking them against my teeth.

"Oh, you tried the porridge. Do you like it? I added dates and walnuts."

She peeled a tangerine at the sink, and popped one section after another into her mouth. "Your family will probably arrive at the new house sometime tonight," she said. "I'm sure we'll hear from them any day now."

She smiled, finishing the last piece of fruit, then ran the peel down the garbage disposal. Between this news and the effect of the candy, my spirits improved so much that I crept up behind and tapped her. Startled, she flicked the switch and the noise of the disposal stopped.

"Sometimes, don't you just want to put your arm down there and chop it up?" I asked her, giggling.

"Tillie! Why would you say such a thing? That's a horrible thought!"

For the rest of the morning, I sat on the towel, embarrassed, fuming, and waiting for the phone to ring.

The next day I woke up feeling sorry for myself. I was out of candy and not looking forward to eating breakfast that was *good for me*. When I left the bedroom, I found Anne pulling clothes from a hamper, folding them and setting them on the coffee table.

"Are those *my* clothes?" I asked.

"I found them under your covers when I checked on you last night."

"They're my property!"

"Tillie, Tillie, it's okay. I just washed them."

But I had already grabbed an armful as I ran back to the bedroom. When I brought them to my nose, there was no smell of home or Momma. They just smelled like detergent. Not even *our* detergent. I squeezed my fists around the ruined clothes and yelled while I threw them.

When Anne came to my room, I was facedown on the bed with my arms out to the sides, furious that Phil was, at that moment, enjoying a long drive with Momma. I imagined him riding behind her, listening to her sing. When they reached the new house, he would be the first to help Momma decorate with books and colorful pillows and the dolls with button eyes.

"Tillie, I was trying to help. I didn't mean to upset you, but you will not behave like this here." She put her hand on my shoulder. "Are you listening to me?"

"When can I go home?" I whined into the covers.

"Just a few more days," she said. "I talked to your father last night."

I turned over to hear better, and also to move her hand off of me.

"You have a great big house with a beautiful yard and a swimming pool in back. The school's just down the street so you can walk or ride your bike to it."

As she spoke, she touched my hair, combing it with her fingers until I covered my head with my hands.

≈≈≈

THE DAYS THAT FOLLOWED were torture. I wasn't used to such calm—Anne's soft voice, her quiet tidying, the droning violins. Even when the music swelled—the one part I liked because it snuck up on you, bold and almost spooky—that was when she lowered the volume. Each day, Anne moved from room to room with a cup of tea, as I moved from room to room with my encyclopedia. After a while, one day was so much like the other, it was hard to know whether I was any closer to seeing Momma.

I missed her—the loud music, the surprise of her moods, the colorful bracelets, even the tears. I missed jumping on the couch and the quick pickup from a package of Ho Hos. I missed all the time on my own when I gave myself dares, like slipping my tongue through the slats of the electric fan or sticking my arm down a hole in the ground, wondering if I'd find the animal that made it.

When she came to my room to call me for breakfast, I asked, "How much longer? Should I pack yet?"

Anne's face looked very serious, and she was slow to answer. "Your father needs more time," she finally said. "You'll need to stay another week."

"No!" I slapped at her, one hand after another, and she leaned backward so I couldn't reach.

"It's not that long," she said, grabbing my wrists. "It's really not that long."

"Stop saying that!" I said, wanting to hit again, but even though she'd let go of me, my arms felt too heavy.

"It's just the way it has to be," she said.

And something in her voice and in my own reaction not to shrug away her hand when she placed it on my back gave me the strongest feeling that things were not right at home.

"It's complicated," said Anne, who'd been talking the whole time, as if, by not giving me space to think or reply, I might forget I was upset. "There are so many unexpected things when you move. You have to get all the utilities turned on. There are broken things that need to be fixed. There's just an awful lot to coordinate." When I started to shiver all over, she paused. "Oh, Tillie, I know you're disappointed."

And she was, too. I could see, every day, that she wanted her house back. She wanted the towel off the couch, wanted to watch her regular shows on TV without my impatient groans, wanted to have back whatever her life had been before I'd landed in the middle of it. When I eavesdropped on calls, hoping to hear news from home, I learned of the friends she wanted to see, of the work she promised to catch up on "as soon as she's gone."

She did try to make my stay more bearable—cutting sandwiches into triangles, adding bubbles to my baths, and offering to fix my hair. At night, she tried to pull the covers over my shoulders, but I pulled them back off and turned over. Anne was not what I wanted.

❧❧

5

Things Beginning with the Letter D

I SAT ON THE TOWEL, bored and uncomfortable, listening to the rain and shifting from one position to another. "Well, there's a fine young lady," Anne said when I'd stopped moving.

Horrified, I noticed in all my squirming I'd settled on a completely prissy and accidental pose—legs crossed, hands folded in my lap. I groaned, flopping onto my stomach.

"Feet off the couch, please."

Two weeks was longer than I'd ever imagined. I moved my feet to the side but stayed facedown until Anne tapped my shoulder. "I know it's pouring outside," she said, "but we need to go to the store. I've run out of tea, and we could do with some more fresh fruit."

When she opened the door, the rain came into the house. "We'll have to really run," she said, giggling, as if there were something hilarious or daring about getting wet. She darted out to the car, and with a scowl on my face, I grabbed my book and sauntered after her, letting the rain soak my scalp and run down the sides of my face.

"Shall I go get you a towel?" she asked after I got in.

I didn't answer, just closed the door and leaned against it.

"You must be freezing," she said, looking at me in my shorts and crocheted poncho. "Are you sure you don't want to dress in long pants or borrow a windbreaker?

My answer was to carefully turn a wet page of my book so it wouldn't tear.

She gave a frustrated sigh and stepped on the gas. The storm clouds made the car dark for reading, but I practically knew the best pages by heart. I'd chosen my favorite dogs (the field spaniel and the wirehaired pointing griffon) and learned to be interested in many things beginning with the letter D—Darwin, deadly nightshade, Delhi, digestive system, Dionysus, Dracula, dulcimer, and dysentery.

The wipers swished mud back and forth on the windshield, and now and then Anne rubbed the fog off the window with her sleeve. By the time we pulled in front of the grocery store, the packed dirt that served as a parking lot was like a shallow lake. When I stepped out of the car, my poncho blew straight out to one side.

"Well, there's Anne's little buddy," the storekeeper said when we walked in together.

"I told her it's an awfully chilly day for shorts," Anne said. "But she's a stubborn one."

"Takes one to know one," the storekeeper said, laughing. "Come on, dear. You come with me."

I walked behind her, trying not to step on her heels.

"I'm surprised you're still here," she said.

I shrugged.

She handed me a store apron. "Here. Put this on. You can help me work while Anne shops."

I slipped it over my head, and it fell to my ankles.

"Follow me," she said. "Just do whatever I do."

And I followed her walk exactly, and stopped when she stopped. She smiled, standing near the cash register, and pointed to the bagging area, where I was to stand.

"On a day like today, it's going to be a lot of standing around," she said.

I laughed and tried to stand professionally as she did, hands on hips, chest out like a bird, listening to the piped-in music and the squeak of Anne's shopping cart going from aisle to aisle.

"I see you like to dance," she said.

I hadn't realized I'd been moving to the music, and was about to freeze in place when she smiled and danced a little on her side of the counter. I smiled back, and spun the way the Pips often spun behind Gladys Knight. She knew the same move, and by the time Anne reached the checkout, we had a whole routine.

"I suppose I owe you for watching her," Anne said.

"Not at all. I enjoyed every moment."

Anne's lips tightened. "Well, she's not like this when I take her home. I try so hard but she's . . . not an easy girl."

She slapped the groceries down on the checkout table, one after another. Outside, the rain came down harder, washing against the windows.

When the storekeeper had packed the groceries into two bags, she said, "How 'bout Tillie stays with me while you pull the car up to the front?" And when Anne had left the store, she reached across the counter to smooth my hair, saying, "Thatta girl."

My knees and shoulders began to tremble. My mother was the last person to use those words, and they stung me. I walked to the window, unable to see past the rain, and poked my fingers through the holes of my poncho.

I hadn't let myself feel it yet, not really, but once I was in the car, thinking of the words again, I imagined it was Momma saying them to me, her bracelets jingling as she reached to caress the top of my head. As we drove slowly through the wet and muddy streets, I curled against the window, knees tucked into my chest, needing her.

"You're shivering," Anne said. "I wish you'd worn long pants and a windbreaker."

I kicked the glove compartment hard with my foot, and it popped open, spilling papers and a box of Kleenex. My toe hurt.

The only sound Anne made was one of her sighs, so confident that I was the one being unreasonable. I could practically hear my father telling me to be nice, to just sit there in my damp poncho and not complain of the itch. As the small yellow house came into view, I tried to prepare myself for the violins and for Anne with her teacup and her prissy laughter, but I couldn't do it any longer. When Anne got out of the car, I slid over to her side and stuck my leg out her door. I closed my eyes tight while she slammed it shut.

6

❧

Knots

M Y SHRIEKING SURPRISED EVEN me. There were sharp pains and throbbing pains, and more nerve endings in my calf than I could have ever guessed. It felt good to scream; it felt good to be able to point to what hurt and call for Momma and to see Anne feel responsible for all of it. I hung in her arms, bawling, while she tried, but failed, to lift me inside.

"Here, you'll have to walk," she said. "Lean on me."

I simply crumbled onto the porch. "Is it broken?" I sobbed. I hoped so; I'd always wanted a cast.

"Stay here," she said. "I'll be back with some ice."

My leg swelled and turned from pinks to grays before my eyes. After what seemed a very long time, Anne came back with ice wrapped in a t-shirt. For once, she could soothe me.

"A doctor's on the way," she said, sitting close and pressing the ice where the car door had left its mark.

Each time I started to cry again, she pressed down on the ice while I shouted, "I want to go home!"

I expected an ambulance with a siren and flashing lights, but when the plain white pickup pulled into the driveway, it was Walter with the handlebar mustache who got out.

"I hear I might have to amputate, so let me have a look. My saw's in the truck if I need it." I yelped when he tried to bend and straighten my leg. "What happened?" he asked Anne over his shoulder.

"She just put her leg out while I was closing the door."

"No wonder her mother went crazy."

"Sh," she said.

I screamed while he pressed along the bone. "I can't think over the noise, Tillie," he said, as if daring me to make another sound while he worked his way to my ankle. "Nope. Not broken."

"But should we take her to the hospital?" Anne asked. "What about all the pain she's having?"

"She'll have a bruise," he said. "That's all. What we have here are some good hysterics."

"Like her mother," she whispered, but not quietly enough.

"My prescription," Walter said. "No coddling. You need me to write this down for you?"

Anne chuckled and then coughed a little to cover it up.

I realized at that moment that my leg didn't hurt nearly enough to keep me there. I stood up slowly and, glad the rain had slowed to a drizzle, trudged through the yard toward a field of weeds and cactus. I was several feet away before I remembered to limp.

"Careful on that leg, Tillie," Walter called after me, laughing. "Don't make me get out my saw."

I found a path and continued into the field, the tall weeds itching my legs and mud sticking so thick to the bottom of my sandals it felt heavy to lift my feet. I kept going. I found a hole in the ground and stomped by it.

"Watch it. Something might crawl out of that hole and bite you."

I spun around and there was the doctor, standing not a foot away. "I'd say that leg's better already," he said.

I stomped my foot near the hole again, but suddenly nervous, I took a step back and then another.

He laughed, pleased that he'd frightened me, and then said, "Have a seat, Tillie."

"No. It's wet."

"You're already soaked. Sit down so we can have a little chat."

I sat on one boulder and he sat across from me on another, shaking a cigarette from a pack.

"Those things are bad for you."

"Lots of things are bad for you. Bratty little girls, for instance." He put the cigarette into his mustache and lit it. "Anne's too nice to say anything," he said. "So I'll say it for her. You've been a burden. I'd have sent you packing a long time ago, but Anne took care of you just as she promised your father she would. She's made a real sacrifice to give you a comfortable place to stay, and you've been nothing but ungrateful."

He stretched out his leg so it reached the rock I was sitting on and kept the other bent, with his arm resting on his knee.

"Don't you have anything to say?" he asked.

"You didn't ask me a question."

He dragged on his cigarette, then tapped it against his boot so the ash hit the rock. "You know what I like about you, Tillie? There's still hope for you. You could march back to the house and tell your host you've been a selfish and unappreciative guest." He handed me his cigarette.

I slid my hands under my legs. "I'm not allowed."

"Next time, maybe." His hand massaged the toe of his boot and then moved to his ankle, where he tucked his fingertips under the cuff of his jeans. I breathed in the smoke, thinking I might like the taste. "So sometime between now and tomorrow when you're on that plane home," he finally said, taking another drag, "I want you to think long and hard about how to be less of a brat."

"I'm going home tomorrow?"

"Is that the only thing you heard?"

"The only thing that matters."

"I'm not sure why I said there was hope for you."

"I'm really going home?"

"You're a terrible, rotten listener, Tillie."

I beamed at him, suddenly wishing I'd taken the cigarette.

❧

BY MORNING THE MUD had baked into a hard crust. I walked through the tire tracks, my mind already wandering through the new house, only guessing how it might look with our decorations—the dolls and wall hangings—and Momma playing the music we liked, turned up so loud I'd feel it thumping inside of me.

"You're up early," Anne said, coming out on to the porch. "And already dressed, I see. But I worry you'll be cold on the plane." She looked at my legs, but mostly at the bruise I knew she wanted me to cover.

"Momma made this for me," I said, smoothing my scooter skirt—a pair of shorts but with a bib across the front, where Momma had embroidered a robin.

"All right, then. But we do have to get you spruced up for your flight. Can you get this through your hair?" she asked, handing me a comb. "I don't want your father to think I didn't take good care of you."

Momma knew how to comb carefully from the bottom, and since she'd stopped getting out of bed, Dad had taken over— the braids not quite tight enough, the elastic tangling at the ends. I'd never tried to fix my hair myself. I took the comb, and right away, it got caught in the knots.

"Let me try," she said, but I never felt the comb touch my head, as if she just stood there staring at my hair, not at all sure where to start. After a while, she simply went inside without saying a word. I was glad to have my last moments there to myself, feeling the sun heat the top of my head and imagining how it would be to run to Momma.

"Hold still," Anne said.

She'd come back out of the house with a pair of scissors. Sitting behind me, her legs squeezed round my shoulders, she began to snip. I sat frozen in place as three- and four-inch pieces fell around me. When she was done, she combed through the snarls with no problem, and I felt my face heat up.

"Much better," she said.

I grabbed my stomach and bent over.

"Tillie. Tillie, what's wrong?"

"You did it because you don't like me," I said, my face pressed into my knees.

"What would give you an idea like that?" she asked.

"The doctor told me."

"Walter told you that?"

I nodded and felt the tears and snot against my legs.

"Well, it's just not true," she said. "Come on. Sit up."

I sat up but kept my face turned away from her, embarrassed that I cared what she thought.

"Your hair looks very pretty," she said. "Let's go inside so you can see for yourself."

There was a long mirror on the bathroom door, and she stood behind me, tucking my hair behind my ears. "See? Didn't I tell you?"

"I look like a boy," I said.

"Well, I don't think you do at all," she said. "Actually, I was thinking we have the same haircut now. I hope you're not telling me *I* look like a boy."

I pouted but kept staring into the mirror because it was an impressive pout. I stuck out my chin a little more and said, "I just want to go home."

"You'll be home by this evening. And I hope you'll tell your father how good the food was. And how much fun you had taking bubble baths."

"I'll show him my bruise."

"Here. I have an idea," Anne said, putting her hand around my shoulder and pulling me away from the mirror. She went to the stereo and turned up the violins. Then, awkwardly, she extended her hands to me while she swayed her hips. "Come join me, Tillie. This is fun. Let's have one good dance before you go."

I stood completely still, so embarrassed for her I had to shut my eyes.

"Maybe not this trip, I guess," she said, patting me on the shoulder. "Here, let's get you packed."

"I just want to go home."

❦

THE PASSENGERS IN THE airport waiting room smiled and chuckled as I hobbled past, and I waved back at them.

"Do you want me to get your book out?" Anne asked, finding a seat.

I shook my head. Swinging my legs, clasping and unclasping my hands, I was too excited about going home. I tried pulling my hair over my shoulder, but it was too short.

"I can't wait to see Momma," I said.

She frowned ever so slightly. "I know, whatever awaits you, you'll do just fine," she said.

"I'll tell her all about my leg."

"It's just a bruise, Tillie. Remember we had a doctor check it."

A stewardess came to my seat and bent down in front of me. "Is this the young girl who will be flying today?"

Anne did all the answering while the stewardess pinned flight wings to my shirt.

"And you've never been on an airplane before, is that right?"

Several times I'd peeked inside the cockpits of fighter jets, but again, Anne answered for me and said this was my first time.

"I think you'll do just fine," the stewardess said.

"Yes. You'll do just fine," Anne agreed. She stood and hugged me into the belt of her dress. And only then, as I gasped for air and tried to pull my face away from her waist, did I understand I'd be flying alone.

When she stopped hugging me, she noticed the panic in my eyes and told me, "You can do it. You can face whatever's ahead."

Something about this statement worried me, but before I could ask what she meant, the stewardess squeezed my hand in hers, saying, "Just focus on who you'll be seeing on the other side."

My mother was on the other side, with her bright orange

hair and watery eyes, and the thought of her waiting for me helped a lot. Soon I was smiling and remembering to drag my bruised leg through the tunnel that would take us to the plane. And behind me, farther and farther away, Anne pleaded, "Stop it. Stop limping. There's nothing wrong with your leg."

❧❦❧

7

National Airport

I FELT POSITIVELY GIDDY. NO one told me flying on an airplane would be like this. I could press a button at will to
bring lovely ladies, all dressed alike, hovering about my seat.
They came with drinks and peanuts and playing cards. They
came with gum when my ears hurt.

Mostly I pressed the button to tell them how delicious the
food was, how the ginger ale bubbles had tickled my nose. I
pressed it to find out where my mother might buy the beautiful
outfits they wore. And I pressed it to ask if I was really and truly
allowed to keep the miniature suitcase they'd given me that was
round and dark blue with a little zipper along the top.

"Really? Are you sure?" I asked. Because when you unzipped
it, there was a needle and colored thread inside, and an emery
board, and best of all, a shower cap! What a marvelous way to
hide a terrible haircut.

For the entire flight, I wore that shower cap, and when we
landed, the stewardess waited with me until all the other pas-

sengers exited the plane before she walked me through the tunnel. "Keep a lookout for your mother," she told me, holding my hand and carrying my suitcase. I carried the smaller one. And though I was anxious to see Momma, we had to go slowly because of my bruised leg, which I dragged beside me, the brave girl walking, miraculously, without crutches. Out of the tunnel and into a waiting room of faces that turned my way, I looked for her orange hair.

"Right here," Dad called.

As I stood with my hands on my hips, searching the terminal, he thanked the stewardess, who smiled and said, "She's a lively one."

"Yes. We're working on that." He nodded thanks to the stewardess, and reached out to take my chin between his thumb and forefinger.

"Where's Momma?" I asked.

"Slow down. The first thing I need to do is check out this leg."

"The doctor almost sawed it off."

"I'll bet," he said. "And it can't be easy walking on a hurt leg when you have your shoes on the wrong feet."

He lifted me up on a low brick wall, beside a couple of indoor trees. "We need to give those shoes a clean while we're at it. Phil, stay with Tillie while I get some napkins."

My brother, who hadn't said hello yet, scowled at me. "Take that off your head," he said. "Don't be so stupid."

I reached up and felt the shower cap. "Anne just cut my hair without asking," I said, pulling it off. "See? She didn't even try to do a good job."

"There are bigger things to complain about," he said, his voice distant and almost chilly. "There's a lot you don't know."

"What don't I know?"

"Just that things are pretty different in the new house."

"What's so different?"

Over my shoulder he saw Dad approaching with a handful of napkins. "Dad says it's not mine to tell," he said abruptly. "You'll just have to wait."

I knew this cautious language. There was something Dad wanted Phil to keep quiet about, and I feared it had to do with Momma.

"What?" I asked again. "Tell me." But I knew to stop talking as Dad came near.

He sat beside me, put one of my feet across his lap and began rubbing the dirt off my shoes. "What did you get into?" he asked.

"Mud."

"I see that. Next time, go around the mud." He gripped my ankle and pulled off one sandal.

"Momma didn't come?"

He shook his head, pulling off the other sandal. My leg relaxed in his grip.

"Dad?"

"Uh-huh?"

"Is something wrong with her?"

"Tillie, that's a big question," he said, buckling one shoe on to the correct foot. "She needs a lot of rest these days." He took my other foot into his lap and went to work.

"I know she's tired, Dad. But why?"

"It's not for you to worry about," he said, buckling the other sandal and patting the top of it to let me know he was all done. "Tennis shoes next time."

I nodded, then showed him the bruise. He whistled as he turned my leg left and right to see the length of it, and it was impressive, much larger than the initial hurt. I giggled when he whistled again, wondering how it was I'd forgotten to miss him while I was gone.

❧❦❧

NATIONAL AIRPORT WAS A blur of men and women dashing past in their tailored suits. I held tight to Dad's hand through the terminal, and then through the enormous parking lot.

I was grateful to see our station wagon again and to have the backseat to myself, where I could curl up against something that smelled like our family. I didn't see any of the scenery during the drive to our new home—not the bridges over the Potomac River or the white monuments standing taller than all the other buildings. I didn't see us race through the beltway with the cars lit up in the dark or the sign as we entered Montgomery County, Maryland. I didn't see the outside of our suburban house before I saw the inside.

I woke up the next morning in a sleeping bag in a bare living room, horrified that I'd not stayed awake to see Momma the night before. As I crawled out of the sleeping bag, I realized I'd wet myself and paused, only a moment, with the embarrassment of greeting her in damp and smelly clothes.

I followed my nose to the kitchen, where Dad stood over the electric fryer, turning slices of french toast. "Where's Momma?" I asked, touching all the knobs and woodwork in the room, trying to feel ownership of the new house.

"Just sit now," Dad said. "Eat."

I sat down on a stool at a corner table in the kitchen, and he set breakfast in front of me. Phil sat on the other stool, concentrating hard on cutting his food into bite-sized pieces.

"Does she know it's time for breakfast?" I asked, forgetting to use my fork and picking up the bread as if it were a sandwich.

I expected her to come around the corner at any moment, but realized just then how silly it was of me to think so. She'd be in the bedroom, whichever room that was. I would stand above her until she opened her eyes, and then she would cry—first the joyous tears of our reunion, and then the buildup of tears it would take many more days to cry out, remembering the misery we'd endured by being apart.

"I think we should eat and then we'll talk," Dad said after a long pause.

"I can eat *and* talk," I said.

"Tillie." He refilled my glass of juice and picked my napkin off the floor. "Your mother will be away for a while."

"*Away?*" I rose to my feet, knocking my stool to the floor. I had waited so long to see her, and she was *away*? I took off, in search of her bedroom.

"Tillie, slow down. You're not understanding."

I ran through the first floor, opening doors and calling, "Momma!" The house felt big and spooky—like we'd moved into an empty museum. "Where is she?"

I dodged my father's arm and climbed the stairs, rushing from one room to the next. "Momma!" A part of me—the strong part, fierce with determination—was sure, absolutely sure, that I would find her. One more door, and we'd have the homecoming I'd been imagining for two weeks. Another part of me, the part that knew I had already opened the room with my parents' bed in it and found no one sleeping there, had become a dead weight I could barely drag to one more room.

"Momma," I called. But I could no longer hear my voice.

And finally I could not move, could not take another step

because as I'd searched the house, I'd been listening—not wanting to—to my father. "She's not here," he'd said. "Tillie, please stop. She's not here."

I stood in the center of a too-big room and sobbed. Dad tried to hold me but I fought him off and, alone with my whole body shuddering, understood that Momma was not there to hold me and welcome me home. She was gone.

I stayed where I was for what felt an eternity, sometimes wailing and rocking back and forth calling her name, sometimes standing stiff and staring at the blank wall. When Dad stepped back into the room, I asked in a hoarse and trembling voice, "Where is she? When is she coming home? Why can't I see her *right now?*"

He spoke softly. "You know your mother was not well. Right now, it'll just be the three of us." Phil stood behind him with his arms folded, not troubling anyone with questions or tears. Dad put his hand on my back, guiding me to the room that would become mine, a room with only a dresser, a small throw rug, and some boxes in it. He told me how much more I'd like it with new carpeting and wallpaper. I cried louder.

"I'll let you get used to your new room," he said. "If you want to open that box in the corner, go ahead."

I stood against the wall, dazed, swaying, not sure if I was hungry or full. I wanted to cry more but wasn't able to work myself up again. My hands touched the bare walls and the holes where nails had been. I touched the large cardboard boxes, opening the one marked TILLIE. There were my toys—stuffed animals, a clown whose arms and legs were elastic bands threaded through flat circles of fabric, my music box with the dancing ballerina, and a hardened chocolate donut I'd hidden inside of it.

A little deeper into the box, I found a photo, only one. We were not a family that took many pictures. Only rarely did we remember the camera. It was always for an event: a parade, a birthday, a day at the museum. And even then, when the event was over, someone would discover the camera in a pocket or sitting on the seat of a chair that was pushed, unused, under the table. Momma always liked to be the photographer, to be sure she wasn't in any photos. I thought she was so beautiful, but she was shy about how she looked in the bright sun or how she looked after her lipstick had worn off. Most times, if you tried to take her picture, she covered her face.

I was not normally allowed to touch our family pictures— Dad said I got fingerprints all over them and it made the pictures wear away—but this was one that didn't make the family album. In the photo, I stood in front of an airplane hangar with hair blowing across my face. I remembered my parents arguing about my hair—Dad telling her to wait until I pulled it back, or to wait till the wind died down. Momma didn't listen and snapped the shot.

Walking home afterward, Dad said, "You won't even be able to tell who it is."

But Momma laughed, saying, "Oh, yes, you will."

When that roll of film was developed and Momma had already studied and then disposed of all the photos she was in, I heard a roar of laughter and ran to see the photo of me with my face completely hidden behind my hair. I stood there with my hands in fists, arms out behind me like I was holding ski poles.

"Is that how I stand?" I asked Dad.

"I'm afraid so," he said, and though he laughed, it was also clear that he was not pleased with this thing about me that the camera had captured.

I set the photo against the baseboard of my new room, where I'd lined up all of my toys, startled by how few there were. In my mind, I tried to walk through my old room to remember what was missing. Where was my Drowsy Doll? Where were the drawings I kept on the shelf beside my bed? I opened the box marked PHIL and began digging through frantically, but found no doll. And where was my ruby cup?

When I heard Dad come up the stairs and knock on my door, I started to cry again, though it gave me a headache.

He gently pushed the door open and asked, "Would you like to see the yard?"

I shook my head, and he did not return again until dinnertime, when he sat beside me on the floor while I ate a tuna fish sandwich and pickle. Afterward, he walked me to the bathroom, where I stood on a stool to brush my teeth. My face had swollen so much from a day of crying that I didn't recognize myself in the mirror; there were only red slits where my eyes would normally be and I looked like I'd been punched in the mouth.

I felt exhausted, quiet, as Dad walked me back to the room, where Phil had brought our sleeping bags. He unrolled them side by side on the floor, pausing at the odor of mine, then continuing to unroll it.

"Phil said he'll sleep in here until the rooms are set up," Dad said, tossing two pillows into the room.

I stood before him, hands at my side and asked him again, "Where's Momma?"

He sighed, kneeling in front of me and gripping my shoulders. "I answered that already, Tillie. The move really tired her out. She'll be away for a while." He tousled my hair and added, "You're going to be just fine."

I shook my head hard, but had such a headache I had to stop. He stayed in the doorway as I crawled into my sleeping bag, which was cold and damp. I thought of the questions I knew he would not answer: *Where did she go? When will we visit her? She's coming back, isn't she?*

"Tomorrow I'll show you around outside," he said as he clicked off the light. "Night, Pest." He saluted Phil from the doorway and then we heard him head downstairs.

I lay there, aching in a way that felt as if I might not live through the night. "Phil? Please tell me where she is."

"Dad says she's gone away for a while."

"I know what Dad said."

"That's all I know."

"Tell me!"

He sat up in the dark. "Okay. She was a mess. After you left, she was on her hands and knees on our lawn, and we had to get her inside because she was making a spectacle of herself."

"Was she okay?"

"You've seen her like that before," he said. "There's nothing you can do. So Dad just went and got the U-Haul and we packed everything without her help."

He picked at the zipper of his sleeping bag. "I was packing as fast as I could, and Dad was carrying the boxes out to the trucks, but he was mad the whole time. I couldn't get them packed fast enough for him, so he just started taking handfuls of stuff and throwing it by the curb so the garbage truck would collect it."

"I'll be so mad if he threw out my toys."

Phil ignored me and continued his story. "When it was time to go, she didn't want to get in the car."

"You didn't leave Momma at the old house, did you?"

"I wanted to. I was that mad. So was Dad. He had to beg her to leave her room and get in the car. And once she was in her seat, she just put her face against the window, and didn't move."

"But you brought her here, right?"

"Yeah. I didn't actually see her get out of the car because Dad took me up to this room and told me to stay here. But I could hear them fighting downstairs. The whole house echoed because there was no furniture in it."

"What did they fight about?"

"I could only hear Dad. He said, 'Get in the house. What's wrong with you?' And other stuff. Stuff you've heard him say before."

"So they *didn't* fight. You mean Dad yelled at her."

"Never mind. You're not listening."

"I want to know where she *is*. Dad says she's away for a while, but where?"

"Maybe she's in the hospital. I don't know."

"Is she sick?"

"I said, 'I don't know.'"

I expected him to say something about the smell of my sleeping bag. I hated when he teased me, but it would mean things were normal and we'd be all right in our new home. Instead he lay back down and didn't speak again that night, though it was a long time before either of us shut our eyes. I stared at the silhouette of my brother in the bare room and tucked my knees to my chest. When I opened my mouth to cry, there was no sound.

❧❦❧

8

Sassafras

FROM THE OUTSIDE, OUR house was grand, like the others on our street: red brick, white columns, and a long walkway lined with flowers. The houses were not identical as they were when we lived on base, but instead had colorful shutters, sun porches, bay windows, gardens full of roses and fruit trees, and the smell of chlorine coming from the backyard pools. During those first weeks, we'd traded in our station wagon for a Volvo, and soon we looked more like we belonged on our street.

But it was the inside of our house that showed what Dad had made of our lives. To walk through our front door gave the feeling of stepping inside a military bunker. The rooms remained barren and impersonal, only containing furniture that was absolutely necessary. Nothing on the walls, nothing so extravagant as a side table full of scented candles. Dad had painted each room a gray-white he said would be easier to keep clean, but it made our house dingy and cold. It was essentials-only living, with unused rooms locked and vents closed to save on energy bills.

Momma had filled our old house with wonderfully useless things: fruits and vegetables made of painted plaster, vases filled with felt flowers on wire stems. Sometimes she stuffed those flowers inside a drawer and replaced them with real ones—purple sage, red Indian paintbrushes, tall grasses—everything bending and lovely. These decorations were not a part of our new world.

When I was alone, I scoured every bit of the house for the items that had mysteriously disappeared in the move. I opened drawers, cupboards, closets, hoping to find Momma's sewing kit, her clothes. Where were these things? I stood outside the locked doors, frustrated and jiggling the handles.

I was so desperate to find anything at all that had belonged to her I even opened the basement door and stood at the top of the long flight of wooden stairs with no backs to them. We were not allowed to play there. Dad had warned us that the unfinished floor was full of nails and possibly rats. What frightened me most was the rickety staircase I feared would send me on a long drop to my death. Still, while Dad and Phil were laying down new carpet in our bedrooms, I put one trembling foot on the first step.

There was a strange, ticking quiet. *Maybe the rats*, I thought, and took another step. *Or maybe the sound of the stairs starting to give way.* I continued down, looking out on both sides of the staircase to see nothing more than cinder block walls. It was colder and darker the lower I went, and my footsteps echoed. When I reached the landing, where the staircase turned to the right, I patted the wall for a light switch, but felt so nervous letting go of the rail, I decided I would brave the dark.

As my eyes adjusted, I scanned the enormous, empty space on the right-hand side of the staircase. Nothing but a single door, painted, it seemed, with only one coat of white, the knot holes showing through. To the left of the staircase, more empty space except for a curious door about three feet above the floor line with a string tied through the hole where there was no handle. I started to take another step when I heard a terrifying rumble, and believing the staircase would collapse and trap me in the basement with no way out, I sprinted back to the top. Only when I was sure I was safe and my panting slowed enough to listen closely, did I recognize the sound of the dehumidifier.

After days and days of searching, one thing was very clear. Momma was not a part of this new house in any way. This was my father's world, lean and orderly. And he modeled for us his strict routine: He shined his shoes every Monday, shopped for groceries every Thursday, had his hair trimmed at the Pentagon barbershop every other Friday. He might have replaced the metal comb and ballpoint pens in his shirt pocket from time to time, but no one ever noticed the change. Every evening at ten he emptied his coins onto the bedside table before clicking the turn switch on the lamp and going to sleep.

He tried to instill in us this same kind of order, giving us lists of chores to do—not that Dad couldn't do them quicker and better by himself, but hard work, he promised, would make us responsible, sturdy, and productive. He oversaw our work like a commanding officer: *Pull that sheet tighter. Put more muscle into it. Be proud of your work.* This was fine for Phil, who was quick to say yes to anything Dad ordered, and took great satisfaction in doing things before he was asked.

While you could bounce a quarter off of Phil's bed, I refused to make that extra effort. When there was something heavy to carry, I whined that I couldn't lift it without his help. In the kitchen, I hid dirty silverware under sponges, in the garbage disposal, in a box of cereal—anything to get the chore crossed off my list. I couldn't—wouldn't—keep track of the rules, or agree to something I didn't want to do.

All that summer, we made the trip to work with him, driving along the Potomac—the suburbs on one side, D.C. on the other—learning the names of the bridges and landmarks, and finally reaching the Pentagon. The beige building with its huge parking lot was nothing like the marvelous five-sided donut Dad had drawn because you never saw it from the air.

Inside, we'd walk through the cement hallways, as men in uniform nodded and saluted and checked ID cards. Everyone there walked so tall, as if they had poles running through the backs of their jackets. They seemed amused to see a girl in the building, though Phil assured me they were laughing at my hair, which was so knotted I could only brush the top layer.

I'd slouch beside Dad as he and his colleagues talked of atomic clocks and spread spectrum radio signals, geostationary orbits and satellites. Listening to these conversations made me itch—first inside my sock, then behind my knee, my nose, under the sock again.

"Tillie, stand still," he would tell me.

Phil, of course, stood perfectly still, eyes on whoever was speaking.

Sometimes I interrupted these men to tell them that I missed our old house, making Dad and Phil nervous, as if I might mention Momma at any moment. I never did. This was a habit as ingrained in me as brushing my teeth in the morning. I had not even considered telling them about Momma. What I wanted, what I needed, was sympathy. Instead, these men, with all their colored bars and fancy pins, recited the many places they'd lived and how it made them more worldly and made their lives more exciting. It is a military brat's life to uproot and readjust, they told me. It would build my character. And while I did not appreciate all of this at eight years old, I would later.

Dad's way of keeping me quiet was to reach into his pocket and give us two quarters. Phil and I would wander the hallways and eventually end up at the snack bar, where we bought powdered donuts.

Toward the end of the summer, Dad led us past the soldier who guarded the room containing the giant computers. The whole room rumbled as the machines pumped out pale yellow cards punched with small squares and reams of paper covered in numbers. He said we could watch how the machines worked as long as we didn't touch.

Sitting with our backs against the wall, Phil passed me a donut, and I licked off the powder, setting the rest down on the wrapper. We weren't supposed to eat in the computer room, but the door was closed and there was no way to hear the crinkling of the package over the noise of the machines.

"Do you think she's coming back?" I asked.

"Don't keep asking me about Mom."

"I miss her."

"I don't."

Phil was sturdy in ways I never tried to be. When Momma disappeared, he did not ask for her, did not search for her or cry under his covers at night. He took in the facts—that there were new chores to divide between us, there would be no one home after school, and we were old enough to tuck ourselves in at night.

"You're saying you're happy?"

He crinkled his nose, as if to say, *What's that got to do with anything?*

I licked the powder off another donut and Phil mouthed, *Quit that*, but he wouldn't fight with me. Dad said the Pentagon was not a place to act like children.

"Tillie?" The door opened slowly, and I recognized her before she was sure she'd recognized me. It was Anne, wearing her fitted blue air force blazer with a short matching skirt. "Well, look at you two here, doing important work like your father," she said.

When she approached, I felt my face flush and strained to keep my lower lip from quivering. She reached out to hug me, and I collapsed in her arms, needy and ashamed. I didn't even like Anne, but seeing her was a crushing reminder of how certain I'd been on the airplane that I was on my way to see Momma.

"I know. I know," she said.

What could she possibly know? I pulled away and stood, shaking with grief and rage, amid the rumbling machines.

"That's right. Wipe the tears."

"Why are you here?" I asked.

"I still work for your father, dear," she said. "It's just taken some time to make the move."

Anne picked up the donuts and wrappers, sliding straight down because her skirt was too short for bending over.

Turning to Phil, she said, "It's good to see you, soldier."

I could see what it was in Phil that made people say these kinds of things. There was something about his face and his posture, despite the chubby cheeks and being one of the shortest in his grade, that made you forget he was a child.

"Well," she said, "I'm sure we'll be seeing more of each other. And I know I won't find you eating in this room again."

I thought of violins, Walter's cigarette, her dumb dancing. I thought of how much my life had changed during that time, while I didn't even know it was happening.

❧

MY FATHER TRIED HIS best to distract us from Momma's absence. There were evenings with board games like Clue and Pop-O-Matic Trouble, hikes into the woods, and picnics with his well-decorated colleagues, who carefully neglected to ask about our mother. Once we even camped out in our backyard, which was crowded with oaks, deep ivy, and a swimming pool—drained long before we moved in—with its blue-painted cement and a large crack running along the bottom. The only time there was water in it was after a storm.

We pitched the tent with the zippered door facing away from the pool so we wouldn't accidentally fall in if we had to pee in the dark. And in a small pit of dirt surrounded by rocks, Dad built a fire where we roasted hot dogs and then used the same sticks to roast marshmallows. I helped Dad dig up sassafras roots, which we handed to Phil, who shaved the tough outer skin off the root with his pocketknife. A pot of water was already heating up over the fire, and we'd take those roots and cook them down into tea.

"Anyone have a Band-Aid?" Phil asked. He'd nicked his thumb and held it up to show off the blood.

"How badly does it hurt?" Dad asked, and I knew Phil had been caught being a sissy. "Do you think you cut into a vein or an artery?"

Phil shook his head no and wiped the blood on his jeans.

"Okay," Dad said. "If you *do* need a Band-Aid, you're welcome to go inside and get yourself one."

Phil went back to work at another root, stripping off the leaves, and I asked what seemed to be the obvious question. "When can *I* get a pocketknife?"

Over a fire surrounded by stones, we made the most fragrant red tea, drinking even the bits of mud that had come off the roots and sunk to the bottom of our cups.

At bedtime, Dad lit the two-mantle gas lantern, the sound like a low and steady gust of wind that filled the tent. He checked my hair for ticks, combing his fingers along my scalp, while I giggled and covered my head with my hands to stop him from tickling. Dad pulled my hands back down to my sides, inspecting again, slowing down whenever he found a scab or debris from our day under the trees. In the end, he did find one tick. He used the tweezers from his pocketknife to remove it, before burning its body with a match.

"Time for bed," he said. "Off you go."

I crawled into my sleeping bag and lay there in the humid, buggy air, thinking of pearl-handled pocketknives and other wants that might fill me. Dad, glowing beside the lantern, took out his work papers.

"You have to work *now*?" I asked, lifting my head off the pillow.

"Go to sleep."

"What are you working on?"

"I'm looking at some test results from one of our Timation satellites. Checking for errors."

"You don't like mistakes," I laughed.

"There can't be any," he said, perfectly serious. "We're making something that has to operate all by itself, and for a very long time. There's no room for error."

I put my head back on the pillow and listened to the scratch of his pen, and then beyond it, into the quiet. When I was still, sometimes I heard it: the sound of Momma singing, and her bracelets clacking against the edge of the pan.

Where is she? Is she okay? When is she coming back? Can we visit her? These were the questions I learned to keep to myself. Though I stopped speaking about Momma, some corner of my mind was always full of these thoughts. I often stood on the lawn, trying to think of the questions that would lead to the right answers.

Up and down the street, neighborhood kids loaded into cars with colorful towels and goggles—off to their last days of summer camp. I walked past them, invisible, until one Sunday I met a girl about my age jumping rope at the end of the cul-de-sac. She was not pretty, but she was extremely tidy in her white button-up and plaid miniskirt, her hair shiny and so short in back that most of her neck showed. She looked like Velma from Phil's old Scooby Doo lunch box. As she jumped, she chanted a rhyme about Cinderella, and when she tripped on the rope, she stared at me as if I'd tripped her.

"What?" she demanded.

"I'm just standing here."

"Be nice, Hope." Her father had come outside, and he put his hand out to shake. "You're the girl who just moved in."

"We've been here a while."

"Well, then," he said, "I'm sure you and Hope can play together."

"But Dad!"

"I'm sure you'll have a fine time playing with . . ."

"Tillie," I said.

"With Tillie," her dad said. "And you need to change out of that uniform. You're not allowed to wear it until school starts."

"Yes, sir," she said, glaring at him. Then turning to me with a shrug, she asked, "Do you like pickles?"

"If they're sour."

I picked up her rope and let it drag behind me as I followed her inside, where we ate an entire jar of pickles, then drank the juice. "What grade are you going into?" she asked.

"Third."

"I'm fourth."

"Do you have brothers and sisters?"

"A brother."

"I'm an only. Which branch is your dad in?"

"Air force."

"Army. What does your mom do?"

I learned from Dad that the easiest way to avoid a question was not to speak at all.

"Uh-oh. Something you can't say? Is that why you're looking so strange?"

There was a lot of shrugging.

I also learned from Dad that if you *must* speak, you could say true and interesting things that didn't actually answer the question. For instance, someone would ask, "Where's your wife?" and he'd describe her hobby of making dolls.

"My mother has orange hair," I finally said. "And a crooked lip on one side where a kitten scratched her. And she's very skinny if she turns sideways but not as skinny if you see her from the front. She's a good singer. She's a good dancer, too, and always wanted my dad to dance with her, but he never would."

"Are you ever going to let go of my jump rope?"

I didn't notice I was still holding it, and I let it drop. She laughed a little and then I did. I laughed much louder and longer than I wanted to. It had been a long time since I thought anything was funny.

"Can I come tomorrow?" I asked.

"I'm only here on weekends."

"Why?"

"My parents are divorced. What do you think?"

And she filled me in on the shouting, the silent treatments, and the one-handed lady who drank with her father all afternoon in the living room and stood behind him with her hands (one being only a wrist, really) in his front pockets. She told me about having to sit on the couch for *the announcement* and how her parents remained standing, and the weird smile on her father's face as he packed, like he'd been released from jail. The worst, she said, was how her mother now stared into the mirror, saying she was too old and too fat for anyone to love her again, and after dinners she vomited up her food because somehow that would make her beautiful.

"Oh," I said.

"I just assumed your parents were divorced, too, because I've never seen your mother."

I told her then. I told her the secrets I'd never told a soul— how Momma would lie on the floor outside my old room crying, and how sometimes I'd sit by her and stroke her hair, or touch the diamond on her ring, wondering if she knew I was there.

I told her how she disappeared. "She was in the car when they came here with the U-Haul," I said. "And then there was a fight—my brother heard it—and I haven't seen her, and my dad won't tell us where she is. He says we should stop asking. I shouldn't be telling you any of this."

Hope stood there with her mouth open. Finally, I'd interested her. She ran to get a notebook and, reminding me of Velma again, said, "I'll write down the clues."

I hadn't meant to tell the family secrets, but once I did, it felt like I had loosened something that had been strapped tight across my chest. And now this complete stranger was going to help me find her.

9

Bells

THE SKY WAS SO thick with rain clouds on our first day of school, it looked like nighttime. Children carrying umbrellas and lunch boxes shouted to each other, acorns popped under tires, school buses rumbled, and cars hissed through the wet streets.

"You're sure this is what you want to wear?" Dad asked.

I'd chosen a yellow t-shirt with an iron-on tiger and flare pants with Dick Tracy comic panels all over them. The pants were too small, showing my ankles, but I wanted badly to wear something Momma had bought for me.

"Tillie, are you listening?"

"Yes. Yes, I want to wear this outfit."

"But I've been talking to you about the lunch money you'll need to bring to school each day. I'll keep it here by the . . ."

This time last year, Momma walked me to school on the first day. It was before things really changed, when she was still leaving the house and going to PTA meetings and bringing cupcakes to my class. On this day, a year ago, dressed more like a teenager than an officer's wife, she whispered in my ear, "Don't worry. I'll stay right beside you. I'm as scared as you are."

The brakes of another school bus screeched past our street, and I gripped my book bag, looking once again at Dad, impatient and checking his watch.

"Sit on the couch now," he said. "Let's get your rain boots on."

"I can do it myself."

"Yes, but we're in a hurry and you're not focused."

Phil had been standing quietly by the door, already carrying his book bag and wearing his jacket with the name of our old air force base printed on the back. When I stood up, Dad slipped my raincoat over my shoulders and pointed me out the door.

The grass was wet, and the cuttings from the last mowing stuck to my boots. Phil and I walked down the hill together, while Dad drove slowly alongside us.

Most of the cars that passed us were filled with boys and girls, wearing white button-up shirts and blue sweaters. Their cars drove in the opposite direction of our school, spraying water at our ankles if they went by too fast. And soon, Dad beeped twice, turned down a different road, and we were on our own.

"You forgot to bring your sneakers," Phil said. "Don't you remember Dad put them in a plastic bag so you could change into them at school?"

"He didn't tell me."

"Sure, he did. You just didn't listen."

"I wish he'd stop telling me things when I'm not listening." I stomped in a puddle then stayed ankle-deep to watch parents on a nearby porch photographing a girl in pigtails. "We forgot to take pictures."

"You would have to comb your hair," he said. "That might take weeks."

I kicked water at him and he pushed me down. Hard.

"Help me pick up my stuff or I'll tell," I said, feeling it soak into my pants.

He picked up my book bag but waited for me to stand up on my own.

As we approached the only major road we had to cross to get to school, we were stopped by a student crossing guard wearing a fluorescent orange belt diagonally across her chest. "I know when to cross the street," Phil told her. "I could have gone just then."

She ignored him, looked both ways, and waved us across. I'd never heard Phil speak in that tone to a stranger, or really, to anyone other than me, but he wasn't used to being treated like he couldn't do things himself. I liked having a crossing guard. It meant I didn't have to pay attention.

Down the hill, a sea of students under colorful umbrellas waited at the entrance of the school. We tried to get spots near the awning, where we'd be protected from the rain, but didn't get that far. We were jabbed by the edges of umbrellas until the doors opened, and then flowed into the building with the current, whether we were ready or not.

Phil headed down the sixth grade hallway, and I went to the "pod," where third graders had carpeted, three-walled classrooms. I found a seat, read my teacher's name on the blackboard, and couldn't help but think that the knot in my stomach wouldn't be there if Momma had walked me to school.

One of the boys had turned to the wall because he was blubbering, his lips puffy and trembling, and I was suddenly glad I could keep my feelings to myself. I got up and walked to the teacher's desk.

Mr. Woodson was bent over a green ledger and a stack of files; his Afro was seven or eight inches around and cast a shadow over his work. My mother used to make felt ornaments—angels, clowns, lions—and she gave all of them Afros larger than their bodies by separating individual pieces of yarn and spraying them with hairspray so they stood straight out.

"Mr. Woodson?" I asked.

He lifted his head. I'd never seen this kind of hair up close. It was not like yarn at all, but tight little curls that I longed to press, the way I would a patch of moss, to see if it would bounce back up.

"You're Matilda, is that right?"

I shook my head.

"I'm wrong? I apologize. Help me find your folder and I'll remember your name forever."

I flipped through the manila folders on his desk, found the one labeled MATILDA HARRIS, took his pen, and wrote TILLIE across the top of it. I smiled at him, then opened the folder and corrected my name on each paper. What I noticed as I did this—besides Mr. Woodson's mouth changing from amused to uneasy—was that my mother was not listed anywhere, on any form. My dad had simply left all sections regarding mothers and spouses blank. And in the section for emergency numbers he'd listed Anne.

"Tillie. Believe me, I will not forget your name again," Mr. Woodson said, placing his hand over the stack of folders. "Now, did you come to see me about anything in particular?"

"I'd like to be excused, please."

It was that easy. He handed me the hall pass, which was attached to the bathroom key, though that's not where I wanted to go. I wanted to find Hope. I hopscotched down the empty hallway, and each time I passed a classroom door, I jumped up and down, trying to peer through the small window. And in jumping I discovered that if I twisted the toes of my boots as I walked, it sounded like there were many more of me, and this was a feeling I liked.

Doing a full circle of the school in search of Hope, I noticed I was back at the entrance of the building. "They're here," one woman called to the other staff members. Several adults walked right past me and toward the main doors as one last school bus pulled into the driveway with brown faces pressed against each window.

"Let's do this right because it will be all over the news if we don't," the woman said before turning to me. "Back to class, dear."

"I'm trying to find my friend," I said.

"Not now."

I followed her eyes to the children who walked cautiously down the bus steps and into the building, their rubber soles squeaking against the wet tiles. Teachers smiled and waved, and when no one waved back, they rested their hands on their hips or clasped them behind their backs. Suddenly the building felt stuffy.

A teacher gestured for me to get back to class, but something caught my interest. One of the girls from the school bus—tall and chubby with braids going in every direction—had small bells tied to her shoelaces, and every time she took a step, she jingled. I couldn't help but follow as she continued down the hallway, and each time she turned to glare at me, I pretended to read one of the welcome posters pinned to the walls. When we both turned in to Mr. Woodson's classroom, I smiled at her and said, "See. I wasn't following you."

"I think we finally have our whole class here," Mr. Woodson announced, and I took my seat. Then he introduced us to Shirley Chisholm Brooks, the girl with the bells. He told us how far her bus had traveled so she could enjoy this fine education and how we could learn from her, too. Then he told us about the real Shirley Chisholm, the first black congresswoman, who seemed to have nothing at all in common with this sour girl except for her name and her brown skin. We all stared at her, and this time, instead of staring back, she laid her head on the desk and studied the wood grain.

I'd hoped people would feel sorry for me at my new school—much as Dad wanted me to be strong—but this elementary was *full* of children living with only one parent. And now there were kids who traveled nearly an hour across town to be there. My brother and I were nothing special with our glum faces and our own house key.

"They laughed at my tooth," Phil said as we walked home together.

"Sorry," I said. "It *is* funny looking."

He tried to kick the backs of my knees, but I jogged out of his reach. "I didn't have a great day either," I said. "There aren't any kids in my class I want to be friends with."

"It's just the first day."

"And I had to borrow sixty-five cents from my teacher to eat. Dad didn't even give me lunch money."

Phil shook his head.

"It would have been better if Momma had taken us to school today. Don't you remember? She always pointed out girls I should say hi to."

"You're too old for that."

The cost of mentioning Momma's name was the immediate silence, the space that grew between us as we walked. Phil reached for the house key tied to his belt loop with a twisty tie. All the way home, he concentrated on detaching that key from his pants.

⁂

HOPE AND I SPENT hours over the weekend listening to a tape recording she made of her favorite Top 40 songs, and we copied down lyrics, rewinding the tape again and again to catch what we missed.

After some jump rope and dares, like flicking water at the electrical outlets and trying to ride the skateboard down her steep driveway, Hope suggested we play at my house.

"There's not really anything to do there."

"We could play run away from your dad, or else!" She put her claws in the air. And when I didn't answer, she lowered them, saying, "So let's play in your backyard."

"I guess we could."

When we walked along the side of my house, the ivy was so deep, it buried most of the steps. "Whoa," she said when she got her first view of the back. "It's like an old abandoned house."

She walked right out on to the diving board, overlooking the empty pool with the ever-growing crack through the cement, and said, "Dare me."

"Don't. I'd get in trouble." I sat on the edge, sticky from the heat, and kicked my heels into the side of the pool. "I tried to find your class at school," I said.

"Well, I don't go to the *public* school," she said. "Almost no one around here goes *this* year."

"Why not?"

"Because of the . . ." and she whispered the word Momma told me never to say. Then she raised her arms over her head and said, "Dare me to do a flip?"

"Don't!"

She bent over laughing. "No, don't, don't!" I thought she might do a flip after all, just from losing her balance, but the outside door to our basement had caught her interest, and she hopped off the board to inspect it. "Let's go in here."

"We're not allowed."

" 'Cause why?" she said, turning the knob, pleased to find it unlocked.

"My dad told me it's not safe," I said, though I'd already followed her inside.

We were like spies, slipping inside, creeping across the entire dark basement without a word, jiggling the closet doorknob, and searching the corners for rats.

I showed her the door partway up the wall, and she pulled the string to open it. We climbed in, found a pull-chain that turned on a single light bulb, and then we closed the door. It was a pipe room with a dirt floor, filled with random furniture that must have belonged to the previous owner. "This will be our clubhouse," she said, hopping into a plaid armchair. "I don't know why your dad thinks it's so dangerous down here."

"Rats and rusty nails," I said.

"Did *you* see any of those things?"

"I guess not."

She reached into her back pocket and pulled out a mini notebook. "I have some more ideas about your mother," she said. "I asked around at my school about people who just disappear."

I had a feeling I was going to have more information than I wanted. Like the nursery rhymes Momma sang to me when

I was little, if you asked what they were about, if you tried to make sense of them, the magic disappeared, and they were no longer something you wanted to hear before sleep.

"I think your father could have put her in *an institution*." She made a grim face as if I should know what that word meant.

"What is that?"

"I read about it at the library," she said. "You take a family member who's causing a problem, and, well, it's not a prison and it's not a hospital. It's where people go and you never see them again."

"But *I* don't think she was causing a problem."

"It's what your dad thinks that counts."

I crossed my arms over my chest, increasingly annoyed at the way she talked about my mother as if we were playing a game of Clue.

"I also found this at the library," she said, and I braced myself for more of her theories, but she had a welcome surprise underneath her jacket—a stolen *Tiger Beat* magazine. We flipped through the pages of teen singers and movie stars, and rated their hair and clothes, one to ten. She ripped a picture of Peter Frampton from the magazine and gave it to me, and said, "But I'm keeping Leif Garrett."

❧

WE'D SETTLED INTO OUR new neighborhood, houses spaced farther apart than they were on base, but following the same daily rhythm: the slap of newspapers on walkways in the morning, cars leaving their driveways just after breakfast, and kids returning in the afternoons. Our lives looked as perfectly normal as our neighbors'.

After school, we let ourselves into the house, and though we

❧❧

10

Hope's Pink Bathroom

WE HAD LOCKED OURSELVES in Hope's pink bathroom all afternoon, staring into the mirror, painting our faces in pastels, and singing Carpenters' songs. When I first got to her house, we'd opened the bathroom window so the spicy scent of lavender that was planted just outside would drift in with the breeze. Now that the sun was going down, it was getting chilly.

For hours, I told her stories about my old home—the blue door that wouldn't open, the bush out front that was covered in ladybugs. I told her about the things my mother sewed that we hung on our walls and how they turned slightly red from the fine dust that was always in the air.

Hope told me about the ring her father had given to the lady with only one hand and how she refused to put it on her finger.

"Maybe it's because she doesn't have a finger to put it *on*," I said, hardly able to finish through my giggling.

"That's the other hand," Hope said, her face serious as she brushed her hair to a side part. "She wears it on a chain around were on our own, we moved around cautiously, as if we could hear Dad shouting. *Don't set that there. Don't eat that. Don't forget to clean up your mess. You missed a spot.* Even our emotions were given rules: *No more crying. No more tantrums. No more prying.*

When our homework was done, we played outside. Phil used his pocketknife to carve his initials and a checkered design into a long stick, and some days, he dug through dumpsters for empty beer cans because he'd started a collection. I simply wandered, sometimes on foot, sometimes on my bike, never with a destination in mind, and often unaware of where I'd gone after I got home.

her neck because she doesn't know if she can trust a man who cheated on his wife."

I shrugged, as if that made sense to me, and opened another drawer. Inside were treasures: barrettes, strawberry shampoo, pill bottles, a green Magic Marker.

"Pass me some matches, would you?"

"Here," I said, finding a matchbook and sliding it down the counter to her.

By then she had a Q-tip in the corner of her mouth and pretended to light up.

"You should smoke," I said, approving. "You look good like that."

"My mom says it helps you keep your figure," she said, her words muffled from the Q-tip. She removed her glasses and took a long drag. "I think I look better when I'm blurry."

"I think my hands look better green," I said, coloring my nails with the marker. We hummed bits of songs while we dabbed on scents and colors, and rummaged through every drawer and cupboard.

"Turn out the lights, Tillie. I know a trick." She pulled a candle out of another drawer, lit this one for real, and held it far under her chin. "You can see what you'll look like when you get old."

She passed the candle, and shadows and lines appeared on my face.

"Does your mom look like that?" she asked. "Did she? Before she went missing?"

"I guess," I said. In truth, I didn't remember. She was more of a warm ache that I didn't want to go away.

Out of the corner of my eye, I thought I saw the streetlights come on. And when I pressed myself against the window to be

sure, I saw the one-handed lady walk across the lawn, ice tinkling in her brown bar glass.

"There she is!" I held my other hand out and tucked my fingers under to make a stub. I tried to hold in a giant laugh. I had never seen her at Hope's before, though I'd seen her around town. She was pretty but not in any memorable way—someone you'd look at a little longer than others, then forget. Until you saw the hand, or rather, until you *didn't* see her hand.

"Eww," I said. "She just put it on your Dad's chest."

"I know," she said. "She's always touching him."

I pressed closer to the screen so my nose was squashed against it. I remembered seeing her at 7-Eleven, trying to remove a bill from her wallet. She was clumsy, and the clerk looked away but then couldn't help turning back to see.

"What's it like up close?" I asked.

"I don't like to get that close to it," she said. "But I saw her lick it once. She made a cake and licked the frosting off her stump."

"Did you eat the cake?"

"Yes, and it tasted like fingers!" We laughed so hard our eyes watered. We made our hands into stubs until our wrists hurt. I could have made that joke go on and on, but it was quickly getting dark.

"I better go," I said. "I'll probably get in trouble."

We both watched our reflections as we left the pink room. Hope may have noticed her barrettes in my hair, but she didn't ask me to return them.

The whole way home I watched my tennis shoes, first in shadow, then glowing under the streetlight, then in shadow again. The cold stung in the place where my mother was always there, always not there. But there was also joy. There were

these perfect afternoons that kept coming, just enough, here
and there.

I caught the scent of strawberry shampoo, still on my
hand. By the storm drain I found a scrunched bird feather and
smoothed its gray wisps before putting it in my pocket. I wondered if people would mistake me for an adult in my makeup.
I felt I must certainly look like my mother walking down the
street. And could she come home, easy as this, someday? Would
she know which house was mine?

That night the details of Momma's face that seemed so difficult
to remember at Hope's came back as clear as if I'd just seen her.
I remembered a time in the old house when she was still well
and getting out of bed during the day. The doorbell had just
rung.

"Hurry, Bear," she told me, dropping to the carpet, where
she would be hidden from view.

Before I joined her, I peeked from behind the curtain at the
lady who sold makeup in our neighborhood. She carried her
salmon-colored tote bag and wore a matching silk scarf around
her neck.

We had let her into our house once, and she sat very lady-
like on our sofa, laying out samples and talking nonstop. There
was not a makeup pale enough for Momma's skin, so after the
woman applied the base, there was a peach colored line where
Momma's jaw met her neck. We tried different shades of eye
shadows and lipsticks on our arms. Momma liked the bloodred
lipstick, but the woman said that her best color was pink.

We bought two items that day. One was a necklace for me
that had a rabbit dangling from it. The face opened like a locket
and had a creamy perfume inside, which I dabbed regularly on

my wrists and behind my ears, though I didn't like the way it smelled. Momma bought a lipstick: bloodred.

But this time when she rang our bell, Momma was determined not to let her in. "Hurry, Bear," she whispered. "Get down." And we lay there with our cheeks squashed against the carpet.

Hope had asked if my mother's face was full of wrinkles, the way mine looked with a candle under my chin, and it was not. It was not smooth, either, but slightly bumpy like fancy stationery. She scarred easily. Paper cuts and scrapes all left permanent marks, but the creases on her face were only on one side of her mouth, the side that showed her smile. Even in photos, and there were not many, one half of her face showed no expression.

"Don't move, Bear. She'll go away soon."

"Is she bad?"

Her answer was cryptic. "I'll protect you," she said. And seeing that smile now, in my memory, I recognize the mischief in her blue eyes, though, at the time, I truly feared that if the woman with the pink tote bag had seen us we'd have been harmed. It was the reason, later that evening, I secretly threw away the rabbit necklace.

We stayed there on the floor, long after the woman had left, talking quietly about things I've forgotten. And eventually I asked if we were allowed to get off the floor. If we could eat dinner.

"Dinner? Have we had lunch yet? Oh, never mind, let's go eat something."

And we stood, laughing again, because our clothes were covered in everything that had been on the carpet: lint, bits of thread, and long orange hairs.

11

※∽✦

School Steps

TIME CONTINUED ON RELENTLESSLY despite my fear that every day forward put me further from the last time I'd seen my mother. The leaves were turning to red and yellow. My hair was turning from dirty blonde to brown. I was still far shorter and skinnier than my classmates, but I had outgrown most of the clothes I remembered buying with Momma. If she saw me today—my two front teeth grown in big and crooked, like a rabbit's—she would hardly recognize me. I used to welcome the new seasons, count down to the next holiday, but now these changes came too fast.

Despite the passing months, I had not made friends at school. Dad said I wasn't trying. Maybe so, but neither were the kids in my class. If there was an empty seat beside one of them, someone would quickly throw a jacket over it and say, "It's saved," and then break into giggles.

In the cafeteria, with tables that unfolded out of the walls, I sat with the other outsiders. Shirley Chisholm Brooks was there.

We were the only two students who had entered the school as third graders that year, though when we stood side by side she looked like my babysitter. There were others from our pod who sat there, as well—the kids with leg braces, weight problems, lisps. We peeled the foil off our school lunches, eating limp broccoli and Jell-O molds with our heads down.

I tried to appear so interested in my lunch and, afterward, in my book that I didn't have time for others. Being alone would look like my choice. I did the same at recess, keeping to the edge of the blacktop, where I drew pictures of Snoopy and Mr. Peanut in chalk. But today we had recess inside because there were reports of a streaker in the woods behind the school. I sat alone at my desk, holding the *Encyclopedia D* in front of my face.

Mr. Woodson put his hand on my shoulder.

"Am I in trouble?" I asked.

He shook his head and smiled. "Here, follow me," he said, and led me through a row of desks. We stopped in front of Shirley Chisholm Brooks, who was busy scratching a paper clip on the cover of her textbook. Without a word, he took the paper clip from her, and pulled up a chair for me on the other side of her desk.

I hesitated before sitting down. I knew very little about her, other than that introduction on the first day, and of course, the bells. What we all knew about her was that she stayed inside for recess every day, but no one was sure what she'd done to get in trouble.

Mr. Woodson set three pennies between us and showed us how we could use them to play a game of soccer. Not once did this plump and moody girl say a word to me or did I say a word to her. But there was an ease when we were together, the ease of two outsiders. And that day, as we tapped on pennies and occasionally flicked them through the goal posts, we did not feel pressure to have a conversation. We just moved the pennies back and forth from her fingers to mine.

The next day during recess, even though the streaker had been arrested, Mr. Woodson invited me to stay inside with her again. He folded a piece of paper into a thick triangle and showed us how to flick it forward. That triangle became our football, and our fingers the goal posts. We made goals, overshot them, and had the paper triangle stick to our fingers—all without expression, without words. Finally she stopped the game, keeping the paper football clenched in her fist.

"There's a school near my house where all my friends go. I don't know why you think this one's so special."

"I didn't say it was special."

"Good, 'cause it's not," she said. "And my name is Shirl. Don't call me anything but Shirl."

I looked her in the eye and shrugged.

"Are you girls getting along?" Mr. Woodson asked when he came in to check on us. I wasn't sure, and neither of us answered.

Phil had discovered a path behind the school that led into the woods and along a creek, and you could follow it all the way down to the Potomac. On days he didn't have a lot of homework, he'd head down to the river where he stood up to his shins in the water and skipped stones. He kept a homemade fishing pole along the way. It was the long stick he'd carved, attached to an old reel and strung with fishing line. He'd fish and climb on the mossy rocks, turning them over to see what was underneath. He'd come home with his jeans and sneakers soaked. I didn't tell on him when he stored a dead copperhead in the bathroom sink or a jar of worms in the towel closet. I could have, except the things he'd get in trouble for were the things I liked best about him.

Phil didn't want me tagging along on these trips, so on days he went fishing I stayed late at school, sitting on the step near the entrance with my face buried in my encyclopedia, which was fatter now, with wrinkled pages that were easier to turn. I'd wait there until Mr. Woodson left the school because I knew he'd sit a while—not long, he always had his car keys ready— but long enough to listen to a story.

"Well, who could it be behind this big book? " Mr. Woodson asked, squatting beside me, and spinning his keys on his finger. "How about a quick story before I head home?"

I considered telling him about dogs with blue coats, and dolmen tombs that looked like they would fall at any moment, but I knew what he liked best were stories about the people I met when I went to work with Dad—the national security adviser, men from the DoD and DARPA. In truth, they were forgettable men with good posture and firm handshakes, but I liked how he listened with such interest.

"Once," I told him, "my dad introduced me to the secretary of defense and, right away, he signed his autograph on a piece of paper for me, even though I didn't ask for one. So I said, 'Do you have another piece of paper? I'll write *my* name down for *you*.'"

"And you gave him your autograph?"

"I *did*."

We both laughed, and I did not tell him the end of the story, how when I started to sign my name Dad took the pen from me and shook his head.

When Mr. Woodson had to go, I walked with him to the parking lot. He must have been seven feet tall if you counted his Afro, and so slim in his flare slacks, he was like a man on stilts from the circus. He put his hand on the top of my head before folding himself into his tiny MG sports car and zipping away. I didn't want to move from the spot where he'd touched me. Dots of sunlight moved up and down my arm, like he'd put them there.

12

The Ways You're Wrong

MY FATHER'S FIRST VISIT to my school was the evening of my parent-teacher conference. I sat at a table in the center of the pod while he and Mr. Woodson, both in suits, talked in my classroom with my school papers and the green ledger between them. The room was still decorated for Halloween, though the holiday had come and gone. Phil and I had dressed as ghosts that year, a last-minute decision to celebrate. We wore white sheets that would later go back on our beds with holes where we'd cut out eyes. It was a somber holiday, the first one without Momma that had mattered to us. We collected very little, calling it quits after a couple of blocks. And when we came home, rather than categorizing our candy and having fierce trade wars over Peppermint Patties and Red Hots, we both went straight to our rooms. I unwrapped one candy after another, in no order at all, just eating to get full.

When the conference finished, Dad handed me the jack-o'-lantern made of faded construction paper that I was now allowed to take home. We didn't speak at all as we walked through the school and then the parking lot, where he opened the door to the backseat of his car and reminded me to buckle. He did not begin the lecture until we pulled onto the road. Then the calm disappeared.

"Your teacher says your behavior in the classroom is erratic," he said. "Some days you stare into the fluorescent lights and he can't get your attention, and other days you're shouting out answers without raising your hand." He passed our street because his lecture still had a ways to go. "Listen carefully, Tillie. You need to choose the right thing to do and then do it *consistently*."

School had been one of the few places I was free from Dad's rules. It was hard enough to stand in the PE line knowing I'd be picked last for sports, just after Shirl, or sitting alone in the cafeteria with my encyclopedia. Now I had to pretend my dad was in school with me, telling me what to do.

"You score just fine on your tests, but your teacher can't predict what kind of work you'll turn in. If he asks you to write two paragraphs, don't turn in ten or fifteen pages. That's ridiculous and burdensome."

Sometimes Dad's talking became like the sound at the end of a record, before you removed the needle. *Fuff fuff fuff.* Everyone likes to tell you the ways you're wrong and ways you can improve yourself and what you should and shouldn't do. Sometimes you have to tune it out or there's nothing left of you that's right.

I pressed my nose and lips against the window, and the world slid by sideways—clouds, guardrails, bumper stickers, and the faces of other children in the backseats of their own cars. I wondered if they had also come from these conferences and were hearing similar lectures. I waved to them, one prisoner to another.

"Wait," I said, sitting up tall in my seat as we crossed the Cabin John Bridge. "Isn't that Phil? There. Down by the water?"

Dad swerved a little, trying to see. "That couldn't be him," he said. "Phil's at home."

It's not like you could miss Phil. His hair had gone curly at the start of the school year—something he felt was as cruel and unfair as the silver tooth—and every morning, after his shower, he put a knit ski cap on his head while his hair was still wet. The idea was to press the curls flat, though they still puffed out at the bottom.

"You don't think that's his jacket?" I asked. I'd never seen anyone but Phil wearing the logo of our old air force base.

Dad tried to look again, then quickly turned off the road and backtracked under the bridge. It only took a minute to be sure it was Phil, ankle-deep and pitching rocks. We parked as close as we could, but we wouldn't be able to get within talking distance unless we got out of the car and stepped across the wet stones.

"He's making a mess of his sneakers," Dad said as he leaned on the horn. "Roll down the window, Tillie."

Soon we were both yelling to him. "Get in the car! What do you think you're doing?"

Phil had gathered everything in such a hurry—the fishing pole, a mayonnaise jar full of worms, and the lid for it—that he had trouble walking without something slipping out of his hands.

"Is that my rod?" Dad said.

"No."

"Leave it, then."

"Dad, the pole's mine."

"I said, 'Leave it,'" and he bolted out of the car so fast, Phil dropped everything he'd been carrying.

Dad had won another battle. He could make Phil leave the pole and the worms, and he could demand that Phil wash the mud out of the car when we got back. He might even make me keep my eyes on Mr. Woodson instead of the lights on the ceiling, though I doubted either of us could control the way my mind wandered.

13

❧

Christmas Lights

I HAD NOT SEEN MY mother through summer or fall, and when winter came, filling our swimming pool with snow and dead branches, it seemed unbearable that we'd spend Christmas without her. Christmas had been Momma's specialty—a time when she decorated every room of the house with a snow globe or a tiny Christmas tree or a tea towel with Santa Claus on it. All of our ornaments were handmade. She cut the patterns from felt, then sewed detailed faces with shiny embroidery thread.

As the holiday approached, Mr. Woodson carefully suggested that we could make cards and gifts for any of the "important adults" in our lives. This was so everyone would feel included. Even someone living in the custody of their grandparents. Or, say, a father who would not tell his children where their mother was.

I spent most of my time on a card for Momma. I drew a picture of my ruby cup and my old bedroom. I drew seventy-two small holes in each ceiling tile, and other details I knew from days I spent by myself, such as the 346 red pieces of yarn that made up the fringe around my bedspread until you got to the clump where I had once spilled some of my drink.

"Tillie, do you think you want to move on?" Mr. Woodson pointed to the red fringe in my drawing. "Maybe it's time to write some words on your card."

I wrote the words with my hands cupped over the paper the whole time. When we were told to put our projects away I quickly cut out a snowflake for Dad.

The next day at school, we were meant to make gifts. There was a basket of crafts on the table filled with yarn, buttons, glitter, pipe cleaners. I removed one of my socks, stuffed it with paper and set about making a sock doll. I glued fabric and glitter to my sock, remembering how Momma could always make something beautiful out of scraps. At the end of the week, when it had finally dried enough to handle, the doll was so hideous, I could not even bear to wrap it.

"It's good enough, Tillie," Mr. Woodson said. "Your father will see it comes from your heart."

There was a Christmas party that day in the empty wing of the school. So much of the building was not in use because most of the children in the neighborhood had enrolled in private school, just as Hope had said. Our classes were small, with the students from Bus 14 carefully distributed, no more than one to a room. The party felt the same as walking into the cafeteria at lunchtime and not having anyone to sit with, so I stayed beside a table decorated in colorful paper, eating cookies.

"Enjoying yourself?" It was Mr. Woodson, picking up a cup and a plate.

I scanned the room more confidently now that he stood next

to me. "How come Shirl isn't here?" I asked. "Why is she always in trouble?"

"Tillie, she's not in trouble," he said, bending low and speaking quietly. "She's just nervous. She feels better staying in our classroom."

"Oh."

"Here," he said, "I was just going to take this back to her. Would you like to help?"

I followed him back through our empty pod and to the classroom, where he unlocked a metal closet behind his desk and took out a record player. Shirl helped him plug it in. That day, while our class stayed in the other wing of the school, we listened to Sammy Davis Jr.'s "The Candy Man" and then military parade tunes. I knew all of the songs by heart and wanted to sing out loud, but was surprised by a lump in my throat that made the notes come out wrong.

As I stood there listening, hands in my pockets, Shirl ran to her cubby and searched inside. She returned with a record of her own—a 45 of the Hues Corporation with visible scratches in the vinyl. She lifted the arm off of the big record, and when it stopped turning, held it by the edges and handed it to Mr. Woodson. Then she set the smaller record on the turntable. When the music started she was so excited every part of her seemed to move in a different direction at once, like a jellyfish swimming.

"Bump your hips into mine," she shouted over the music. "Like this."

"Ow!"

I tried to bump into *her* and somehow missed. The next try was too hard. By the middle of the song, we had it down. We both sang along with the chorus:

Rock the boat, don't rock the boat, baby. Rock the boat, don't tip the
boat over.

When the music began to fade out, we kept singing at full
volume. Maybe it was the influence of living in a mostly Irish
neighborhood, but I thought the words were "Rockin' on my
shamrock."

It was the first time I saw Shirl smile, her teeth too bright
against her skin. She grabbed my sleeves as if that would keep
her from falling to the floor. "No!" she laughed. "It's 'Rock on
wit yer bad self.'"

It was then, as we were laughing and holding each other, that
our classmates walked back into the room. I did not hear what
they said, only the sound of Shirl smashing the record, two-
handed, against the table.

"In your seats!" Mr. Woodson shouted, and we all ran because he almost never raised his voice.

Shirl sat at her desk, the record still in her hands. It was
broken into five sharp pieces, held together only by the record
label at its center. When Mr. Woodson turned his back, I whispered to her, "If you're not going to keep it, can I have it?"

Leaving school, I heard Shirl behind me. It was not just the
sound of her bells but also the whispers of the other students.
When she came up beside me, she opened her book bag and
handed me the broken record.

"You said you wanted it."

We walked as far as her bus together, where she got in a line
and said, "My mom showed me in the newspaper how people
drive through your neighborhood to see all the lights."

"Yeah," I said, surprised to know she'd talked to her mom about me.

People often drove up our street just to see how our neighbors had framed their houses and hedges with strings of color. You could look through the living room windows and see their huge decorated trees. And when they opened their double doors, you'd hear holiday music. But that wasn't the case with our family. There were none of the details that had once come with Christmas—no reindeer hand towels, no marshmallow snowmen with pretzel sticks for arms. I wasn't even certain we'd celebrate this year.

"Tillie," she said, "why don't you invite me over some time?"

I stood there, holding my first vinyl record, hoping it wouldn't break into any more pieces before I could tape it back together. I looked at Shirl, trying to imagine her sitting in our empty living room, and said, "Get permission, I guess."

Dad had never specifically told us not to have visitors, but he didn't encourage the idea because visitors tended to ask questions that were tricky to answer. Still, the next day, with a note from her mom, we set off for my house—Shirl with a hood of spotted fake fur framing her face and bells ringing with each step. I'd never walked home from school with another classmate before. And other than Hope and the Orkin man, who sprayed for bugs, we'd never had a guest in our home. It felt nice, imagining my neighborhood through Shirl's eyes—the neatly raked yards, the groomed gardens under burlap until spring, the painted mailboxes, and of course, the Christmas lights.

"I feel like people are staring at me," she said.

Once she said it, I noticed, too: housewives and elderly couples pressed against their windows or walking very slowly down the sidewalk. They looked for too long, and one woman smiled so hard her lip stuck above her teeth.

"I'm nervous," she said.

It was such an odd thing to imagine anyone being afraid in my neighborhood where many kept their doors unlocked at night. And while other communities were in the newspaper for fires or shootings, ours was more likely to be featured for charity drives and garden club awards.

When we got to my street, I noticed Dad's Volvo in the driveway. Normally, we used Phil's key to get in, but it wasn't unusual for Dad to come home early. If his meetings were done, he could do his paperwork at home.

"Well, this is my house," I told Shirl, and we stood, admiring the neighborhood lights from my porch.

"Why didn't *your* family decorate?"

I shrugged. It was more apparent at night when you drove up the street and felt you were inside a tunnel of lights until you got to our house. Our porch was lit by a single bulb and stood out like the broken strand of lights on a Christmas tree. Your eye went straight to it.

"Well?"

"Well, what?"

"I'm freezing."

"Oh. Well, I didn't ask if you could come inside."

"Can you?"

"Okay," I said, leaving her on the porch.

I found Dad in the formal living room, wearing the itchy cardigan sweater he always wore around the house this time of year, struggling to place a Christmas tree in its stand. I was surprised; I'd begun to believe we wouldn't make time for Christmas.

"Stay back, Tillie," he said, when I came close to help. "It's too heavy for you."

"Dad? A girl from my class wants to come over."

"Can't you see I'm busy?"

"But Dad, she's on the porch."

"Tell her to go home. It's not a good time," he said, grunting and wrestling with the tree.

I went outside. "My dad says it's not a good time. Sorry. You have to go home." I looked at Shirl shivering and said, "Well, hold on a minute."

This time, when I came back outside, Dad came with me, distracted and pulling pine needles out of his pant legs. "Here, my dad will drive you."

Shirl saluted him, holding her hand all wrong. It has to be stiff and touch the eyebrow. We got in the backseat, and while Dad waited for us to buckle, Shirl gave him directions, starting from the YMCA across town.

I'd heard whispers about the neighborhoods the bused kids came from, how it was a place for robbers and drug deals and kids who brought down the scores on our county's tests. As we drove, I worried that the people out my window carried guns, and if I looked for too long they might shoot.

"Left here," Shirl said. "Another left. Now a right. Okay, turn at the next light."

The houses on Shirl's street were larger than I thought, but they didn't have the columns or bay windows that you'd see in my neighborhood, and there were no trees anywhere. When she got out, Dad locked the doors and waited for her to get safely inside.

As we drove home, I passed him the snowflake I'd made at

school, and considered asking him if he'd deliver my card to Momma, then decided against it. Something about his refusal to talk about her was beginning to feel scary.

When we got home, the tree was up and Phil, in his knit cap, was under the branches tightening the screws of the stand.

"It's tilting toward the kitchen," Dad said, setting the snow-flake in a pile of bills.

My brother stayed under the tree until he got it straight. And when he stood up, he seemed taller and moodier than the brother who chipped his tooth one winter ago.

I could still see him trying to close the door in his slippery wool mittens, then heading down the street behind the bigger boys with his Flexible Flyer. Watching him slip and fall behind the others, his breath blowing out like smoke, I remembered how glad I was to be inside. Though Dad was strict about keeping the thermostat low, Momma had turned the oven to the broil setting and kept its door open to heat the house.

We never heard the crash of his sled. We had the music turned up, and I had just convinced her to put a pat of butter into the hot stove so our house would smell like cookies.

The first knock at the door startled us. Momma didn't want to answer it because she was in her bathrobe—though she could have, it was before she'd painted it shut. The knocking continued, and when she finally did open the door, we heard Phil's wailing at the bottom of the hill. Even before the stranger could tell Momma what had happened, she was running down the snowy street in her robe and slippers. I waited by the window, mad at the interruption and at the cold coming in through the open door.

Boys were crowded around the parked car he'd run into.

He was jammed underneath it, up to his waist, and practically squealing. Momma helped him up by placing her wrists under his armpits, the broken tooth lost in the red snow. When she passed the sled, she told me she kicked it hard for running him into that car.

Dad handed me a sandwich and I admired the lights he'd hung on the tree. After we ate and washed our hands, he brought out the boxes of ornaments. When he took the lid off that first box, I smelled the old house. Not the smell that used to make us open the windows, but one I hadn't noticed until just then—something faint, like wallpaper paste. Each ornament was wrapped in tissue, and through the paper you could see the colorful fabric and animated faces Momma had sewn onto angels, Santas, and snowmen. I slowly took an ornament out of its paper and held it, overwhelmed with the sorrow I could not express. I didn't hang it on the tree. None of us did. We just stood there, holding pieces of Momma.

Finally, Dad rummaged through the box for the Afro'd angel that always went on the very top of the tree. When he found it, he paused for only a moment and then showed us how to soldier on by marching to the tree and hooking the angel to the tallest branch. Phil and I went next, and after an hour of hanging Santas and angels and Frosties, the tree—so colorful and whimsical in our otherwise spare home—said all we couldn't say about what we were missing.

꧁꧂

IT WAS A SENSIBLE Christmas. Our stockings were filled with school supplies, and there were very few presents under the tree—a hat from me to Phil, a scarf from him to me. He gave Dad a package of drill bits; Dad gave him thermal underwear and mittens. Phil could have told him that no boys in the sixth grade of our school wore mittens—they only wore gloves—but he kept quiet. Then, wincing, I gave Dad the present I made him. And when he held up the hideous sock, sharp with dried glue, I wondered why I thought he'd want a doll.

I could not help but imagine the lovely, impractical gifts Momma might have given: mirrored sunglasses, clogs, Pet Rocks, a mood ring. As Phil and I threw the last pieces of wrapping paper into the fire, Dad disappeared for a moment. When he returned, it was with the kinds of unreasonable gifts we'd been hoping for! There was a rock tumbler for Phil, with bags of rough, unpolished rocks and the chemicals that would smooth and shine them. Then, for me, he wheeled in a Schwinn Sting-Ray with curved handlebars, and a banana seat colored red, white, and blue for the bicentennial.

I put on my coat and pedaled hard and fast into the wind until everything burned. I rode round and round the school, and when I was out of breath, stopped behind it at the edge of the woods. There, I pulled the card I'd made for Momma from my coat pocket and read it out loud as if she might hear me: *Dear Momma, Where are you? I look for you every day, and I know you're looking for me. Every night, I wish for you to hurry home. You know who this is from.*

For a while I stood listening for her, and when it was too cold to wait any longer, I put the card on the highest tree branch I could reach, where she might find it.

I got back on my bike, riding past the lit-up houses and the sounds of piano playing and children laughing until I was home.

We had survived Christmas without all the decorations or the piles of wonderfully unnecessary gifts. Still, I could not shake the feeling that I'd find her. Sometimes she felt so close. And that night, when I closed my eyes, I could swear I heard her singing Christmas carols.

14

Careful

I T'S NOT A GOOD sign that she didn't send you a card," Hope said. We sat in the basement clubhouse on the worn furniture—Hope upside down, me scraping my feet back and forth through the dirt floor. "No, that's not good. That brings up other possibilities."

"Like what?"

She shook her head as if to say, *Poor girl*. "I don't know. Can you think of anyone who wanted to *murder* her?"

A chill worked its way through my body, knowing that both of us, right then, were thinking of my father.

Again she shook her head. "I'm only putting together clues. I think the fight they had, the one Phil overheard, could be when it happened."

"I don't know," I said. When I shrugged, my shoulders stayed up by my ears.

"You said he has a temper, right? Do you think she could defend herself against him?"

Her questions made me feel like Alice falling down the long hole, and the world I knew disappearing too fast to grab hold of it.

"But what did he do with the body?" I heard Hope ask. "That's the question I have. Where's the body?"

Unable to stand even one more of her ideas, I was suddenly on my feet. "What time is it?" I asked in a voice that was both too high and too loud.

She looked at her watch. "Quarter after."

Panting, as if I really had climbed back up out of that hole, I said, "It's almost my dinnertime. I have to go."

She stood up and put her hands in her pockets, her shoulders arched high like someone who knows a lot but isn't saying it all. "You'll have to be careful," she said. "Don't let him know how much you understand."

I nodded as we both jumped out of the door in the wall and closed it again. "Careful," Hope said, whispering from behind me now. "You're leaving footprints." She bent down and wiped them with her sleeve.

"Sorry. I didn't notice," I said, my heart beating faster.

"I'm just saying you have to be real careful." She followed me out the basement door, and from there we split up. She snuck from my backyard through the neighbor's, and I walked up the side steps to the front of my house.

I peeked inside through the gold mail slot, listening for my father. I knew if he heard me come in, he'd already be mad about something I did or didn't do. There were so many rules to remember: Never climb the kitchen doorway, never put dirty dishes to the right of the sink rather than the left, never ride bikes through wet grass without drying the spokes with a towel afterward, and never sit in the barely furnished living room reserved for grown-up company, even though we'd never had a grown-up visit our house.

But now I questioned whether there was a darker side to him. What if he was not just picky and controlling? What if . . .

"I see you there, Tillie." Dad spoke through the mail slot from the other side. "Are you going to come in for dinner?"

I tried to answer, but my mouth felt frozen.

Dad opened the door. "What did you get into this time?" he asked, looking at my feet. "Hold on, there. Leave your shoes on the porch."

"Okay."

"Socks, too. I should start buying you brown socks."

"Okay." The cement was so cold I stood on tiptoes, hopping from one foot to the other.

My dad was not a large man, but he spoke as if he were. "Into the bathtub," he said, finally letting me through the door. "Dinner will be ready soon, so make it quick."

"Okay."

As I started up the stairs, he called after me, "Hustle now, Pest."

I took my time. I didn't mean to, but I hardly felt I was even inside of my body. It took effort to move, to remember where I was. I filled the tub with water that was hotter than I was allowed, poured in Prell shampoo to make bubbles. When I got in, my legs turned bright pink and the water turned a muddy brown.

"Are you out yet, Tillie?"

Out yet? I hadn't even gotten my shoulders under the water; it was still too hot. I added some cold water and more shampoo until it foamed.

"Tillie. We're waiting for you."

There was an insistence in his voice that made me believe Hope's theory. A feeling in my gut that he could go too far. I sunk into the bath, as the water continued to get colder and higher, and imagined him approaching Momma in the dark bedroom, and—seeing the plate of food he'd cooked tipped upside down on the bedspread—placing a pillow over her face to smother her.

After dinner, I went straight to my room, closed the door, and huddled on the floor with my covers. I missed her. Wrapping my arms around my shoulders, I felt her there with me. It gave me some relief from the constant and hollow feeling of wanting to tell her something during the day, something completely insignificant—about a cat whisker or a heart-shaped rock I'd carried all day in my pocket or a story I'd overheard as I sat by myself in the lunchroom. The things untold, unshared—they added up.

I wanted to tell her that I'd auditioned for the school play. It was Shirl's idea; she talked me into it at recess and said all I had to do was stay after school and sing "Over the Rainbow." We practiced in the corner of our empty classroom, and I tried to sound just like Judy Garland. I thought if I could show talent, maybe the girls who ignored me day after day might think, *We were wrong*. Maybe we'd begin to sit together at lunch and trade snacks. But when we gathered in the auditorium after school and I took my turn beside the piano, I couldn't make any words come out. The tune started again, from the beginning, and after a long delay, I sang in a strained and trembling voice, stopping before I got to the chorus, and simply sitting back down in my seat.

This was a story I could never tell Dad or Phil. As I sat absolutely still on my bedroom floor, I found I could hold my mother there, could see her long orange hair and watery eyes, and feel how she took her time when I needed her.

There you go, Bear. There you go.

I didn't hear my dad open the door to my room. Only when I saw him standing there, holding a dirty sock, did I realize I'd been talking out loud. I sat up, feeling physically cold and groggy, my arms heavy like sandbags. I thought I was in trouble, but he said in a soft voice, "Why don't you get yourself ready for bed. I think you could use some extra rest."

I could not answer him, could not even move. I closed my eyes, not ready to leave my mother.

MAY 29, 1991, 9:31 AM

A BEARDED DOCTOR, WITH *G.W. HOSPITAL* sewn over the pocket of his lab coat, sticks out his hand. *"Matilda Harris?"*

"Yes," I say, trying to sit up, but first I have to arch awkwardly to sweep my hair from under my hips.

The doctor's shoulders tilt back just a touch, forcing his chest out, and he takes a deep breath and sighs as if I'm holding him up. *"How are you feeling now?"* he asks with some impatience in his voice.

"A little better." Finally we shake hands. *"Lying down helps. And the water, I guess."*

"Very good. Well"—and his pointer finger taps against his beeper— *"I've made contact with your regular doctor."*

I catch the slightly parental tone in his voice, the very subtle twist at one corner of his mouth. It's something I'm sensitive to—being judged, written off. I can only imagine what my doctor shared of our private talks or my too-frequent visits, usually with a sense that something's wrong that I can't quite name or locate in the body. I'll have trouble breathing, but everything sounds fine through the stethoscope. I lose my *voice but have no strep. I have pains where there are no bruises or frac-tures. And I'm sent home, the doctor irritated with me again.*

This was actually one of the bonuses of moving—a chance to start fresh with a doctor who will listen and not dismiss my complaints.

"I appreciate that a woman who's pregnant for the first time can feel a little nervous."

The hair stands up on my arms like spikes. It makes me touchy when people try to tell me what's real and what's not.

Dad speaks up. "Her husband's out of town, and she just moved. That would cause a person some stress."

"Dad, stay out of it." *And turning to the doctor I ask,* "Why are you talking to my dad when I'm the patient?"

"It's understandable that you'd feel some anxiety right now," *he says,* looking directly at me as he folds his arms across his chest. "Some people even get what we call 'phantom pains,' which sometimes can be a per-son's fears becoming so big, they feel real. A person like this wants reas-surance, something friends and family could probably provide better than doctors. You just have to be careful not to use the emergency room as your first step."

And Dad is alert. This is language that concerns him, signs of being off-kilter, not coping in situations where others do fine. I can see in his face that he believes the doctor over me and thinks these pains are in my head.

"I am not making this up!"

"Okay, Tillie, settle down," *Dad says.*

I hold my belly and wince for another pain, this one so forceful it burns, even along my spine. I bend over, but nothing eases.

The doctor twists the corner of his mouth again, and Dad gives me a look that says, Tillie, stop doing that. Don't you understand what he's saying?

"I'll take her home," *Dad says.* "She can lie down there."

"It's not that easy," the doctor says, reaching to scratch his beard. "Since she checked in, we can't release her without an exam. I just want to be clear that the ER is for emergencies."

"Do you really think I have time for this, to just come here because I want reassurance? I'm supposed to unpack. I'm supposed to get a new driver's license and license plates and hook up the telephone. . . ."

I can't talk without crying, mascara dripping onto my enormous belly. The doctor puts his hand up like a cop stopping traffic. And it's this sweaty, talking-too-fast state I've worked myself into that makes people tune out.

"Let's just get this exam done," he says, starting to put his hand on my shoulder, and then wisely deciding against it. "Here. I'll take you to Room 8." And from the doorway of Room 8, he says, "The gown ties in back. I'll send a resident down to give you a full exam."

"A resident. Great." Just before he shuts the door, I work up enough courage to say what I think of him. "Asshole." And the latch clicks.

As I get undressed, I hear the ranting drunk in the next room. I tie the gown in back but leave my shoes and socks on because I can't reach them.

"Can I come in?" It's a short, round nurse with a kind face who sees me behind the bed in a gown and high-tops. She smiles. "Can't bend down to get those shoes off?"

I shake my head.

"Here. Climb up on the bed, if you can."

She removes my shoes and socks, opens a package of foam slippers, and puts them on my feet. She's quick: thermometer under my tongue, finger on the pulse at my wrist, blood pressure cuff on my upper arm, cold stethoscope in the crook of it, gently moving my hair out of her way, and writing down numbers.

"How far along?"

"Thirty-four weeks."

She writes that, too, and then says, "Okay, just lie down on your back," and pulls out stirrups for my feet. We both recoil at the sound of the drunk retching in the next room, and then the nurse is paying attention again. "Feet here. That's it. Now, bring your bottom down to edge. A little more. There you go." And she takes a folded sheet and covers me from my waist to the top of my thighs.

I reach down to feel if my baby is moving, but the rustle of the paper sheet and the gagging next door makes it impossible to concentrate on any of the delicate kicks and flutters.

"Dr. Young will be right in," she says and practically bumps into him when she opens the door. "Speak of the devil."

"Ms. Harris?" In blue scrubs with a white doctor's coat overtop, baby-faced Dr. Young arrives so quickly I assume this is their attempt to hurry and get rid of me. He takes my vitals again as he asks, "What brought you to the ER today?" His voice is stern, as if the other doctor has already poisoned him against me.

"I've been having contractions all morning, and I'm only thirty-four weeks."

"Let's not be too quick to call them contractions," he says, wrapping the blood pressure cuff around my arm. "Pregnant women often feel some good kicks and tugs, especially this far along. Here, I'm going to take a look at your abdomen."

He presses and taps his fingers against my belly. "And I need to see how everything looks from the inside," which is my cue to study every tile, every water stain on the ceiling. I'm trying my best to ignore his gloved hand, his forceful probing so close to my baby's head—Be careful, I think—when the pain grabs hold of my back again.

"There's another," I moan.

The doctor is quiet, moving the wet plastic glove from one side to the other. "Okay," he says. His voice has a hint of surprise in it. "You're four centimeters dilated, and your cervix is about seventy percent effaced."

These are terms I know from reading ahead in my What to Expect book. He's telling me I'm right. That I did feel contractions all morning. This has happened before—people trying to talk me out of my instincts, like they did when my mother disappeared—and then, like now, it would be easier if I were wrong.

When Dr. Young leaves the room, I think of the question I wish I'd asked—What now? The door, partially open, reveals a bathroom at the end of the hall. I can't believe I have to pee again, and at first, I try to wait it out. Without clocks, the only way to count time is the rambling of the drunk next door, a man expressing what I'm feeling silently, which is we've been forgotten back here in our rooms.

With some effort, I roll out of the bed, which slides a little as I try to plant my feet on the floor. Luckily, no one is here to see that I've flashed the room. I sweep my hair out of the way and hold the gown closed in back as I make my way down the hallway. The floor is ice cold through the thin foam slippers, which feel like they may disintegrate before I even reach the bathroom.

I'm glad to find it empty, feeling I've waited to the last possible second to go. But after a long wait, still feeling my bladder is full . . . nothing. I'm just about to stand when something falls into the toilet— a small foamy clump, like something a truck driver would spit out of a window. I try to get a better look at it when someone bangs hard on the door.

"Hurry up in there!" He bangs again.

With difficulty, I manage to stand up, steadying myself with my hand on the wall when there's more pounding on the door and an awful sound of belching. It startles me so much, I flush the toilet out of habit, and helplessly watch as the stringy mass swirls down, down until it disappears.

"Just wait!" I yell, but then put my hand on my belly, afraid my shouting will hurt the baby.

Another belch from the hallway, and I wash but don't dry my hands. The second I open the door, the drunk, reeking of hard liquor and maybe a hamburger, pushes past me and locks me on the other side. I hear the splash of vomit.

Frozen in place, my mind races through the baby books I've read. Could that have been a piece of the baby? The mucus plug? What an idiot I was for flushing.

Scanning the room for someone who can help, I'm grateful when I see the nurse who's been kind to me moving down the hallway. I'm about to follow her when I'm whipped backward, a strong pull at the base of my neck. I turn around toward the endless sound of vomiting and realize my hair is locked in the door.

"Nurse." At first I say it timidly, overwhelmed by the embarrassment of being stuck here. "Nurse!" I shout, this time for the baby.

She turns around. "Oh, honey, you should really stay in bed the way everyone rushes around here. It's so easy to get bumped into. Which room are you supposed to be in—eight?"

I start to cry and she comes closer, puts her arm on my shoulder to lead me back, when I tell her, "I'm stuck."

"What do you mean you're stuck?"

And as the vomiting continues behind us, I trace the length of my hair with my finger until it disappears on the other side of the door.

"Please," I say, "I'm afraid I might be going into labor."

"I think you're right," she says, squeezing my shoulder.

"You believe me?"

"M-hmm. Unless you're peeing on the floor, I think your water just broke."

And my belly tightens again as the warm stream moves down my leg. "But it's too early!"

"One thing at a time," she says, and pulls a pair of bent scissors from her lab coat pocket. She cuts me free from the door, wraps her arm through my elbow and hollers, "Wheelchair! Let's get this woman up to maternity!"

꙳

15

Fever

I DIDN'T WANT TO GO to school now that the cast list had been posted for *The Wizard of Oz*. Most who had really bad tryouts were cast as munchkins. My tryout had obviously been much worse. I was so upset about facing my classmates I didn't even finish my homework.

When I woke up achy and hot, it seemed I'd been given a gift. My brother thought I was faking, and I wasn't entirely sure that I wasn't, but Dad took my temperature. "Yep," he said. "You have a pretty good fever."

He shook the mercury down on the thermometer and then found a little bell I could ring if I needed him. As he went downstairs to call the school, it occurred to me that I was in the care of the man who may have murdered my mother. I wasn't even opposed to being in his care. How does that happen? How could someone do something so horrific and I could still look forward to spending the day with him?

Out the window, kids walked down the hill with their lunch

boxes and book bags. Snowy tulips stood tall and opened to the sun; winter and spring were in a battle that spring would win, which would mean another season without Momma. I turned my pillow over to cool my face when Phil came in, holding his stomach and moaning, "Oh, I can't go to school. I'm *dying*."

"Be quiet," I said, ringing the bell to send for Dad.

"What are you calling him for?" he asked.

"I need a glass of water."

"So go get one yourself."

"But I'm sick."

Finding pleasure in others doing favors for you was not only something he didn't understand, but the whole idea made him angry. "Never mind," he said, and went downstairs for breakfast.

I rang my bell again. I didn't need water because I was thirsty, but because I wanted to paint. I decided to illustrate and watercolor a stack of poems I had written. This was the exact thing that Dad had lectured me not to do—to take a school assignment and simply change it into what interested me—which was why I'd hidden the paints and brushes under my covers.

Throughout the day, Dad came to check on me—every hour, like he'd set a timer—and each time he brought something: a couple of Saltine crackers, a small bowl of SpaghettiOs, a few sips of ginger ale, a *Ranger Rick* magazine. Sometimes he felt my forehead with the back of his hand, and if I was lucky, there was enough evidence of a fever to get another orange-flavored aspirin, which was better than candy.

By the afternoon, however, the satisfaction of staying in bed and being waited on had run out. I was tired of the color of my bedspread, the sound of the ticking clock, and having to get attention on Dad's timetable. I set off, a little lightheaded, down the stairs, but before I reached the bottom, there was Dad with a ballpoint pen between his fingers.

"Back to your room, Tillie."

"But, Dad."

I tried again when Phil returned from school. I would have been happy even to hear him turn the pages of his textbooks, but once more, Dad stood at the bottom step, shaking his head.

"Can't I eat at the table?" I asked when he brought me dinner.

"You're being a real pest," he teased.

That night, after he said good night, my legs felt restless in the hot and tangled sheets. I had turned my pillow over, but both sides were sweaty, and I'd been lying down all day and couldn't stand the idea of not moving until morning.

I walked downstairs, my legs not as sturdy as I thought, and I needed the handrail. The stairway was cooler, and I walked slowly so my nightgown wouldn't rustle. When I reached the bottom, I felt the relief that my father wasn't waiting there to send me back to bed.

All the lights were out for the night, and I found my way to the kitchen. I quietly opened cupboards, looking for something to eat, when I heard a creak below the kitchen floor, and then the sound of water running through the pipes. I froze in place, first not wanting to be caught, and then, and more urgently, not wanting to be alone. My father had been so adamant about not going to the basement that to hear him down there, and so late at night, made me curious. I grabbed a butter knife, remembering the rats.

I opened the door that led downstairs, surprised to find no light on. Knife in hand, I stepped onto the cold, wooden stair, and walked into the dark. I continued to the bottom and felt the shock of the cold concrete floor. The noise seemed to be coming from behind that lone door with the knot holes showing through the paint. But in the dark, it was hard to see anything at all so I slid quietly along the drywall, feeling for the handle.

My shoulder was the first to hit the door, and the noise behind it became louder, more certain. I tried the handle, but it was locked. I knew it would be; I'd tried every door in our house. I felt hot, woozy, and didn't want to turn around and climb those stairs again.

"Dad?" I called, hoping he'd open the door, call me Pest again, and carry me back to bed.

There was no answer. And then I remembered—how stupid of me to only remember now—that in our old house, when Phil and I chased each other, I often locked myself in one of the rooms to catch my breath. I learned quickly that Phil could always get in by turning a knife in the keyhole.

I inserted the knife and heard the button pop out on the other side. When I slowly pushed the door open, there was a flickering blue light. This was not a closet at all, but a room with no windows. And as my eyes adjusted, I noticed shelves stuffed every which way with books. Another step inside, and I discovered a couch, lamps draped in scarves, a side table, and on top: sticky jars of Pond's cold cream, Oil of Olay and ivory makeup, cups filled with pens and makeup brushes.

The floor was full, too: stacks of books, junk food wrappers. And in the corner, on top of an ottoman, providing the room's only light: a TV. Though the sound was turned all the way down, I was sure I heard a very faint and high-pitched hum, and the picture on the screen was nothing but bright-colored vertical bars.

Behind a second door was the noise I'd been searching for—definitely water running, then the shriek of a faucet and the water was off. It sounded very much like someone taking a bath.

Someone is here, I thought, though somehow I no longer expected my father. That would have been reason enough to hurry up the stairs, but instead I took a step closer, compelled by something stronger than logic, stronger than fear. A color had caught my eye, a color barely visible in the weird blue light, until I took another step into the room. I stared long and hard at the kelly green fabric slung over the arm of the couch. Momma's sweater. And scanning the room again, I began to recognize other items that had belonged to her: the sewing basket, a Raggedy Ann doll lying on its side on a shelf.

Behind that inner door I heard water draining, and my heart pounded. I pressed close against the wall, not hidden by anything but the shadows of the room. And when the inner door opened, someone thin and ghostly pale walked into the room. A woman in a bathrobe, leaving a trail of wet footprints.

Only now did I let myself think it: *Momma.* I didn't realize I'd said the word aloud until I heard my own voice. I quickly covered my mouth, afraid she'd heard me, too, but she continued on toward the couch, and clicked on a small lamp on the side table. The lampshade was covered with a scarf, so that corner now glowed warm like a fire.

Momma.

Her face was not as soft or full as it had been, but there was the orange hair twirled on the top of her head and held there with bobby pins. It was her. And still, I could not move, feeling I'd now waited too long to know how to begin.

My mother. I found her.

Again, the dizziness. I swayed a little and held to the wall, wondering what exactly I had stumbled upon. It was all stranger and more terrible than I had imagined. She propped a magnifying mirror on top of a pillow and leaned into it to cover her face with cold cream. But soon, her hand froze in place as her eyes slowly opened wide and found me.

"Momma," I whispered, feeling so nervous I thought I'd collapse. "Momma, it's me."

It seemed to take a very long time before she answered in a trembling voice, "Of course, oh darling, of course it's you." She frantically wiped her face with a washcloth, and cold cream smeared in her hair along the edges. "It's okay, darling. It's such a wonderful thing to have you here. It's just that you surprised me. You were so quiet."

I smiled, finally—a shy smile with my shoulders hunched. Momma closed the gap at the top of her bathrobe, covering her sharp collar bone. "I wondered when you'd find me," she said, and she tapped the far corner of the couch. "Come sit here."

This was the singsong voice she used when she tucked me in at night, and I remembered her holding me tight, whispering as she spun above me, *I don't deserve you, Bear. All I can do is ruin you.*

"Come on over. I have a spot for you right here." She moved a few items onto the floor to clear a spot. "Here, I want to fix my face," she said. "I look like such a mess." And with shaky hands, she fumbled through several clear plastic bags until she found the one she wanted.

I held my hands in my lap, feeling afraid, glorious, ashamed— all of this.

She dug into the bag filled with makeup, then colored in her eyebrows with a copper-colored pencil. She shook a container of liquid black eyeliner and drew a line along the inside of her bottom lashes.

"I stayed home from school today," I said, realizing the

strangeness of mentioning an entire world she'd not been a part of. "I'm feeling better now," I added, and smiled into my lap, watching her out of the corner of my eye.

"That's good. That's very good." She painted her lips a shimmery pink inside the red lines she had drawn, then asked, "Would you like to try some lipstick?"

I nodded and cupped my hands. Momma set the lipstick in them and closed my fingers over it. Her touch was warm like bathwater.

"We're having such a nice visit, but soon it'll be time to run along." She took the lipstick from my hands, uncapped it, and colored in my lips. "You'll need a note for school, right?"

I wondered if she thought it was daytime. How could she know in this room without windows? And what was happening here?

"We had a splendid time," she said, reaching for a pen and notepad among the stacks on the floor. She wrote something down and then looked at me very seriously for a long while. "Now, you can't mention this to *your father*. This has to be our secret."

I'd been waiting to hear if she'd mention his name. Something about the way she said the word *father* gave me chills, as if she were warning or protecting me. There were questions forming deep in my gut that I couldn't yet put into words, a feeling that I was on the verge of learning something terrible that would change everything.

She handed me the note. "Remember: Not a word to your father."

In perfect handwriting, she had written: *Please excuse Tillie from missing her classes. She was with her mother. Mara Harris.*

I read the word "mother" and the name "Mara," and felt an

emotion so strong I wondered if it was joy. But it seemed more complicated than that—something that rumbled deep down, like the dehumidifier right outside the door.

Back in my bed, I lay there, restless, thinking and not thinking, staring and thinking again. *My mother lives in our basement*, I thought. *How long has she been there? And what did she mean, "Don't tell your father?"*

My head hurt. I felt hot and kicked off the covers, then immediately felt too cold and curled up by the pillow, my legs shaking. I had to tell someone.

I crept down the hall and peered into my brother's room, which was darkened by an American flag draped over his window. I wanted badly to see him—his schoolbooks on the floor by his Eagles and Bad Company 45's, and on a shelf over his head the pyramid of beer cans he pulled from dumpsters.

"Phil." I could barely hear myself.

If I could just see him, I'd know this moment was real, that my mother was real, that this whole strange night was true. I took another step into his room.

A little louder I said, "Phil?"

At first, he only turned over as if he'd go right back to sleep, but then he woke up, startled. "What are you doing in here? Get out!"

"Phil, I found a secret room that lights up blue, and Momma's in it."

"Would you get out of my room!"

"It's blue because of the TV, and she put makeup on me and said she knew I'd find her."

"Stop bothering me," he said. "I mean it. Get out of my room."

"Phil, listen!"

"You're sick," he said. "And I mean sick in the head."

"No. I saw her."

He turned over, threw the covers over his head.

"Phil, you have to listen to me!"

And then he sat up violently, the covers falling to his waist. "You *didn't* see her," he said. "And you know why? It's because she's *gone*. Because she left us. Get it? It's why we don't visit. She didn't want to be here."

"You're wrong!"

I took a step backward, moving away from his doubt, as if it might find its way into me. He had always been the smarter one, the one you could believe. Maybe it was all too impossible, too strange to be true.

"I said, 'Get out!'"

I felt my face heating up again. When I was back in bed, weighing his words against mine, I didn't know which to believe. I rolled it all through my mind—the blue light, my pale mother, her voice, the perfect handwriting on her note. The note! I searched on the floor and all around my bed, felt in my pockets, checked the hallway, but it was gone. And rather than searching anywhere else, I crawled under my covers while the memory of our time together was still fresh, so I could fall asleep, believing.

16

❧

Poem about the Moon

I GATHERED THE POEMS I'D watercolored and took hesitant steps down the stairs for breakfast. I tried to remember how to walk like an eight-year-old getting ready for school, how to hold in the electricity of knowing things I wasn't supposed to know, of doing things I wasn't supposed to do. When I walked into the kitchen, I didn't look at my father, in case this wonderful, terrifying secret showed in my eyes.

"Feeling better?" Dad asked.

I nodded, looking only as high as the bars on his uniform, then poured some Grape-Nuts into my palm and stuck my tongue out until it was covered with little nuggets. At the sink, I filled my hand with water and took a slurp, my mind straining to understand what I'd uncovered.

I think the fight they had, the one Phil overheard, could be when it happened.

Hope was right: Whatever crime my father had committed must have happened just after the fight Phil told me about. But what exactly happened, and how did Momma survive it? Had he locked her in and left her to die? Did she play dead, and he closed the door, believing he'd hidden her body? When did she give up trying to escape?

"Did you hear me?" Dad asked. I turned off the tap, noticing the sink was now filled with water. "I said, 'Don't forget to empty all the wastebaskets before you go to school.'"

"I know."

"Did you finish your homework?"

"M-hmm. I did it."

When my brother walked through the kitchen, Dad's spoon stopped short of his mouth. "Trash day, Phil. Don't forget to take the cans to the street."

"Right," he said, but bristled because he took pride in doing his chores without a reminder. He grabbed a stack of books and used them to push open the screen door.

"Wait for me," I said, sprinting into the living room.

"Not so fast, Tillie."

"I know. I know. The trash." I heard the screen door close behind Phil, so I hurried through each bare but spotless room, grabbing paper bags.

"Hurry!" he called. "You have to get those bags on the street before the truck comes."

I whispered it as I went through the house and out the door, bags in hand and bare feet mashed into my sneakers: *Villain*. I threw the bags by the curb, and chased after Phil, calling, "Wait up!"

He slowed only enough for me to know he'd heard me, but kept walking.

"I said, 'Wait!' Dad says you're supposed to walk me to school." I was out of breath by the time I caught up to him.

"You're old enough to walk by yourself, you know."

"Just tell me something," I said, panting as I spoke. "Do you think Dad was angry enough at Momma to try to kill her?"

Phil stopped and finally turned around. "Do I think *what*?"

"Well, what if he tried to kill her but she survived? What if he *thought* he killed her, but he *didn't*?"

"Do you even know how retarded you are?" He shoved me hard. I slipped off the curb and fell on the street, scraping my leg. I didn't cry. Tears didn't come easily anymore.

"Stop running to me with all your crazy ideas," he yelled. "She's gone. And you know what? I don't care where she's gone to, either. She could be lying on a beach working on her tan for all I care."

I thought of the windowless room, where no sun could touch her. How dare he think she was lying on a beach. How dare he forget she couldn't tan but only sunburned.

"You know what else?" he said, starting toward the school again. "Stop tagging along all the time. You're starting to get really strange."

I stared at every bump of gray and black in the road until I could see patterns. I bit down hard, wishing I had something between my teeth. Phil didn't deserve to know any more about my time with Momma. He had given up. Believed the worst about her. And since that was how he wanted it, I would keep her to myself.

I took my time straightening my homework papers, then boldly I stood up and walked to school. Phil was out in front, and I let the gap between us grow. I concentrated, instead, on showing my poems to Mr. Woodson—sorry I couldn't also show him the note from Momma.

. . .

"We missed you yesterday," Mr. Woodson said. "How are you feeling?"

There were no words I knew of to answer his question. I stood there, silent, and after some time, I simply handed him my assignment. The school bell rang, but he didn't make a motion to start class. He read each page, studied every picture, turning very slowly to the next. I watched closely when he got to my favorite poem. It was about the moon, about trying to catch it with a string and pulling it down to see if the face was friendly or more like a goblin's. Mr. Woodson's face was tense with concentration, and I waited where I was until he reached the end.

"Well, it's a good thing that you're standing right here," he finally said. "I was thinking of writing 'See me' at the top of your . . . report . . . and now I don't have to."

"Am I in trouble?"

"No. You're not in trouble. But you understand this wasn't exactly what the assignment was, right?"

I nodded.

"Because this was meant to be a one-page science report," he said. "You wrote down the assignment, didn't you?"

I nodded again.

"Tillie." He sighed and flipped through the pages. "I'd like to hold on to this and give it a more careful look. Right now, my thinking is that even though you didn't follow the assignment, not even close, actually, I'll simply have to give you an A."

When he started to smile, my whole face burned like the fever had come back. "I was with my mother yesterday," I blurted out. "She wrote you a note, but I can't find where I put it."

And now another sigh and the crooked crease that showed between his eyebrows when he was thinking hard. "You have a tremendous imagination, Tillie. There's a great deal going on inside that head of yours." He drummed his fingers on top of my poems. "I think it's time I start class. What do you say?"

I nodded, beaming.

"Next time, let's see what you can do if you read the directions a little more closely."

I nodded again and turned to walk back to my seat. Some people, not many, can reach the most tender spot within you and hold you there—sometimes without even knowing that's what they've done. As I made my way between the desks, I felt so good I thought the sound of the bells was coming from me. But it was Shirl, clapping her shoes together under the desk.

I'd been unable to explore the basement during the day; someone was always home. And I just couldn't make myself stay up late enough at night to avoid Dad. Instead, I paced the house, trying not to look suspicious. Sometimes I wondered what our neighbors thought—if they knew anything about us beyond our comings and goings. Had they seen my mother that day she went into the house and never came back out? Did they wonder where she'd gone or what had happened to her? I supposed these questions—like asking who you voted for or how much money you made—were the kind polite people didn't ask.

When Friday finally arrived and I'd finished school and my chores, I raced my bike up the street to talk to Hope, who was drawing on the sidewalk with chalk. "I saw her," I said. "My mother! You'll never believe where I found her. Come see!"

Hope finished the bubble letters in her name, each one connected. "You found her?" she asked, setting down the chalk.

"Yes! Come on!"

"Where are we going?"

"My house. The *basement*."

I pushed off, and now she jogged alongside. "Dead or alive?" There was an excitement to her question, and I could tell she wanted a gruesome discovery.

"Alive," I said, irritated. "She's been locked in the basement closet. But it's not a closet. I'll show you where it is."

"Who would lock your mom in a closet?"

I dragged my feet until the bike came to a stop, then threw it to the curb. I led Hope down the side steps to the basement door, feeling sick with too many thoughts, all terrible and implicating my father.

As we approached the basement door, Hope hopscotched on the walkway.

"Sh!"

"O-kay!"

"Don't let the door slam."

"Okay. Okay."

We walked cautiously through the basement door, as we always did, because we knew we weren't allowed down there. Now, the danger seemed greater, something darker than rats or stepping on a nail, a danger harder to identify. I tiptoed along the drywall. "That's the door," I whispered, pointing, but not going close.

It seemed impossible that Momma could be in there, behind the door that so clearly seemed to lead to a closet or storage space.

"Well, let's see," she whispered. "Open it."

I paused, thinking of how Momma hated visitors, and how pale and thin she looked. I worried that Hope wouldn't find my mother as wonderful or pretty as the stories I'd told of her. She might even regret all of our searching.

"I don't know if we should go in," I said. "Momma gets very nervous with company, and I don't want to upset her."

"Wait, she's still in there?" she asked. "You found her and left her there?"

Hope always came up with the most horrifying thoughts, things I never considered.

"Don't you think she's probably starving to death?" she asked.

"I'm going to feed her tonight," I said, panicked and angry that I didn't think to set her free when I'd had the chance.

"It's awfully quiet in there," she said, and gave a grim but smug expression, as if pleased that she was right.

"Well, I'm not going to let you in to see her," I whispered more loudly. "You can forget about meeting her."

"That's because you made it up," she said.

"I did not!"

I grabbed her arm, squeezing hard, and pulled her to the other side of the basement. I tugged on the string to open the door to the clubhouse, and we climbed into the damp and dusty room, where Hope wrapped her hands around the fattest pipe and swung her legs back and forth.

"It's all a bunch of BS," she said. "I don't believe a word of it."

"Why don't you just go home?"

"Sure," she said, jumping down from the pipes.

"And you're not in my club anymore."

"Fine," she said. "Then I'll take this with me." She removed a package of giant Sweet Tarts from her pocket and held it in front of my face.

"I don't care," I said, and stupidly added, "I don't even like candy." After she stomped out of the clubhouse, I wrote "Hope stinks" in the sand.

. . .

For days after our fight, I tried to sneak to the secret room, but I was frightened I'd be caught and only got as far as the basement door. Standing there, her room eerily silent, Hope's words haunted me. *It's all a bunch of BS. I don't believe a word of it.*

I felt desperate to prove her wrong, and angry I hadn't just opened the door and let her see Momma for herself. As the week rolled on, I felt more panicked, needing to find a way to visit, needing to see her again with my own eyes and prove to myself that she was real.

I began collecting food, a handful at a time, so I'd be ready. But I needed a plan for waking up at night that didn't also wake up Dad or Phil. I couldn't use my alarm clock. I had to be clever. My bedtime was eight and Dad was always in bed by ten, so I needed to pretend to sleep until ten, and then somehow keep myself from nodding off during the wait.

Just after my bedtime, I drank a pitcher full of water, and in the middle of the night, woke up urgent. I peed, but did not flush, and then put on my bathrobe, which already had the pockets stuffed full with carrots, salami, and Saltine crackers. I crept through the house, butter knife in hand. Down the last set of stairs, I held the rail with both hands so I wouldn't fall into the black. And when I reached the bottom, I felt along the wall for the door and then the handle.

I was afraid of what I'd find—Momma starving, or worse, nothing more than a closet, just as Hope believed. I inserted the knife into the keyhole, and slowly let myself in. There. The blue flickering light. Something glowing in the corner of the couch under the small lamp. It was her. I breathed a sigh of relief to find Momma sitting up in her bathrobe, books crowded into her lap, and the television showing the same picture on it.

"I didn't tell him," I whispered.

"Good girl," she said. "Come sit with me. I was just about to read."

It felt like something the size of an acorn had just become lodged in my throat. I inched toward the couch, wanting badly to hear a story, and when she scooted the books out of the way, I curled up beside her. I'd often thought about the last chapter in *Alice in Wonderland*, wondering which way the story turned. I could have checked out the book at the library and simply read that final chapter myself, but it was Momma's smiles and tears for Alice that I longed for, and how she always read until I drifted off.

Remembering the food I brought for her, I reached into my pocket and placed it between us. She smiled and then opened a book with the odd word "PLATH" written across it and started to read out loud:

The claw of the magnolia
drunk on its own scents
asks nothing of life.

I had no idea what a "magnolia" was. The other words I knew, but they seemed like they were in the wrong order. Still, I loved how she read the poem into the top of my head, her lips touching. It was a feeling of being in a brand new world and wondering how I'd ever tolerated the old one. "Read some more," I begged.

Momma read from other books that night—strange, serious books that were nothing like the ones I'd read before. Each time she finished, she passed me the book, warmed from her hands, with her favorite passages underlined perfectly in felt-tipped marker.

When I was so tired I didn't think I could make it back up the stairs, I waited for a space in Momma's talking, where I could say good-night. She seemed to sense I was about to go, and whispered, "I love you the best." She said it with a kind of fierceness.

"Do you want to come with me?" I asked as I opened the door. This was a test to see if she wanted to escape, or if she was too afraid.

"I better stay here," she said, and smiled with her lips closed, one side of her mouth curling upward, the other side flat and guarding her secret.

At the bottom of my pocket, I felt for a piece of paper that had been folded over and over into a small square. I dusted the cracker crumbs off of it and handed it to Momma, my hand shaking. It was my poem about the moon.

꒰ ꒱

17

Chair Legs

MY FATHER'S WORK INVOLVED creating some kind of navigating system in which things on earth could be tracked, and possibly even directed, from space. Sometimes at breakfast he tried to explain this idea to me, describing satellite geometry and signal frequencies. It sounded like science fiction, and I found it hard to be interested in space and in the future when more important things were taking place right here in our own house.

Still I nodded, saying the occasional "hmm" so as not to raise suspicions. But what I really thought about were his lies. Even the times I remembered as good ones—camping in the backyard or going to the Pentagon with him—were different now because of what I knew. When I was missing Momma and begging to know where she was, he could have told me.

My head could nod. My mouth could smile. My body could rise and collect my book bag and find its way to school. I could do all of this by rote, though my mind was somewhere else entirely. Sometimes it was churning with questions: *Why did he do this? How could he be so cruel?* Most often, my mind was far away in the secret room, reliving favorite scenes with Momma over and over, but revising them so that my words were smarter and there were fewer pauses in-between.

I walked down the hallway at school, wondering where the day had gone. Students were packing up to leave for home, and those of us cast in *The Wizard of Oz* headed to the cafeteria for our first rehearsal. The janitor had transformed the room into an auditorium by putting the lunch tables back into the walls and setting out rows of metal chairs. I sat in back, slumped in my brother's Baltimore Colts shirt, since none of mine were clean, and tried to work up the nerve to quit the play.

"We're going to play a little get-to-know-you game," our director, Mrs. Newkirk, announced. "Everyone, pull your chairs into a circle."

The game involved a ball. You had to say your name, your part in the play, and then throw the ball to someone you hadn't thrown to yet. The ball went back and forth between the popular students who shouted out lead roles. At last, out of necessity, someone threw the ball to me. I said my name, and my voice sounded small, the way I sounded when Hope and I recorded ourselves on her cassettes. I was meant to keep up the rhythm—name, role, throw—but I stalled. I couldn't say the name of my part, even when the other students laughed and said it for me. I felt desperate to return to Momma's blue-lit room, and when I threw the ball at another student, I threw it like I was playing dodge ball. The next time the ball came to me, I threw it even harder.

. . .

When I returned from school, Phil, sitting on the front porch, said, "I heard you got sent to the principal's office."

"Don't tell Dad," I said.

"I'll bet they already called him at work."

"The principal said he wouldn't because I was so sorry and my grades were good."

My brother grinned and said, "Still might have called."

At dinner that night, I braced myself for a lecture, one that would end with the question, *Why? Why would you do such a stupid thing?* And I would only be able to say, *I don't know.* Because the more truthful answer—*It just felt good*—was something I'd have to keep to myself.

I swung my legs back and forth—it calmed me to concentrate on the rhythm—and as I did, I thought, *She's there, right below us.* She would understand why I'd thrown the ball at those girls. She would cheer me on. And could she hear my feet banging into the chair legs?

I wanted so badly to see her, but it wasn't easy to wake myself in the middle of the night, even with my many methods. Some part of me fought it—the part that wanted to rest and stay warm, to have a full night's sleep the way other kids did.

"Would you please pass the salt?" Phil said.

Dad and I both looked up at the same time and said, "What?"

There was something so quiet and formal about my brother that he could just blend in to the background and you'd forget he was there. When our family used to walk together on the air force base, rare as it was, sometimes Dad would say, "What a lot of traffic. They should create another lane so it doesn't back up like this. Do you smell that exhaust?" Or Momma would say, "Listen to the birds chirping. Don't you love their songs?" And until they mentioned traffic or birds, you were completely unaware of them. It was like they didn't exist until someone reminded you.

And it was like that with my brother. Except no one tended to say, "Do you notice the curly haired kid with the silver tooth who eats his vegetables and uses his napkin? Do you see him there, sometimes pressing his fingers to his front teeth, moving from the regular tooth to the funny one?" No one tended to point him out the way they pointed out traffic and birds, so when he spoke up and asked for salt, it was kind of like, "Oh, yeah. You."

"The salt," he said again, but mumbling because, lately, he tried to talk without letting the silver tooth show.

"Phil, speak up. If you're not clear, people will think you're weak."

My father would not pass the salt until Phil apologized. Then he let it go, and we all found something on our plates to spear.

This sudden focus to Phil doing something wrong was good news to me. It was obvious the principal hadn't called, and I could relax again. There was never a worry about Phil telling on me. The one thing you could count on was my brother following Dad's rules, and he knew Dad didn't like tattlers. I kicked the legs of my chair again—a secret hello to Momma.

❧

18

Great Tap Root

I FEARED THE VIEW OUT my window when I set out to be with Momma. At that hour, the glow of streetlamps shone only enough to reveal the endless span of night. I crept slowly through the house, sure I could hear my father's breath behind me, sure that I'd turn a corner and he'd be there.

Down the wooden stairs, gently tiptoeing to avoid splinters, I made my way to the bottom. The cold of the cement floor worked itself into my feet as I unlocked the door and entered the hum and the blue light coming from the TV set. Momma had her head on a pillow, eyes closed, legs stretched across the couch and glowing blue. Only my footsteps on the carpet made any noise.

"I'm here," I whispered, but there was no answer.

I sat near her feet. My corner of the couch had a hole in it, and each time I sat there, I pulled out stuffing, twisted it into thin ropes then stuffed it back in. Most visits I was so nervous about being discovered even our whispers seemed too loud, but now it was the quiet that left me feeling afraid. I turned the sweaty ropes in my hands.

"I'm here. I'm here," I said. "Please wake up. I came to see you."

I noticed a sock sticking out at the end of the blanket, and with my shoulders held stiff, I touched it to see if she would move, if her body was warm. It was. I breathed out. I let my fingers wrap themselves gently around her foot, squeezing to wake her.

"Momma. Momma, it's me."

Very slowly, she breathed more deeply under the blanket. She stretched and turned until after a moment, she was sitting up, groggy.

"Will you read to me?" I whispered, and I reached to touch the cover of Sylvia Plath, which had been shoved between the cushions.

She rubbed her face in her hands and took the book from me. Then she turned on the lamp beside her and spent some time finding the page she wanted. A rosy color moved from her chest to her face when she found the passage to read aloud:

I know the bottom, she says.
I know it with my great tap root:
It is what you fear.
I do not fear it:
I have been there.

Momma's voice was wonderful and dramatic, not at all like mine or Phil's or Dad's, the way we sounded so plain. I practiced the words in my mind as she closed the book.

"Do you understand it?"

I nodded my head as if I did.

"The very bottom of the elm tree roots," she said. "As low as you can go."

"We learned about roots in school," I said. "Each student got a plant in a Styrofoam cup."

"But in *this* story, the roots are filled with disease and sorrow, and they spread though the whole tree. It's about a sadness so deep you don't know how you can go on. I understand that feeling."

I nodded again. Her face was happier when I seemed to understand, and I was ashamed I'd mentioned something so stupid as a science project.

"She will die with her head in an oven."

"Who?"

"This poet. She's so sad that the oven is a relief."

I was stunned. My father never told me these kinds of secrets, darker and more thrilling than anything I could have invented in my own mind. "Someone found her with her head in the oven?"

"That's right. She killed herself because life was more painful than death. It was a short life, but not a shallow one."

I sat speechless on my sagging end of the couch as she hummed again and placed small objects in my hands: a painted figurine, a tiny key to turn a tiny lock, a lotion she rubbed into my skin until I smelled like peaches. We shared the pleasure of details—the smell, the texture of anything within reach. Momma called us poets at heart.

She passed another object, this time carefully because it was loaded with pins: a cushioned tomato from the old sewing kit.

"Oh, Momma," I said, remembering how I used to sit on her lap while she pinned crinkly patterns to fabric and made them into miniature shoes and vests. I thought of us around the Christmas tree full of Momma's ornaments, and was she down below even then? If I was right about Dad, she *was*.

"Are the pins hurting you?" she asked.

"No," I said, pausing, choosing my words. "It's just, I missed you so much at Christmas time."

"I heard you playing." She put her hand on my arm. "I always listen for you."

I couldn't respond to what she'd said. I felt sick that I hadn't found her sooner. Sick knowing I had opened presents and ridden my new bike while she suffered. If I had discovered her any later, she probably would have died.

"How long will you be down here?" I asked, though my real question was, *Momma, what should we do? Because I don't know, and I'm scared.*

"Whenever you want to visit, I'll be here," she said.

I understood then. What she meant was that it wasn't safe for her to leave this room. I repeated her answer over and over in my mind so I wouldn't forget to write it down in the notebook where I kept details about our visits. On paper, I was trying to put together the puzzle, but I was careful about gathering information. I didn't want to ask questions that would upset her— not after all she'd been through. I wasn't going to be the one to make her curl up on the floor and cry. And something deep inside made me careful, as well. There was a sense of danger in knowing too much at once. Sometimes the edges of conversation are like the dim edges of the streetlamp's light. You know better than to wander past its glow and into the endless dark where you could find anything at all.

She touched the blanket where my legs were nestled beneath it and announced, "Time for you to go to bed."

Of course I knew it was coming, the journey back through the dark house before I was ready and the shock of cold on my legs from not being under a blanket with her. Our closeness was always followed by distance—days apart, maybe weeks—and afterward, I'd think too much. Had I been as interesting or smart as she believed me to be? Had I said anything to bore or upset her?

I returned to my room without showing the items I'd stuffed up the sleeves of my nightgown, things I thought I wanted to show her, like my collection of animal erasers and a black light bulb that made your teeth glow and showed the dust you never knew was on your face. But the items from my world seemed silly and trivial when I was with Momma, and I kept them hidden, and scolded myself later for bringing them at all.

I read from the notebook I'd been keeping: *Very thin. Door locked. "Don't tell your father." Won't follow me. "I better stay here." "It's our secret."* I added some new notes: *Leave childish things in room. Read more of Momma's books. Understand them! Don't say dumb things! Remember Sylvia Plath.*

I held the notebook to my chest, my mind stuffed full with questions, fears, and secret joys. I knew things about Momma that no one else in the family knew. I felt almost tingly, with the pleasure and agony of not speaking a word about our time together.

On another page in the notebook, I had drawn her room—everything I could recall of it: the magnifying mirror, the makeup-stained pillow, so soft and flat that you could fold it in half. I added the pin cushion and the book she read from that night. Then I wrote her name, over and over in my best script. I wrote *Momma*. I wrote *Mara*.

☙❧

"LOOK WHAT I BROUGHT!" I stood in the middle of the school playground, raising a bottle of Flintstones chewables in my fist. "I have been to the bottom of the root and I do not fear it! Are you with me?"

I felt bold, like I was showing some new and secret part of myself in public, bringing something from my hidden world into school. "I do not fear it!" I shouted as I worked at opening the cap.

Most kids played on, ignoring me, though I heard one say, "That girl's crazy," when I pretended to eat a handful of the vitamins. I fell to the ground, coughing and kicking my legs in spasms.

"Tillie?"

I knew it was my teacher's voice even with my eyes closed, and I slowed my legs to a stop, feeling not as great as I had hoped to feel.

"Come with me, Tillie." Mr. Woodson held me gently by the arm and walked me closer to the building and our classroom window. "I've been doing some thinking about you," he said, gently pressing down my hair where I'd forgotten to comb it. "Here, let's sit."

We sat down on the grass so he no longer towered over me. I dug my nails into the dirt as he spoke.

"You're a very bright girl. I wonder sometimes if I need to give you ideas for better ways to spend your time so you don't . . . well . . . alienate your classmates."

Shirl had her face pressed against the window to see if I'd join her inside.

"I've been trying to think of something that will give your

mind a challenge. Like a book report. Why don't you find a book that really excites you and then write a short paper on it?" he said. "I think you could have a lot of fun with it. You could even read your report in front of the class. Maybe find some friends that way."

I wasn't sure why it had taken Mr. Woodson so much thought to give me more homework or how he thought it was any different from the work he already assigned. But I liked that he had thought about me. And I liked the way he smelled up close, like talcum powder.

He held out his hand. "Why don't you let me hold on to those chewables? I'd be awfully upset if you got sick from them."

I passed him the bottle. "I couldn't get the cap off anyway."

Walking home from school that day, a crowd of boys stayed right at my heels, calling me names.

"Batty!"

"Out of her mind!"

"Bananas!"

"Cracked!"

"A real nutjob!"

I crossed the street, and when I reached the other side, I turned to them with my hands on my hips. "You act like a bunch of children," I yelled. "Are you proud of your shallow lives?"

There was hysterical laughter, but it stayed on that side of the street so I felt I'd made my point. I jogged to catch up to Phil, who was further along the walk home.

"I see you're making friends, as usual," he said. At least he was talking to me again.

"They're stupid," I said.

"Maybe. They can be stupid and right at the same time, Nutjob."

"So be it."

I imagined how we looked from farther away—me and a sixth grader, walking side by side. That would show those boys.

When we got to our house, I continued on to Hope's. It was a Friday and I was ready to accept an apology from her. Maybe I'd tell her what I'd figured out about Dad, though I'd keep the visits with Momma private.

Her father seemed surprised to see me. He called for Hope, and when she came to the door, she asked, "What?"

I reached into my book bag and handed her a crumpled paper filled with song lyrics. "It's the words to 'Afternoon Delight.' Whenever Phil's out of the house, I listen to his radio until this song comes on. Here, take it. I got all the words."

We sat on the front porch together while she read the lyrics. "It's not 'Thinking of he's working on an apple tight,'" she said. "That makes no sense."

"I guess. I'll listen to it again."

Hope had a purse now, and like the older girls at *my* school, needed to carry it with her at all times, even if she was just sitting on the porch. We said nothing to each other as she took each item out of her purse and inspected it: a bottle of nail polish, Bonne Bell Lip Smackers, a small Snoopy notebook, and a very fat ballpoint pen that had a dozen different colors of ink in it.

"Can I see this?" I asked, pointing to a keychain viewer with the words "Spring Break in Ocean City" attached to the strap of her purse.

After she unhooked it, I held it up to the sunlight to see a picture of Hope and three other girls I didn't know, huddled together in colorful towels with the beach behind them. Somehow, during our time apart, I assumed she was moping and waiting for me to forgive her.

The screen door opened and the one-handed lady stepped onto the front steps. "Almost ready?"

"I'm ready," Hope said. When the screen door closed again, I waited for a burst of giggles about the stump, but she simply handed back the lyrics. "Here. I have to go to pick out a clarinet for orchestra."

She popped the top off her Lip Smackers and rubbed back and forth over her mouth until she smelled like strawberries. I was about to ask, "Can I come, too?" when I realized what she meant was I should go home.

I gave back the keychain viewer with her new friends inside of it, and she worked at attaching it to the strap of her purse without saying good-bye. As I walked away, I noticed a sign on the edge of her lawn that said for sale. How did I miss seeing that before, and why didn't she tell me?

By the time I'd reached my house, my jaw hurt from pressing my teeth together too tight. Phil was by Dad's car, trimming the hedge that lined the driveway. My shoulder bumped him as I walked past.

"What's *your* problem?" he asked.

"Leave me alone."

"Dad wants us to help in the yard," he said.

"What'll he do if I *don't* help him? *Kill* me?"

❧

19

Good Lies to Tell

I'D PERFECTED WAYS TO wake myself in the middle of the night. With my door shut, I arranged the sharp objects in my bed—soccer trophy, salad tongs, hole puncher. I set a pitcher filled with water on the nightstand. Before bed, I would gulp it down, and after I was asleep, if my bladder didn't wake me, I'd eventually turn over and stab myself. Sometimes, however, I wet the bed instead of waking up, and I'd head to school, bruised, red-eyed, and with wet hair from a last-minute shower.

I was consumed with thoughts of being with her again, wanting to hear her praise and to have her tell me I was a poet and more mature than others my age. The world outside the blue-lit room—away from Momma and our secret talks—just felt so ordinary.

Sometimes I kept something from our visits so I could feel like I had her with me: eyelash curlers, a sock that had slipped off her foot, a damp washcloth covered in makeup and smelling of Noxzema, worn so thin that I could see my fingers through it. I kept these objects hidden among my things: her washcloth in my sock drawer, her book on my shelf. I needed her there.

I made my way to the kitchen, intent on finding the pyramid cheese grater. It had worked well before. It woke me immediately, cutting right through my nightgown and leaving a scrape on my side. More and more, Dad noticed the disappearance of these objects, so I had to return them after each use, and then steal them all over again.

I stopped in the doorway of the kitchen—its counters crowded with mixing bowls and measuring cups. Phil was by the sink, pouring oil, while Dad stood behind him, shoulders hunched. "Watch it. Not so fast," he said.

Phil stiffened, and oil dribbled down the side of the bottle.

"Oh, come on!" Dad said, and handed him a dishtowel. "Quick! Before it drips to the floor!"

"What's everyone doing?" I asked with my back to the drawer I needed to open.

"Baking a cake," Dad said.

"Oh, right. Happy birthday, Phil."

He was concentrating too hard on carrying the cake mix to the oven to give an answer.

"Careful," Dad reminded him, and Phil tensed up again.

You could look at my brother's face and already see all the places he'd have creases when he got old. I wondered sometimes if Dad knew that telling him to stand so straight and act so grown-up wasn't making him popular at school. Phil reminded me of the palace guards in London that we learned about in social studies, the ones in the bearskin hats who didn't smile or react to anything at all. When he was teased about his silver tooth—and he was teased every day—he didn't change his expression or the pace that he walked. He didn't cry or shout back. Once a boy followed him so closely chanting "metal mouth" that he stepped on the back of Phil's sneaker. And when the shoe came off, he simply picked it up and continued on his way, so serious and controlled, like there was no kid left in him.

"You dripped," Dad told Phil, who didn't argue. They both hurried for the sponge, and that was all the distraction I needed to grab the cheese grater from the drawer and slip away.

Phil's birthday, since Dad was in charge of it, had none of the decorations, games, or guests that would make it feel like a celebration. Just a cake after dinner with twelve lit candles, and singing that ended after the first verse because we all got embarrassed.

I forgot to give Phil a present, but Dad said the set of barbells was from both of us, and wouldn't he look a little sturdier if he used them each day? His big present would come when Dad had time to schedule an appointment with the dentist. Now that Phil was twelve, the silver cap could be replaced with porcelain.

Later, while Dad instructed Phil in the art of building muscles, I cut a quarter of the cake, put it on a paper towel, and, unable to wait any longer, snuck away to the secret room.

"Ta-da!" I whispered as I unlocked the door. "I brought birthday cake!"

She seemed surprised, unable to speak. I closed the door slowly so it wouldn't make a noise, worrying I'd hurt her by reminding her of the life she was missing.

"I wanted you to have some," I said, putting the cake between us. The television was on, and for once there was an actual show on the screen, featuring a very short brown man with his much larger wife.

Momma began to sing quietly over top of the TV show—her voice cracking as if she might cry. "Happy birthday to you . . ."

She thought it was *my* birthday.

She continued singing. "I have presents for you . . ."

At first I believed she'd forgotten my birthday was in June, always the final party of the school year, and one of the last things we did together in the old house. Then I realized she didn't know what time of year it was or how much time had gone by. How could she? There were no windows, no clocks, no calendars.

"Okay," she announced, her voice getting bolder. "Close your eyes!"

I only squinted, first distracted by pictures on the TV—an argument or a love scene, it was hard to tell—and then by the surprise of Momma pushing off the arm of the couch. I hadn't seen her stand since I first discovered her in the basement. Her hair was matted in back, and her legs seemed weak and cramped as she walked to the closet and searched through a heap on the floor.

When she came back, her hands were full. "Now open." And she brought out gifts, one by one: a hairbrush with orange hairs in it, a lipstick that was practically new, and a necklace with a gold letter M on it. She did not yell at me when I accidentally smeared frosting on the brush.

"It's a perfect birthday," I said. "Now it is, anyway."

"You don't need all of those hats and noise blowers, do you? To tell you the truth," she said, "I never did like parties and holidays for the very reason of decorations."

"You didn't like the decorations you made?"

"There was always so much competition between the

mothers—so much time and money spent trying to get the decorations just right," she said as she put perfume on my wrists and then clasped the necklace around my neck. "And why? Why was that so important to us to have theme parties, or cookies shaped like snowmen, or a red, white, and blue cake on the Fourth of July? Isn't that ridiculous, the things we spent our time on?"

I nodded my head, as if I didn't like those things.

"You didn't understand this before, but you're old enough now."

I nodded again.

"Imagine you dream of the things you might become— maybe a doll maker or a singer or you just want to travel one way to another country and see what it's like to live there. And at some point, you notice years have gone by, years of spending your days doing these trivial things you aren't even interested in. And you wonder, *What happened to your dreams? What happened to the you who might have been?*"

My eyes widened. Momma never said anything I expected her to say. She played with my hair—brushing it from the ends, never pulling.

"I was picked to write a very special book report," I finally told her. "I'm the only one in my class who got this assignment, and I can choose any book I want."

"That's because your teacher understands how special you are." And she reached for a book. "Your teacher will love this."

She handed me a book with worn and dog-eared pages, and I read the title: *The Feminine Mystique.*

"He will?"

"Yes, and it will be perfect for a report. You can skip right to the chapter called 'The Forfeited Self.' It's what we've been talking about. Of course, you should read 'The Comfortable Concentration Camp,' too. Unless . . ." Momma rummaged through the books by the couch. She slowed when she found the book of magnolias and tap roots.

"That one's great, too," I said quickly. "But I think this other one will be just right. I'm too excited about it to switch now."

Her smile was triumphant. "We're just the same," she said. "We're the best of friends because we understand each other."

I didn't understand her at all, but I wanted to. Mostly I was glad for the way she saw more in me than was actually there. She started to make small braids, just near my face, keeping the rest long, working so gently until suddenly she froze. I did, too. There was a noise in the distance. My father's footsteps? We sat there, saying nothing. We did not talk about my father or our fear of him. We didn't have to. We did not talk about what he'd done to her because our time was so cozy. I wouldn't dare bring up anything that would upset her.

When the noise stopped, we waited a little longer still. Then Momma breathed out again and her fingers finished another braid. "It's pretty like this," she said after she'd wound an elastic band to the end of it. And the next time I prepared to see her, I knew I'd be conscious of my hair. I'd think, *Will she like this?*

Momma smiled at the cake between us, then used her hands to split it in half. We giggled, eating with our fingers, proud that we followed different rules. We could eat with our hands. We could eat until we groaned in pain. We could lick our fingers to get clean.

"I'm sorry our birthday party has to be so short," Momma said, tasting the last of the frosting on her fingers.

"I'm just glad we could spend my birthday together."

Something fluttered in my stomach whenever I said things that weren't true—pretending it was my birthday, pretending I was okay leaving so soon—but these were good lies to tell. They would make my mother happy. She leaned in and held my shoulders, squeezing so tight my arms hurt where we were touching.

My brother, bare-chested, pumped his weights at the top of stairs. "Where did you go?" he asked, not moving out of the way.

"I don't know."

"I know where you were," he said. "Somewhere pigging out on my cake."

I smiled and held up the butter knife, glad if taking the blame right away kept him from knowing I had Momma's lipstick and hairbrush inside my sleeve, and her book behind my back.

"Dad's looking for you," he said. "And he's not happy." Phil took a step back and pumped the weights again. His shoulders, biceps, and the seriousness on his face were like a man's, but his smooth chest and round cheeks still a boy's. "You look weird," he said, staring at my hair.

"You do, too," I told him, turning toward the staircase when I heard Dad call my name.

"I told you he wasn't happy," Phil said.

Tucking the necklace under my shirt and the book into the waist of my pants, I went downstairs to face my father.

"Where were you?" he called from the kitchen.

"Outside," I said, the lies coming easier. I wondered if I smelled of Momma's perfume.

"Don't you think it would have been more appropriate to stay with Phil on his birthday?"

"I'm here now."

"The day's practically over," he said. "And don't you think you took more than your share?"

"It was really good cake," I said, setting the knife on the counter.

"Well, it's drying out now because you forgot to cover it."

He was right there and could cover it himself if he didn't have to prove a point all the time. Momma never bossed me around this way. I set the lid over the cake, made an exaggerated effort to clean the counter, then turned to leave.

"Just a minute," he said.

I froze, the brush bristles jabbing into my arm, sure that he smelled the perfume or noticed the book bulging at my waist. I could not risk reaching to my collar to feel if the necklace was showing.

He stared for a long while before he said, "Don't you have something to say?"

There were words I didn't like to say. Words like "thank you" and "sorry" just stayed there like a fist in my throat. After some thought, I said, "I'll get ready for bed now. Good night," and waited a little longer to see if Dad would accept that.

"All right," he said. "Go on."

When I went to my room, I set the gifts from Momma on my desk and itched my arm where the bristles had poked me. Then I cleared all of the items out of my bed. I no longer had to wake myself in the middle of the night. Instead, I could fall asleep, thinking how she called us the best of friends. I wondered if that meant she would eat candy with me in the clubhouse or listen to the same song over and over until we got all the words right. I wondered if she would come upstairs someday to see my room, if she'd like the things I kept in it.

As I dressed for bed that night, admiring the tiny braids in the mirror, I noticed red marks where Momma had held me. All night I touched what I knew would become bruises, hoping they'd be slow to fade.

20

❧

Spare Key

I RECORDED EVERY MEETING WITH my mother by placing a small checkmark on my calendar: five visits in March of 1976, daily visits for the first week of April, a series of skipped days, a day where I'd visited twice, and now, at the beginning of May, a long gap of almost a week since I'd seen her.

During the time in-between, I studied anyone and anything I believed would impress her. I remembered the names of her heroes: Nikki Giovanni, Bob Dylan, James Agee, Martin Luther King Jr., Golda Meir, Ralph Nader, Desmond Tutu, and Mary Hartman, Mary Hartman. I listened to her stories about showers built to trick and poison people, penniless families in swirling dust, a lonely painter who cut off his ear for love.

My mind was more and more with my mother. *What is she doing right now? Is she thinking of me? What could I do today that she'd like to hear about later?*

At first, I loved the secrecy. I liked the yearning—how waiting to be together built to something almost unbearable.

But something had changed. It began to prick at me—how our time was always cut short at its height. I'd become more reckless about seeing her, standing near her door midday, tiptoeing downstairs before I was sure Dad was asleep. I read the books she gave me in broad daylight, left my notebook of clues lying about. I was no longer satisfied seeing Momma here and there in the middle of the night; I wanted her in my daily life.

And I had a plan. Every time I passed Phil's room and found it empty, I stole a coin from his silver dollar collection. I didn't feel guilty about taking his coins because he no longer counted them or added any new ones. When I began taking them, the box was so full it wouldn't latch. Now I could see the bottom.

❧

I'D SPENT MOST OF my effort on the cover page of my report, and that was because reading Momma's book had become painful. Even on the first page, I got stuck on words like "statisticians" and "Freudian sophistication." The story picked up with girls eating chalk to stay thin—if I wasn't already so skinny, I would have tried it myself—but after that, the book became dull again, so dull that whenever I opened it, the words swam around on the page, and I couldn't make myself read them in the right order.

"Mr. Woodson?" I loved standing by his desk.

"What do you have there, Tillie?"

"*The Feminine Mystique*. It's taking me longer to do my report than I thought."

Mr. Woodson put his long fingers on the cover of the book.

"And I was wondering if maybe I can just do the chapter on 'The Forfeited Self.'"

"Tillie." He said it quietly. He didn't say anything else for a long time. His brown shoes sighed up and down as his toes curled inside of them. "I was hoping you would choose a book that you could discuss with your peers. I wanted you to pick something all your own and have fun with it."

"I'm having fun." I showed him a smile, but was pretty certain it was the kind I gave the camera—a look that said, *Quick! I can't hold it much longer.*

Mr. Woodson leaned over and put his elbows on his legs. His face was beautiful up close. I'd never looked at it straight-on before. "Please tell me who gave you this book."

"My mother."

"Your mother." Mr. Woodson took a deep breath. "Tillie, I have never met your mother. Does she live with you?"

I said nothing. How could I? If I told about our time together in the middle of the night, if I told him how I snuck food to her and we spoke in whispers so Dad wouldn't hear us, he might call my home. And if he did, Momma would be in danger.

Mr. Woodson breathed in deep again, held it there, and after a long while, his breath came through his nostrils, smelling like coffee. "Sometimes," he said, "I feel like the Tillie I know doesn't come to my class anymore."

He seemed to be waiting for me to say something, but he hadn't asked a question, or not one that I understood, so I just watched him tap his fingertips together. I liked his hands, which were brown on the back and pink underneath. "Tillie," he finally said, "don't get lost. Don't lose that thing you have."

"Thing?"

"Forget the book report. What happened to your poetry?"

"You like my poems?"

"I think you'll make a very fine writer some day."

He palmed the top of my head like a basketball, and left his hand there as I counted to seven in my head. I wished he'd kept it there longer, at least so I could have counted to an even ten.

⤳⦉⦊⤝

I SCOURED MY ROOM until I found the pages of watercolored poems I'd created two months earlier. I'd chosen colors I preferred more than real life: magenta skies, lime green trees, pink-and-orange checkered birds. I had written those poems the day I had my fever, the day I discovered my mother. I turned page after page of wrinkled papers and found where I'd ripped out the poem I'd given her about the moon.

The last page was a painting of the ladybugs I knew so well from the days Momma didn't wake up. I knew all their shades of red—some deep, some faded like fabric left out in the sun. I knew how they could unlock their red shells and release the little wings that were sheer as black pantyhose. I must have drawn a hundred of them here: red blobs with the paintbrush, not bothering to make them into circles. The black spots were sometimes on their shells and sometimes just nearby, as if I'd been painting too fast to care.

At the bottom of the paper was an arrow. And when I turned the page over, I discovered a note from my teacher that I hadn't noticed before: *What I know about the young poet, Tillie Harris: She signs autographs. She knows about dandelions, Darwin, and Denmark. She laughs with her whole face.*

When I read this, I felt the way I did with Momma— important, noticed—and I decided: *This is the day. This is the day I'll free my mother.* We'd escape to who-knows-where, she'd read to me from her books, and tuck me in somewhere far from here.

· · ·

Outside, Dad pushed the reel mower across our lawn, mowing squares inside of squares, with a rhythmic *Cha cha cha. Cha cha cha.*

In the old house, I'd sit on the porch while he mowed, and whenever he came close, I'd ask him a question: *Why is the sky blue?* Always, he gave a long, scientific answer before mowing another square. When he came close again, I had another: *Where does the sky end and space begin?* His answers, which I paid almost no attention to, made me giggle, simply because I'd found a way to get his attention. *If the earth is round, why don't the people living on the bottom fall off? And why aren't they upside down?* At some point, he'd call me "Pest," and a smile would spread across my face.

When my father got to that final strip of grass, the very middle of all of those squares, he'd stop. That was my cue to hold the handle of the mower myself. And because I was not strong enough to push it without his help, he stood behind me, his hands on the outside edges of the handles, and we'd walk the last strip together. That was a long time ago.

I stood by the screen door, hands in my pockets, where I fingered the last of Phil's silver dollars. My plan was almost ready. To my father, this was just a day like any other with ground beef thawing on the counter for dinner and a call placed to the dentist. He'd made an appointment for Phil to have the silver cap replaced with porcelain, something I was curious to see, but Momma and I would be long gone by then.

While my father mowed smaller and smaller squares, I snuck to his room and slipped his car key off the wicker table. Then, for no reason except curiosity, a good-bye, maybe, I opened his closet to see everything so tidy: shoes lined up in pairs, ironed slacks hung over hangers. I would be leaving behind this orderly world with rules for how everything must be done.

I rummaged through his drawers next, and beneath his socks I found handfuls of medals he'd won, and behind those, the pitiful doll I'd made for him last Christmas, along with old cards I'd written even before we moved here: HAPPY FATHER'S DAY, BEST DAD. I didn't know he'd saved them, and something ached where I didn't expect.

As I stood back at the screen door again, seeing that Dad had finished mowing and now wiped the blades dry with a hand towel, I reminded myself: He wasn't the same man. I felt the coins in one pocket, the key in the other, knowing I couldn't stay in two worlds any longer.

21

Silver Dollars

PHIL, WHO NOW EXERCISED dutifully before bed, curled weights to his chest, fifty reps on each arm, grunting with every one of them. Dad washed the last of the dinnerware, closed the creaky door to the dishwasher, then emptied his pockets onto the wicker table beside his bed. These were the sounds to listen for as our family called it a day.

Sitting on my bed in the dark, I counted the silver dollars, passing them one at a time from my right hand to my left, waiting for the quiet. My clothes pinched at the waist, and I couldn't bend my knees very far because I'd dressed in layers—my biggest pair of jeans over pajama bottoms over shorts, and on top, a t-shirt and pullover sweatshirt—so when we made our escape, I'd have a change of clothes. I loaded the coins, my dad's car key, and the butter knife into the pouchlike pocket on the front of my sweatshirt, and when I was certain Dad was asleep, I walked stiff-legged down the stairs.

Each step clanked, just slightly, but I was so jittery, I couldn't slow myself down. I'd had enough of my father's gray world. I slowed past his room, remembering the sock doll in his drawer, knowing that when I left him behind I would have to leave the good as well. I breathed in, held it tight, and kept going around the corner. Down the last flight of stairs, a coin dropped from my pocket and landed with a loud *plink* before bouncing to another step. I started to bend down to find it when I barely caught the others from sliding out the same way. I had to leave it and go on.

As always, I turned the knife in the keyhole, but this time I paused. The doubt had crept in: Phil calling me crazy the night I found Momma, Hope calling me a liar as we stood outside the secret room, Mr. Woodson telling me I had a tremendous imagination.

I'd been in trouble so often for talking to myself, for simply disappearing. An entire class could go by in school and I wouldn't remember any of it. A knot formed in my gut as I wondered, *Could I have imagined everything?*

And then a tougher question: *Could I possibly survive going back to my room, just lying there with my eyes on the ceiling tiles, letting tomorrow be the same as today?*

More certain than ever, I turned the knife just a little more until I felt the lock release. I pushed on the door, entered the blue glow, and there she was. My muscles relaxed, and I let out my breath.

"Momma," I whispered, closing the door only partway. "I have good news."

She leaned against her usual side of the couch, but tonight she had a jewelry box and other trinkets spread across the cushions. "Try something on," she said, holding out a satin-lined box filled with costume jewelry.

When I reached for bracelets and clip-on earrings, she dabbed perfume behind my ears.

"Take another," she said, pointing to a bracelet. "When you dress up, your jewelry should make a little jingle."

I grabbed the first thing I touched, anxious to get going. "I have a plan," I said, trying to sit beside her, but my pants were so tight I couldn't bend in the middle. I stood up again. "It's something that's going to make you very happy."

"What's this plan you're talking about?" she asked, rummaging in a pile beside her, tossing colorful scarves, shawls, and hats my way.

The way she said "plan" showed that she didn't understand. I wasn't talking about a simple to-do list or homework strategies. This was about escape, about changing our lives. I pulled a silk shawl over my shoulders, feeling the coins shift to the other side of my pocket.

"Let's just say it's the best night of all for us to dress up." In fact, it was perfect—making our escape a real celebration.

She smiled and put a beret on her head and a handful of bracelets over her wrist so they lined her entire forearm. She put on every scarf and necklace I passed her.

Once we were dressed, I paraded in my shawl, taking long, dramatic steps like a model. She laughed again, but it was the empty kind of laughter that meant she was tired. "I think it's time for bed," she said.

"No! My plan. Remember?" I pushed both hands in my pocket, searching for the key.

"Tillie, it's late. We'll do this another time."

"But you don't understand." I fumbled more furiously, not

feeling the key. "Wait," I said, getting on my hands and knees, patting the floor for it. "This will just take a second."

With poor lighting and impatient fingers, I felt along the ground, moving scarves and hats out of my way, when I heard more coins fall. I growled in frustration, and the silence that followed made me realize how very loud I'd been—and foolish. We'd have to hurry.

I recovered what coins I could, then patted the floor more frantically until I finally found the key, which I held up to show Momma. Her eyes were wet as if she suddenly understood I'd come to save her. It was the kind of beautiful moment to stop and enjoy if we had the time, but there wasn't a minute to spare.

"Come on," I said, reaching for her wrists, not letting the key go this time. I didn't mean to shout, and didn't mean to grab her so hard, but once I did, I wouldn't let go.

"You're hurting me," she said as I walked backward, pulling her off the couch and toward the door, the key digging into my hand and her arm.

"We have to hurry." I didn't have time to explain and could hardly speak my teeth were chattering so much. We could talk in the car.

"Don't be scared," I said. It was an expression I knew people used when you have every reason to be scared—an attempt to trick your mind into bravery, though you hear footsteps up-stairs.

We didn't have far to go, but we had to be quick, and I needed her to walk with me instead of pulling back. I turned to give her a reassuring smile, one that said, *Please don't be nervous. I've thought this through.* But beneath the beret and scarf and dan-gling jewels, the troubled expression on her face quickly grew to one of alarm.

I could feel the danger in the room, and turned to face the dark shape filling the doorway.

My father.

He stood there in his briefs and his thin undershirt, blocking the door. And a strange sensation worked its way from my stomach to my throat.

My ears thumped with the sound of my pulse as he stepped into the room and flipped on the overhead switch. The harsh light revealed a mess of open drawers, clothes, and soda cans thrown everywhere, and my mother in the middle of it all, white and startled. My father seemed to mouth, "Quiet!" And when the sound returned, I heard my own voice—high-pitched, desperate—and realized I'd been screaming the whole time.

When I stopped screaming, in the awful silence that seemed to go on and on, I reached for Momma, not sure when I had let her go. And standing just too far away, I swiped at the air, my bracelets clinking together. I tried again, finally grabbing hold of her sleeve.

"I found her!" I shouted. "I found her, and we're leaving right now!"

More footsteps overhead, and soon Phil rushed down the stairs and stopped short on the landing, where he stood with his arms limp. There was no way to know what he was thinking or feeling except for it was a lot of something, and he was not letting it out.

"Tillie, you're confused," Dad said.

I shook my head back and forth until I felt lightheaded, hoping to shut out his words.

"Tillie, get a hold of yourself," he said.

And I didn't want him to tell me that my mother wasn't here. He couldn't take her from me again. He tried to grab my hand but I pulled it away, hysterical and thrashing. "Stop him, Phil! He's going to kill us!"

Phil, on the landing, did not move. There was only the sound of us panting, until he spoke—only a whisper. "Someone tell me what Mom's doing here."

MAY 29, 1991, 2:30 PM

M Y UNDERWEAR, SOAKED WITH *amniotic fluid, drips in a trail until the nurse who's been kind to me lowers me into a wheelchair. She spreads a blanket across my wet lap and we're wheeling fast down a hallway, past the numbered rooms and lines of cranky, coughing patients.*

A powerful contraction grabs my lower back and squeezes forward, but this time it stings so deep at the base of my spine I start to hyperventilate.

"Take a slow breath if you can," the nurse says.

And I choke trying, my eyes watering with the pain.

"Slow breath out," she says.

"I can't have this baby!" I say, gasping. "I'm not due yet. You have to stop the labor!"

"I'll take her from here." This new nurse is all business, and I feel the panic of losing my only sympathetic ear.

Before she's gone, the one I like whispers, "I'll check on you after my shift," and I'm wheeled away, down another corridor.

"Please! I'm not ready. Someone listen to me."

We stop at the closed elevator. "Honey, you may not be ready, but the baby is," the nurse says, and drops a rubber band into my lap. "I suggest you tie your hair up while there's time."

The doors open, and we roll inside, my belly tightening again, and I start to pant.

"One slow breath," she says. "Remember your Lamaze class. You practiced the breathing techniques, didn't you?"

"Yes, I practiced them. When it didn't hurt!"

What we'd prepared for sounded so peaceful. Almost romantic. Simon had planned to rub my back, and feed me ice chips. We were going to play classical music. We were going to pick out a boy's name and a girl's name. He was going to hold my hand throughout.

The nurse puts her hand firmly on my wrist, and I jerk my arm away from her, shouting, "I can't have this baby! I'm not ready!"

Someone's finger presses the number three, as if I'm just some crazy person talking to myself in the corner. When the doors shut, I hear the nurse whisper to another, "We may need the social worker on this one," which is all wrong. She's not understanding. Simon would never put up with people talking to me like this.

"Tillie." My father's voice comes from the back of the elevator.

"Oh, God, what are you doing here?" I crumble into tears.

"Tillie, don't get yourself worked up," he says.

The nurse nods her head in agreement. "You need to focus on the baby, Ms. Harris. You're going to have to get yourself ready."

And how does this happen? Even when he's not wearing his uniform, and though there's no way for the nurse to know that this slender man is largely responsible for nearly ninety thousand tons of bombs dropped this winter in the Persian Gulf War, my dad is giving orders and people just carry them out.

The elevator doors open again, and I'm wheeled into a dim room, muddy pink with teddy bear wallpaper only along the ceiling.

"Here, ma'am. I need you to stand up." A technician holds one of my arms at the elbow, hoisting me out of the chair.

I feel air on my backside, and move my hand to close the gown, when the nurse says, "Hold it right there." I feel the cold wet of an alcohol swab just above my butt. "Okay, you're going to feel a little stick."

"What is that?"

"This is a corticosteroid to help speed up the development of the baby's lungs."

"Please," I squeak, my nose stuffy from crying. "Please, stop the labor."

"Okay, let's get her on the bed. One, two, three, lift your hips now."

I don't lift at all, but somehow I find myself on top of a bed with wheels.

She lifts my sleeve and swabs a cotton ball on the inside of my arm. "Some extra fluids for you," she says, inserting an IV tube, then hanging a clear bag on a metal pole beside the bed.

"Would you like—is this your father? Would you like him with you?"

"No!" I shake my head so hard I'm dizzy. "Dad, get out of here! Oh, God, here comes another one." I take a deep breath as if I'm about to get dragged underwater.

"Here, let me tie up her hair," the nurse says, finding the rubber band on the floor.

She's rough, snagging strands that cause me to reach for my head, but the pain returns to my back and my belly, and I don't have enough hands to hold everything that aches. I simply moan, looking up to the tiles and the sprinkler system, hoping for any distraction from the pain. Nothing helps. I can only live through it and try to recover my strength during the few minutes in-between.

Clear liquid flows down tubes into my arm. And now they've attached a belt to my abdomen with wires that dangle between my legs, connecting me to a fetal heart monitor. I hear continuous clicks—like my brother opening and shutting the ashtray in our old car—as a strip of paper rolls on and on with the jagged mountains and valleys of the baby's heartbeat on it. There are so many wires, so many different machines I'm attached to, I can hardly move in any direction without feeling a tug. I've lost track of who is in the room with me, and it seems like everyone here has looked between my legs and stuck a hand inside. Any sense of modesty I had is long gone.

Another contraction grabs hold and I'm too exhausted to cry. I just cover my face and feel the utter despair that the pain is inevitable, that my protests make no difference. I wonder if this was how my mother felt in her blue-lit prison, face-to-face with what she couldn't control.

I grip the damp sheets through the next round of contractions, which come so fast, one on top of the other, that all I can do is blubber miserably. I can feel the baby moving down, pressing on my lower back, like it's going to come out of the wrong hole. When Dr. Young enters the room, wearing a mask and blue scrub cap, I tell him this, though it comes out as cursing. He only nods, then turns on a huge round light, like an eye that swoops down from the ceiling, and I feel someone place my feet in stirrups again, and someone else breaks down the table so, without me having to move, my legs are open wide at the very end of it.

"Ms. Harris," he says, "the baby's ready. I want you to push as hard as you can while I count to ten."

"No," I sob. "I'm too tired."

"I know. It's tough. It's tough," the nurse says.

"Push!" he commands.

"No!"

"Push!"

"Stop yelling at me!"

22

The Ghost of Momma

IN THE CENTER OF the school playground, there was a teth-erball pole. Just the pole. The ball and the rope it hung from were never replaced after a weekend of vandalism, and so the pole was mostly used for base during games of tag, and occasionally for boys who wanted to show how fast they could shimmy up to the top. Today it was free.

With one hand holding the pole, I walked in circles, leaning out toward the ground, watching my shadow. The pole burned, but I held on, listening to the squeak of my hand against the metal and telling myself, *I got my wish. I got my wish.*

It had been one week since I was caught trying to escape with Momma. One week since we all stood in the basement with the lights on and Dad shouting, "Go to your rooms!" I ran as fast as I could in three layers of pants and Momma's long shawl, tripping all the way to my room, where I shoved myself under the bed. It hurt, and I wanted it to. I felt hot and cramped, unable to lift my head. The perfume Momma had dabbed behind my ears was too strong, and I wanted air.

Phil came up the stairs slow and steady, as if still considering all that he'd seen. When he got to his room, I heard the first crash. He'd taken a swipe at the pyramid of beer cans he kept on the shelf over his bed, and the cans clanked against each other as they tumbled. Then there was another crash, and another, and the sound of him kicking the ones that had already fallen against the wall.

My hand squealed against the pole as I spun faster.

The woman my father brought up from the basement was a ghost of my mother. She slumped on the couch in the formal living room like a person with no bones, her orange hair brittle and knotted. The makeup she wore the night before was faded but still visible on her face—a ring of lipstick, a trace of rouge, mascara smudged below the eyes.

"Your mother hasn't been well," Dad said, standing right in front of her. Though his voice was calm, the veins stood out in his neck and forearms. "She wasn't well, and I was caring for her."

"That's not true," I argued. "She's well. And *I* was caring for her." I held her limp hand as she stared forward. The sunlight from the window was cruel, revealing loose skin, dull eyes. I squeezed tighter.

"Tillie," he said, "there's a lot you're not understanding."

"You're wrong," I told him, but under my breath and without any courage.

"She would be embarrassed if people knew she'd been living in the basement," he continued. And then he repeated the rule I knew so well: "This is a family matter, and we won't talk about it outside of this house." But we weren't talking about it inside of the house, either.

The only real sound of protest came when Phil dragged his feet through the beer cans. There were sixty-eight cans in his collection, sixty-eight cans still lying on his floor a week later. No one mentioned them, but every day, the sound of Phil going in or out of his room sent a shiver through the house.

I spun so fast, the world began to blur. I didn't realize my eyes had been closed, but when I opened them, they stung from the brightness of the sun. Turning my head toward the pole, I saw a brown hand just above mine. I didn't need to look behind me to know it was Shirl because she always wore a ring made of wire and shaped like a butterfly, and she had the cleanest fingernails, like she never once clawed into the dirt to pick up a worm.

"Why are you outside for recess?" I asked, still walking in circles. My jaw hurt when I talked, as if I'd been biting down too hard and for too long.

"You've been going around the pole for a half hour," she said, staying with me.

"So?"

"So what's your problem?"

I slowed and considered telling her everything. I could feel the words in my throat and in my chest—heavy as stones—but something stopped me. Maybe the habit of keeping secrets. Or maybe the shrieks of laughter on the playground, reminding me how badly I wanted to be like the other kids.

"I don't know," I mumbled. "Just feel like spinning, I guess."

Though I felt queasy, I kept on turning until the bell rang to go back to class. When I finally stood still, the monkey bars, the field, the slide all turned in circles and smashed into each other as if I were viewing them through a kaleidoscope. I let go of the pole, and my arm ached at the elbow. My hand, its palm sore from rubbing for so long against the metal, would not straighten. It stayed scrunched up like a claw, like I could grab something and strangle it.

⌘

IT WAS THE QUIET that bothered me. It was everything continuing as usual as if nothing had happened. It was walking through the hallway at school, and seeing the same kid cut in line at the water fountain, the same one do a lay-up to touch the EXIT sign. It was sitting in my seat, pulling one of the chewed pencils from my desk, and writing $9 \times 3 = 27$. How had all the screaming and crashing cans come to this? Where were the police asking if I wanted to keep my father with us or send him to jail? Where were the crowds of neighbors wondering how I survived?

I tried to remind myself: *I got my wish. I have my mother back.* But she wasn't the same person I had known in secret—handing me trinkets, whispering stories, and calling me a poet. In the week since she'd been upstairs with us, I only saw her leave the couch once, at Dad's insistence, to join us for dinner. She took painfully slow steps to the table, the sash loose around her bathrobe, exposing the bones above her chest. She bent over a serving of chicken and broccoli, her makeup washed away so her face had become faint—lips as pale as her skin, eyes like faded blue dots. She only put food into her mouth when Dad ordered her to do it.

I knew we weren't supposed to talk about private family matters, but the secrets felt right there at the surface. They were tangled in my mind with math problems and spelling. And when the school bell rang, they rattled inside me as I walked down the hallway. I looked toward the glass wall of the main office, where the teachers and principal stood, fighting an urge to tell.

But telling wasn't so easy to do. I didn't know where to begin, for one thing. Would I just blurt out that my mother was locked in our basement for almost a year? Because if I said this, they'd call home, and the only one who answered our phone was Dad. He could show them my mother sitting right there in the living room, not in the basement at all.

As I continued out the main doors of the school, Phil was ready to take the path into the woods that led to the river. I jogged beside him, but he sped up, trying to lose me. Frustrated, I simply stopped where I was, put my hands on my hips, and shouted, "Are you going to tell?"

He turned, his face stretched tight. "I'm no whiner," he said. "And what do you think would happen if you told someone?" He dropped his book bag and put his hands in the air, wiggling his fingers. "Do you think things would just magically get better? Mom would stop being a crazy person?"

He picked up his bag again and walked fast toward the path. I didn't try to catch him. I turned up the sidewalk toward the patrols waiting at the top of the hill. Sometimes the easiest thing to do is nothing. You just make do. Keep your mouth closed and hope all the rattling goes away. You walk home from school, pretending everything's the same, running your hand along the hedges and fences, like there's nothing waiting for you but your homework.

❧

23

A Note on the Fridge

ONE OF THE TOYS that never made it to the new house was my Drowsy Doll. She had a plastic head and plastic hands and eyes that were always halfway closed, but the rest of her, the part wearing pink footed pajamas, was as soft as a bean bag. And what I liked best about this doll was how, after months of carrying her around, she got even softer and smelled like a real person.

Drowsy Doll had a pull string on her hip, and she'd say, "I'm sleepy" or "I want a drink of water." But I wasn't careful with my toys, and after too many times left in the rain and too many times of being carried by her string, she stopped talking.

Eventually, she sunk to the bottom of my toy box and stayed there until one day, for no reason at all, she started to say something in a slow and muddled voice. By the time I dug her out she was silent again, even after I shook her hard. Dad said I should throw her out, and I guessed that's what he did the day he packed the U-Haul. He didn't understand that even if she never talked again I would miss her smell, her soft belly, and the way she always fell asleep at the same time as I did. Now something was breaking inside my mother that I wasn't sure could be fixed again. Though Dad had moved her upstairs, she didn't become a part of our lives.

⁓

DAD CARRIED A CARDBOARD box filled with Momma's belongings up from the basement, and I hoped this would help cheer her up. I set out her favorite trinkets and books. I set out her makeup but hid her mirror. I thought when the room was friendlier and more familiar looking, I'd see a sign of the mother I knew in private.

"Phil, why don't you help, too?" Dad said, heading back downstairs with a bucket and sponge. "Help unload that box."

Up until then, Phil had been sitting in a corner of the room with his *Mad* magazine, turning pages faster than he could read them. But when Dad gave the command—because Phil always did what he was told—he came right over to the box. At first, he reached inside and picked up Momma's beret with just two fingers, as if it was something disgusting to touch. Sneering, he looked around for a place in our home where her things might belong. And when he didn't see anything obvious, he simply dragged the entire box to the hallway closet, where he dumped it upside down and shut the door.

Momma turned her head away—never willing to fight with Phil or tell him what to do—but I knew she didn't want to see him hurting her, either. I scooted close beside her, patting her leg. I was happy with the display I'd made of her favorite things and waited for her to feel better. I waited for her to tell me one of her stories or pass me some object we could admire. I sat till the edge of the couch dug grooves into the backs of my legs. The whole time she hardly moved.

I sat with her like this each day—after school and after dinner, sometimes with the TV on, though we didn't really watch it, and sometimes with a book opened in her lap, though she didn't look at the words. I often passed time by flipping my eyelids inside out, which made the room blur and darken. It was like the fade-out of a TV show, and I could roll my eyelids back down if something started to happen again.

It was another night eating dinner in the front of the television—the easiest way to bring us together. I liked listening to Walter Cronkite, who was always calm, just sitting with us in the living room and telling stories. He told about a peanut farmer who wanted to be president and a high school football team that didn't like the bused kids joining it. Phil sat on the floor because there was no room on the couch, and Dad, rather than watching TV, spent dinner glaring at a dirty fork Momma had dropped on the floor.

"Dad," Phil said, "isn't that your research they're talking about?"

The TV showed protesters on college campuses, waving signs that said: STOP THE WAR MACHINE. BOOKS NOT BOMBS. NO CLASSIFIED RESEARCH ON OUR CAMPUS.

"Zealots," Dad muttered. "Why wouldn't they want more accurate missile strikes?"

He grabbed his plate and Momma's fork and took them into the kitchen. "Am I the only one who cleans up after myself in this house?" he yelled, like he'd been in the middle of an argument with someone. "I work all day, and then I come home and work some more—dinner, dishes, trash. And now we're practically out of groceries, and I suppose I'm the one who has to go shopping."

He came back into the room and turned off the TV in the middle of a story about porpoises who died tangled up in fishing nets. "Phil. Tillie. In the car," he announced. "And Mara, I don't want to see you lying on the couch when we get back. I'm not kidding about this."

We drove to the commissary, though there was a grocery store not five minutes from our house. Dad always made the thirty-minute trek to shop at the local base, not just for the military discount, but because the world there was orderly. Customers moved through the aisles in a quiet, disciplined fashion. Unlike Safeway, parents at the commissary didn't open a box of cookies before they paid for them, just to quiet a baby's crying. And here, no child dared to put one foot on the bottom metal rack of the cart and push off with the other.

Phil strolled the cart down the aisle with excellent posture, stopping whenever Dad found something from his list. He was as polite and distant as a stranger since Momma had come back.

"Colonel Harris?" A soldier slowed his cart near ours in the produce aisle and saluted. "I've been following your research, sir," he said, and they shook hands.

While they talked, I searched a nearby apple bin, turning each one to see which was best.

"Leave those alone," Phil said. "Don't put your fingers on everything." But I kept touching them until I found one that was huge, without a flat side or a soft spot, and so red it looked painted.

I walked over to Dad as the soldier said, "Now tell me, what part of the missile are you actually involved with? The payload?"

"No. It's a navigation system that will be accurate to within a few hundred yards."

"Spare some lives?"

"It will be more efficient."

"Well, keep up the good work, Colonel Harris. Don't let the critics stop you."

I held up the apple. "Dad, can I get this?"

"Sh. Don't interrupt."

I mouthed, *Can I get this?* And he nodded.

Phil would never have gotten away with the same thing, and to show he noticed, he turned the cart just enough so I ran into it. But I held tight to the apple, all the way to the checkout. I even requested for it to be put in its own bag, ignoring Phil's groans.

We left the store, past the salutes, past those who smiled as if congratulating me for being Colonel Harris's daughter. When we were on the road again, I rolled down the window and let the wind blow my hair. The sun had almost set, and in the towns between the commissary and our house, flyers stapled to trees and telephone polls seemed to glow in the dark: STOP BUSING. SAVE OUR NEIGHBORHOODS! I'd seen these signs pinned to the bulletin board at the library and at Robertson's Five and Ten.

There were no such signs as we turned onto the streets closer to home, just neighbors walking their dogs and polishing their cars with Turtle Wax. It was against the community rules to hang any posters at all. If you wanted to advertise a yard sale or post a notice about your missing pet, you had to use the bulletin board near the nature center. Our neighborhood always looked peaceful, just as we did, stepping out of the car with our bags of groceries—and no one could tell what we returned to when we opened our door.

· · ·

There were overturned books and a loaf of bread left open on the couch. A trail of scented powder led across the carpet, stopping at Momma. She stood by the bay window overlooking the swimming pool, filled with rainwater and broken branches, ivy creeping through cracks in the cement.

I put my hand on her back and asked, "Do you want to go outside?"

She shook her head, didn't even look at me—only closed her bathrobe tighter.

Dad slammed the groceries into the fridge and cupboards, and finally shouted, "Mara, don't you think you can give us a hand?"

"I'm not feeling well," she said, still focused outside.

"Okay, so you're not feeling well again." He stomped into the room and pointed to the couch, where Sylvia Plath, Anne Sexton, and Virginia Woolf lay upside down with their spines broken. "But you have time to read these books, is that right?"

I stood between them. "*I* can help with the groceries."

He ignored me. "If you can't help in the kitchen, maybe you can help Tillie with her homework?"

She bent over as if she'd been punched, but Dad made no effort to comfort her. He simply put his hands in his pockets.

"I don't really need any help," I told him, and with that, he sent me to bed.

That night, Momma cried like an animal caught in a trap. In-between sobs, she listed the reasons she hated my father. "You don't care. You don't care. You don't care."

"Do you want me to make that call?" he said. "Because I'm this close."

I couldn't hear my mother, only the sound of pleading and whimpering, and imagined this was like the fight Phil overheard the night they moved in.

"You're a disgrace. That's what you are," Dad said, so sure he was right. "Your being here doesn't add anything to their lives. In fact, you're a burden to them."

Momma said nothing—maybe feeling as I did—frozen and holding the pillow.

"I'm telling you right now," Dad continued. "I need to see a change, and soon. Get dressed. Take a bath. Do something for the children. Because if you can't pull it together, I've got the number right here."

And the next time I came downstairs, I saw a number for St. Elizabeth's taped to the fridge. I knew from my talks with Hope that it was one of the places people went into and never came back out. He was asking too much of her—things I knew she couldn't do—and I thought of my doll again, how, when a piece had broken, he threw her to the curb.

24

❧

Porcelain

"T ILLIE." MR. WOODSON KNELT beside my desk with his hand on my shoulder. "Don't you want to put your things away before you take your seat?"

I hadn't remembered getting to class at all. I sat there, wearing my jacket and book bag and holding a large paper sack with my apple inside of it. I looked up at him, not speaking, and walked, groggy, to the coat closet.

"Tillie, are you ready to find your seat?"

I had been standing by my coat hook, and though I heard him, I just couldn't move yet. My mind was full and blank all at once.

"When you're ready," he said.

The flawless apple was still cold from the refrigerator. I scratched a smile into it with my fingernail, on the bottom, where Mr. Woodson wouldn't see. And when I passed his desk, I gave it to him. He held the apple like it was easily hurt, and set it down gently beside his pencil holder as he called for us to sit on the rug.

We sat in a half circle. He sat in a kid's chair, his long legs bent like a grasshopper's, and told us the continuing adventures of Ed and Edna, two children who had gotten lost. That day they were stuck in a dungeon and we listened to find out if they'd escape. I could see the apple over his shoulder as if it levitated there.

I sat closest to him, and sometimes I touched my finger to his brown shoes, wishing he could know how much it mattered to me those times he tried to help. All through the day, I checked Mr. Woodson's desk to see if he'd eaten the apple. I imagined the smile I'd carved floating inside of him, all safe.

At play rehearsal, I moved my lips to the songs as the janitor in his blue jumpsuit pushed his mop down the length of the cafeteria. When Mrs. Newkirk called for a break, I realized I did not even know what scenes we'd run through. Everyone took seats at the tables throughout the room, and kids unwrapped their snacks—pretzel sticks, Little Debbie cakes, sunflower seeds. I'd forgotten to bring one, so I sat at the emptiest table and opened the *Encyclopedia D*.

Out the window, my father's car pulled up to the front of the school. Who'd ever believe the man coming to take Phil to a dental appointment was also the kind of villain who'd lock our mother in the basement and scare us into silence? I knew he expected Momma to get better, and quick, but it seemed like we were waiting for something horrible to happen.

Phil left the building with his hood pulled over the top of his head and got into the backseat, though he was allowed to ride in front. When I heard the sound of bells, I turned to see Shirl coming toward me with a lollipop in her mouth. She dropped a note and another sucker on the table in front of me before heading back to her seat.

I unfolded the lined paper, and over my shoulder, some classmates read it out loud: *You can come to my house. I asked. You can ride the bus home with me if your mom writes a note. SCB.*

The students who'd read the note started to laugh. "You'll never be found alive again!"

"Better not cross the tracks."

"My dad says they shoot white people over there."

I kept my eyes straight ahead and unwrapped the lollipop.

"Ooh, you're going to eat that?"

"You know why their skin is brown? It's from *you-know-what*." The student pressed her lips on the insides of her hands and blew. Everyone was cracking up.

I folded the note again and tucked it in my front pocket, thinking of Momma hugging the sofa pillow and Phil kicking his feet through the beer cans on his floor. Maybe it would be nice to spend an afternoon at Shirl's house.

"Okay, listen up, cast," Mrs. Newkirk announced. "I need to work on that last scene, but just with the leads. If you'd like to go home early, you can. And if you need to wait for your ride, you're welcome to play a game quietly in the back of the room. Everyone clear?"

The leads groaned, "Unfair." But it was only to draw attention to themselves as stars.

I started to leave when Shirl caught up with me. "Did you read the note?"

I nodded and said, "I'll have to ask."

She walked to the door with me, though she'd have to

stay for the whole rehearsal if she wanted to catch the late bus home.

"I wonder what our costumes will be," I said.

"I don't want to talk about it."

"Yeah, we got sucky parts. I thought you'd get cast as Dorothy."

Shirl was naturally dramatic, always standing with her hand on her hip and speaking in a voice so loud she didn't need a microphone. She even had the braids.

"Mrs. Newkirk isn't going to make someone like *me* Dorothy," she said, rolling her eyes. "She's kind of a—" I could tell she wanted to say a cuss word, but she got nervous, had probably never said the word out loud before.

"I don't know," I said. " Sometimes she'll look over her glasses, like this"—I made an exaggerated sour face—"but even that day she walked me to the principal's office, she wasn't mean about it."

"Well, I *know* she's going to be nice to *you*," she said. "All the teachers favor you because . . ."

I crossed my arms and waited for her to say it was because my skin was pink, and lump me together with all of the other kids in the auditorium. "Go ahead. Say it."

"Because of your dad," she said.

And now I moved my hands to my pockets because maybe she was right, and maybe I didn't want her to be.

A number of teachers had taken to calling me "the little academic," only because I carried an encyclopedia everywhere, and they seemed to expect that I might, at any moment, stop being so much like me and start being more like my father.

"I have to go," I said.

"Don't forget the note."

When I was a good distance from the school, I practiced singing "Follow the Yellow Brick Road" in my thin voice. I hadn't been cast as a yellow brick for nothing.

When I got home, Momma was seated on the edge of the couch with a plastic bag, a roll of wrapping paper, and some scotch tape beside her. She looked at me with red, puffy eyes, and smiled briefly. "We're going to have a party," she said, in almost a whisper.

"What do you mean? For what?" I put down my book bag.

"Your father bought this present," she said, handing me the plastic bag. "It's to celebrate Phil's new tooth." She started to cry.

"But that's good, Momma," I said, sitting beside her and taking the plastic bag from her lap. "Do you want me to wrap this?"

She rubbed her thumb back and forth along the jagged edge of the tape dispenser. "We're going to have Phil's favorite dinner and then one of those family nights. Don't you think this will be fun? It's like a new beginning." Her bottom lip trembled, and I took the paper and tape from her.

As I wrapped, Momma, holding a pen and a tiny card, hung her head over her lap. I thought of all those days and nights she was alone in the basement, before I'd discovered her there. She must have seen those TV commercials with families cheering for each other over games of Yahtzee and Electro Shot Shooting Gallery. I couldn't imagine us ever being like them.

When I finished wrapping, Momma uncapped the pen and wrote very slowly. The ink didn't show on the parts of the card where her tears had fallen.

"Do you want to get dressed up for the party?" I asked, taking the card and taping it to the package.

Her pajama bottoms were stained with food, and the robe didn't smell very good. "Here," I said, answering myself. "I'll pick out something you can wear."

I looked through the hallway closet, where Phil had dumped her things into a deep pile, glad to do something that would keep Dad from yelling at her again. The first piece of clothing I found was her kelly green sweater.

"That's fine," she said, reaching for it.

"In May? Are you sure?"

"It doesn't matter."

I handed her the sweater along with a necklace that had a tangled chain. And while Momma used the TV screen to apply her makeup, swirling the brushes in a kind of a daze, I continued to dig for a skirt or a pair of slacks.

By the time Dad's car pulled into the driveway, the living room floor was covered in clothes, scissors, tape, and cuttings of wrapping paper. Momma had put liner on one eye but not the other. She joined me in the foyer, her face half done, and wearing the sweater over her pajama bottoms. Even through his mustache, I saw Dad's disapproval, but I ran to straight to Phil.

"Show me," I said. "Let's see the new tooth."

He headed for the stairs and wouldn't turn around, so I followed him to his room and stood outside his door as he stared into the mirror.

"Let's *see*," I said again.

"It's just a tooth." He touched it with his finger.

I stepped over the cans to get closer. The *Dr. Demento Show* played on the radio, turned down so low I heard the laugh track but not the jokes. I stared along with my brother.

"I thought I'd look . . . you know—"

"Yeah," I said.

We could both see the problem. It was as if fixing the tooth called attention to the fact that his front teeth were too big, that his nose was still too small and round.

Dad called from the stairs. "Come on down, Phil."

"Wait!" Phil shouted, and then mumbled, "I just want to be by myself."

"We've kind of been planning something," I said.

"Dad told me." He tried looking at his mouth with his lips closed. "I don't want to have a party for my tooth."

Downstairs, Dad complained about the mess. "Pick this up. And this. Don't just set it down on the couch. That's not picking it up."

"Just do it for Momma," I said.

"It was easier when she was gone."

"Don't say that. She's been through so much."

"You don't get it," he said. "You didn't drive from Albuquerque with her."

Every time we really talked, he had to say something about that drive out here with the U-Haul and put her down one more time.

"You should be nicer to her. You said yourself she wasn't well."

We could hear Dad crumpling up wrapping paper and shoving it in the trash. "And your face," he lectured her. "What are you trying to do—scare the kids?"

"Come on," I said. "If you come downstairs, they'll stop fighting."

"Why should I care about that? Every one of you lied to me about what was happening in this house."

"*I* didn't! I told you the day I found her, and you didn't believe me! You told me I was crazy!"

On the radio was more laughter and the sound of a bicycle horn.

"Phil!" Dad was at the bottom of the stairwell again. "Phil, are you coming?"

"Come on, Phil," I said.

He turned up the volume on the radio to hear the song about worms by Captain Rock.

"Okay," I said. I stared one last time at the new tooth, which was pure white, making the others seem yellow, and then I went downstairs, where my parents stood uncomfortably at each other's side.

"We can start without him," I reported. "He thinks he looks ugly."

"Oh, that's ridiculous," Dad said. "Phil! Now!"

We all waited at the bottom of the staircase, Dad occasionally nudging Momma to stand up straight, like he was training her.

At last, my brother came down and stood on the bottom step, not raising his head.

"Don't just stand there with your eyes glazed over," Dad said to Momma under his breath. "Do something."

Momma took a small step toward Phil. "I'm sure the new tooth looks very good," she said. "Now you'll be more handsome than ever."

He scowled. With his unruly hair covering his eyes, Phil was anything but handsome, and he knew it.

"There's a present on the table for you," Dad said.

Phil stared at it, but didn't move from that bottom step.

"I'd like you to open it," Dad said more forcefully.

Momma reached out her hand to touch Phil's arm, but the moment she made contact, Phil jerked as if he'd been given an electric shock.

Dad snatched the present off the table and shook it hard with both hands, so Phil could hear it was a jigsaw puzzle. "Look," he said, pointing to the card. "It says it's a celebration for the whole family."

Phil said nothing, but turned a deep shade of pink, while Momma wrapped her arms about her waist.

"Open it!" Dad yelled as he ripped off the wrapping paper. "Like this, see? Just cooperate. Say, 'Oh, good, a puzzle. Let's put it together tonight!' "

With his hands balled into fists, Phil snatched the present from Dad and stormed outside. My pulse pumped in my neck when he slammed the door. For that split moment before the door latched, Momma reached out her hand—maybe to open the screen—but pulled it back again while Phil marched between our neat rows of marigolds. When he reached the middle of the street, he set up like a punter and dropped the puzzle toward his foot. With the first try, he missed completely and had to pick the box back off the ground. The second time he hit. It was a lousy kick.

❧❧

25

Wading into the Potomac

S O AFTER ALL THAT complaining about his tooth, he decides he likes it better silver," Dad said, clearing our plates. "I should have saved my money."

When Phil didn't come back inside to apologize, we taught him a lesson by finishing the celebration dinner without him. Dad said you can't reward temper tantrums, and if Phil chose to be left out, that was *his* problem.

Dad squirted the table clean, and soon all that was left on it was the puzzle he'd picked off the road hours earlier. Though Phil had kicked it, the box was hardly damaged.

"I'd like to put this together," I said, hoping to change the mood for Momma's sake.

I expected Dad to shake his head, but he opened the box and emptied the jigsaw pieces onto the table. Momma organized them into piles of like colors, her hands shaking, while Dad grumbled continuously about the importance of listening and respecting your superiors.

"I'm sure he snuck in the side door," he said, keeping his eyes turned toward the puzzle. "He's probably in his room, pouting." But of course this wasn't true, or we would have heard the cans.

After a while, Momma left the table to sit alone on the couch. Dad got up next, but I continued to stare at the puzzle because I wanted to finish the edge of the sky.

I could hear Dad opening a Hefty bag, and soon he moved from room to room, collecting trash. Each time he left a room, he turned off its light, and after he left the living room, he turned off Momma's light, too, not even seeing her there.

"Dad, wait," I said. But I could hear he was already moving to another floor of the house.

I got up to hit the switch, but Momma said, "Just leave it off." And she began to cry.

"It's okay, Momma," I said, finding my way to her side. "It's okay." Though we both knew it wasn't.

At first I could only hear her sniffling and feel the thin terry cloth of her robe, but light from the dining room helped me gradually see her and the tears streaming down her face. I sat beside her and didn't move, though my neck ached. When she wiped her nose with her sleeve, I uncurled my fist, not even realizing my hand had been in a fist, and inside was a sweaty puzzle piece, the slick side peeling away from the cardboard. Dad would have to mark another game box with masking tape and a note that said: *Missing piece of sky.*

We heard Dad move through the different floors of the house, heard him go out a side door and then come back in. Steadily, his pace picked up, opening and closing doors with more force, until finally I heard him grab his car key off the wicker table beside his bed. He burst into the living room and threw on the light.

"Tillie, get your jacket."

"Why? What's wrong?"

"I need your help finding Phil."

Momma covered her mouth, her blue eyes wide open with worry as Dad walked out the door. I hurried behind him, forgetting my jacket, hardly able to keep up.

"I think you upset Momma," I said, starting to jog.

"We can't worry about that right now. I won't have this kind of disobedience from your brother." He unlocked my door. "Get in."

We drove slowly past the school, the 7-Eleven, the small park with the bent basketball rim. We drove beside a boy who scuffled along the sidewalk in a hooded sweatshirt, hands in his pockets.

"Is that him?" Dad asked.

I rolled down my window. "Phil," I called, and he walked faster.

We stayed with him and I continued to shout, "Phil!" until, finally, he turned around to give us the finger and to show we'd been following the wrong boy.

"What if we don't find him?" I said, facing forward in my seat again.

"We'll find him, and he's not going to do this again."

The sky, always true to my box of sixty-four Crayola crayons, had turned from Ocean to Midnight Blue. Dad drove slowly up and down the blocks Phil liked to walk, and then, as if an idea suddenly came to him, he sped up, drove through several stop signs and across and then below the Cabin John Bridge. He stopped the car so the headlights shone on the bank where Phil liked to fish. It was too dark to see anything at first and then our eyes found the shadow on a nearby sandbar.

"Phil!" Dad called, jumping out of the car.

Whoever it was on the other side of the river wasn't moving. Dad started to cross the rocks toward the shadow, but his shoes slipped underwater. He shouted back for me to stay on the bank, but I followed.

Each slippery step brought us farther into the dark water, the shock of cold seeping into my shoes. I could barely see the shadow slumped against that huge rock, but I just knew it was him.

"Phil!" Dad called again, and there was no answer. "Tillie, go back," he told me. Then, seeing how far I'd come, he said, "Okay, come with me. Stay close."

"Is he dead?"

"Tillie, hush."

"Oh no, I hope he's not dead."

Dad hurried across the rocks and jumped onto the sandbar. I could now clearly see Phil's wet and motionless body, his knit cap with hair curling out of the bottom. Dad had just about reached him when my legs refused to go any closer. I didn't want to see. I didn't want to drive home with his body facedown across the backseat.

Dad slowly bent down to touch his shoulder, and my brother went wild, punching and screaming, "Get off of me!"

He'd only been sitting there, brooding. I almost wanted to laugh. My father grabbed him by the shoulders and rolled him on his back. "Phil, get control of yourself!"

My brother kicked again. "You can't make me!"

Both of their voices were strange and high-pitched. I slipped off a rock and stood shin-deep in the water as they wrestled on the ground, Phil swinging his arms and Dad sticking his knee on Phil's chest, pinning him there with all his weight.

"Get. Off," Phil said.

You could see how much force Dad had put into his knee, my brother struggling for air. Finally, when Phil had stopped thrashing around, Dad stood up. And never taking his eye off of him, he said, "Get in the car."

My brother didn't move, except for he was shivering so hard. We all were.

"Phil, just do it," I said, up to my knees in the river. "I'm freezing."

Phil's face showed how cold and exhausted he was. I knew he wanted to be in the car as much as I did; he just didn't want it to be Dad's idea.

Dad took my hand to help me back across the rocks.

"I'd rather stay here and freeze," Phil said, but all the while, he followed behind us.

Dad seemed to understand that Phil's cooperation counted on him being quiet and not turning around to look. He made no comment when Phil got into the back of the car and kicked the passenger seat as we drove past the black water. Dad only spoke when we pulled up to the house, telling us to shower before bed or we'd catch colds.

The house was dark, and Momma lay with her face to the back of the couch. I couldn't tell if her eyes were open or closed. Phil and I sulked up the stairs, smelling of fish and mud. When we got to the hallway at the top, Phil stared at me with his mouth stretched tight so that his lips disappeared into a thin line. Then, with no change in his expression, he punched me hard in the ribs.

I gasped for air, trying to punch back, but he palmed my

forehead so I couldn't reach him. "This family's a joke," he said, shoving me to the floor.

There was no point in getting up. It would just encourage him to knock me down again. I stayed there, level with his soaked jeans and shoes, until he walked away, each step oozing water. I waited to hear the clanging of cans, and when it was finally quiet, I crawled to my room and into bed with my wet clothes. I could still feel his fist in my ribs, and it felt good, like the truest thing that had happened in months.

26

Hush Now

ALONG THE SIDE OF the house, I sat on one of the stone
steps, pitching rocks into the ivy. If the ivy ever died back,
you would see the many things I'd buried there: school exams
with disappointing scores; Halloween candy I refused to eat—
Almond Joys, caramels, Raisinettes; even silverware I didn't
want to wash because something gross was stuck on it.

"Well, there you are," Dad said. "I've been looking for you."

"I've been here." I pitched some small rocks and let them
disappear into the green.

"I'll get right to it," he said. "Your mother and I are having
trouble making this work, and we have some difficult decisions
to make."

"Dad, no. We just got her back."

"I'm sorry, Tillie."

"I'm going to go see her," I said, rising to my feet.

"No, you're not." He tugged me back down by my belt loop.

"I need to go to the office to get some work done, and you're coming with me."

"I want to stay here."

"Your mother needs some time alone," he said, and mumbled something about the complicated world of adults. Then he picked up a rock. Pitched it. Picked up another, and so did I. As soon as he released his, I tried to hit it down. The next time, I threw a whole handful.

"You're just going to give up on her?"

"We haven't made any decisions yet, but we're running out of things to try."

"You never even tried being nice," I whispered.

"What? I didn't hear you."

"Never mind," I said, throwing another rock.

"Okay, then. I'm going to get my briefcase, and I'll meet you at the car."

As I stood by the Volvo's back door, Phil rode down the cul-de-sac on a plastic skateboard, banana shaped and neon yellow.

"Where did you get that?"

"When your friend moved, they dumped all kinds of stuff on the curb," he said, hopping off and scooping it into his hand.

I reached out to touch the nicks, spin the wheels. It felt good to have something of Hope's.

"Want to ride it?" he asked.

I remembered how it tickled the bottoms of my feet when I rumbled down Hope's driveway, always jumping off before I got going too fast.

"I can't. I have to go to Dad's office," I said.

"Too bad. I'll be riding this down to the school."

"Why don't *you* have to go?"

"I guess he's not worried about leaving me with a crazy lady."

"Shut up." I tried to stomp on his foot, but he moved it.

"Don't get so touchy," he said.

"Did Dad tell you?"

He hunched one shoulder toward his ear. "Doesn't surprise me."

Phil changed after that night on the Potomac and not in the way I expected. I thought he'd start blasting his music; he played it softer. I thought he'd skip meals; he was there right on time, then cleared his dishes afterward. In some ways, he seemed more agreeable than ever, except there was always a twist: He'd clear the dishwasher but put things back in the wrong places. Or Dad would suggest we eat a vegetable for snack, and Phil would bite into a head of iceberg lettuce.

Dad closed the front door, hurrying down the steps with his briefcase in one hand and a blazer draped over the other arm. "Why doesn't Phil have to go?" I asked him.

"Oh, he's coming, too." Dad turned the key in the driver's side door. "Come on, Phil. We're going to spend a few hours at my office."

"I'll be ready in just a minute," Phil said. "I just have to clean off my shoe. I stepped in something pretty bad."

I didn't see anything on his shoe, though he scraped the bottom of one across the grass. Dad checked his watch and opened the door to his perfectly clean car.

"I'll just give it a quick rinse with the hose," Phil said, and when he turned on the water, he made noises like the smell was killing him.

"Why don't you stay and clean it right?" Dad said, just as Phil knew he would.

"Are you sure?" Phil asked, pretending to hurry, but Dad was already in the car, reminding me to buckle.

Phil bent over by the hose until we backed out of the drive-way. But before we'd even driven around the corner, he was rolling down the street, pumping his arms in the air.

I didn't mind spending the day at the Pentagon because once Dad shut himself in his office I had Anne's work area to myself. Her chair had wheels, and when I lay my stomach over the seat, I could race across the floor until Dad told me I was making too much noise.

I moved along to Anne's desk, peeking through all her neatly organized supplies: colored paper, Wite-Out, index cards. I made a chain from the paper clips I found in her drawer and was about to turn it into a necklace when a voice startled me from behind.

"Comfortable?" I turned around to find Anne with her hard-to-read smile. "How about just use three paperclips? That way I can still do my work on Monday."

I began to unhook the chain while she moved every single item on her desk, even the things I hadn't touched—turning the paperweight and the letter holder as if correcting a wrong I had done.

"I see you've been enjoying the typewriter, too."

She usually kept it covered, but I liked typing my name so fast on the noisy electric keys that it sounded like gunfire.

"My dad's going to replace the ribbon," I said, trying to explain why there were parts taken out. "He was trying to figure out how to do it but had to get the phone."

"It's a good thing building missiles is so much easier than fixing typewriters," she said, finding a new ribbon and inserting it into the machine.

"I'll put these back," I said, hurrying to detach each link.

"That's a good girl," she said, now using her friendly voice. "I heard Phil had a little flare-up this week. Is that right?"

I paused, feeling trapped by the question. Slowly, I nodded as I slipped the paper clips back into her desk. Even after I shut the drawer, I kept my eyes to the floor.

"Well, I'm glad he pulled it together. I'm sure *your situation* at home hasn't been easy on him."

I felt tight all over, wondering just what Dad had told her, and knowing she would only have heard his side of the story. She put her hands on my shoulders. I started trembling, and was angry my body had given away that something was wrong.

"Hush now," she said, though I hadn't been crying or whimpering at all; she only seemed to fear that I might.

She pulled the other chair close to hers and said, "Here. Let's have a little chat." We sat with our knees touching like I'd seen the popular girls do at school. "I know your mother hasn't been well. That it's a delicate situation."

I wondered *which* delicate situation she knew about. "She's just tired," I said, immediately wishing I'd kept my mouth shut.

"That's a very generous way for you to phrase it," she said. "We certainly hope she'll get better, but that just may not be the case. Your father's tried all he could."

"He *hasn't*!" I said, clenching my teeth together and standing so my toes pressed against hers. "He's mean to her."

She tipped her head upward just a little. "It's not easy to help someone who's uncooperative," she said. "But I know your father will find the best solution."

"My mother's not going anywhere," I said, my nose so close

to the top of her head, all I smelled was hairspray. "If she does, I'll go with her."

"Well, these are not things to be decided by a seven-year-old."

"I'm eight."

"Watch your talking back."

"Eight isn't a bad word."

"Tillie," she said, standing, so I was shorter than her again, "you don't have to trouble yourself with any of these decisions. They're for your father to make so you can be free to enjoy school and talk on the phone and ride your bike."

I almost laughed, trying to imagine myself waving to kids in the hallway at school and then running home to chat on the phone. Sometimes I noticed my bike leaning against the porch, but I hadn't ridden it in weeks.

When Anne grinned again, I recognized it as the same expression she had when she accepted Momma's invitation to dinner almost a year ago.

Sometimes when I thought about Anne, she seemed the easiest to blame for all that had happened. If I'd fought harder to get out of her car, I could have run back to Momma. I could have fallen asleep under her arm and ridden in the U-Haul to our new house. I could have been there to stop the big fight.

She pointed for me to sit back down. "Here now," she said, sitting in her own chair again and placing her hand on my knee. "You know you can talk to me about anything that's bothering you."

It was so hard to keep it all down. I didn't like or trust Anne, but I longed to confess *something*, and finally blurted out, "My friend just moved. My best friend, Hope." I could tell Anne this because she wouldn't question whether Hope was still my friend.

"You'll make another," she said, pleased, as if she'd solved my problems just like that. "Tillie, look at me. You're a soldier's soldier. Whatever happens, you won't dwell on the past when you can march forward."

My face heated up before I even realized I was mad. In the other room, I heard Dad load his briefcase and then snap the locks.

"Well," he said, coming through the door. "Here's a surprise."

"We were just discussing bike riding and making new friends," she said, and he gave an approving nod.

Dad put on his blazer and said, "I just had a productive phone call with a congressman who thinks there's some potential backing for our missile project."

"Now that's very good news," she said and patted my head.

"I just have to send over a proposal, renaming it a *navigation* project and exploring some nonmilitary uses for the technology."

"Must appease the zealots," she said, "or they'll get busy with their signs and petitions again."

"I'm going to start on the proposal as soon as I get home," he said, buttoning the jacket at his waist. "I think," he continued quietly, as if talking only to himself, "if we add NUDET sensors to the payload, that would satisfy the DoD's need for a joint program."

"It's all very exciting, don't you think, Tillie?" She put her hands on her knees to speak closer to my face. "One day, I'll bet you'll be a famous scientist, like your father."

"I'm going to be a poet."

She paused for a minute as if trying to figure out if I'd just told a joke, then said to my father, "I'll be ready to type up your proposal the moment you need me."

"Can we go now?" I asked him.

"Yes, yes, Pest, we can go now."

I was almost out the door when Dad called me back. "Remember your manners."

And eyes on my sneakers, I muttered, "Thank you for a very nice time."

"You'll have to come closer," Anne said. "I didn't hear you."

Standing in front of her chair, I repeated, "Thank you for a very nice time."

"It was my pleasure, Tillie." She brushed my hair behind my ears. "You're a soldier's soldier," she whispered. "No more feeling sorry for yourself. It's time for you to march forward."

All through the cement hallways of the Pentagon, I walked with my fists clenched, remembering Dad's words on nights he cooked lasagna. *Swallow, Tillie. Just swallow!* It was a food I could hardly force myself to put in my mouth—it was just too many flavors at one time—and I'd try holding my breath and swallowing without chewing it first. Most times I could get it down, but I wasn't at all sure that it would *stay* down.

27

Apple

MY PILLOW WAS HOT and damp. I turned it over to the cool side, and flipped my body to face the wall. I still couldn't sleep, so I put on my robe and walked down the stairs, first one flight and then another. I shut my eyes and held the rail so it felt like before, walking into the black, electric with fear and longing, my pulse thumping in my neck.

I knew what I was doing, that I was only pretending everything was how it used to be. That she'd be there in the blue glow—mine alone—and we'd share sodas and books warmed by her hands.

I love you the best. I'm always listening for you.

Eyes still closed, my feet could feel that I was on the landing, where the staircase turned to the right, the door just at the bottom. I patted the wall for the cold metal knob. The door was open, but I could make myself forget that. I closed it behind me, and felt my way through the dark to my side of the couch. It was my first time back to the secret room since our failed escape.

"I'm here, Momma."

Have a look through this box. See if there's anything you want.

If I let myself stay sleepy and focused only on the memory, she was there, on her side of the couch, a plastic bag filled with makeup sitting between us.

I uncapped a lipstick and circled it round and round over my lips as Momma looked on, amused. She reached over with a Kleenex and wiped where I'd missed my mouth. Then she pointed to where I'd misbuttoned my robe and fixed it for me.

All better.

I rubbed my fist over my mouth, thinking of the cool, smooth lipstick. I buttoned and rebuttoned my robe, trying not to let myself believe I was alone. Over and over I let her fix my face, my buttons. And when I was ready to sleep again, I told her, "I'll stay here tonight."

I took my robe off and folded it into something that felt like her lap. I lay my head down and combed my fingers through my hair.

"I'm going to stay here. Is that okay? I'm going to fall asleep right here."

❧❀❧

SOMETIMES I BORROWED THE hall pass at school just to take a walk. When the halls were empty, I'd zigzag from one wall to the other or try to hop on only the white tiles. If there was no one in the bathroom, I'd take handfuls of paper towels, wet them under the sink, and fling them to the ceiling to see if they'd stick.

Today I just walked from one end to the other, remembering my confusion when I woke up this morning in the basement, hearing Dad call for me. I rose before I was ready, angry at the cold. My neck hurt from sleeping with my head propped up too high, and I wasn't sure where I was at first. The secret room had changed so much—no sense of Momma there at all.

I started to jog because I wasn't sure how long I'd been gone from class. If you take too long with the hall pass, you lose your privilege. I hurried down one hallway and turned down the other when I found myself walking right behind Phil. I slowed down to avoid his seeing me, and the angry glare that would follow. It was hard to get more than a glimpse of him anymore. You heard him, of course, before school, kicking through the cans, and sometimes you saw the back of him ducking through an old chain-link fence—the new route he took to school. It was twice the distance, and a real trek through tall weeds and poison ivy, but he'd do anything to be left alone.

It used to be that my brother would walk down the hallway at school with one arm brushing the wall, but now he walked down the center, his shoulders broad from pumping weights. I doubted anyone noticed he had the silver cap removed because he still kept his mouth closed in that same grim expression, but you could tell something about him had grown strong. When a group of kids approached, he didn't move out of the way. *They* had to.

Mr. Woodson waited outside the classroom for me. "Did you get lost?" he asked, taking the hall pass and guiding me back and through the rows of desks.

Ever since I'd found the note he'd written on the back of my poems I would read it over and over. I even pinned it on the wall near my pillow because it made the days not hurt so much.

"Mr. Woodson," I asked, "when are you going to eat that apple?" For a week and a half it had been sitting on his desk in the heat—now bruised and leaning to one side.

"I'll have it after school, Tillie, but right now you need to get back to your seat."

I followed him to the blackboard, where he began to write our spelling words in a list that sloped to the right.

"Please sit," he said.

But I didn't want to sit. I wanted to stand near him while he read my poems and ate my apple and asked how I'd found one that was so red. I wanted him to tell me again how Ed and Edna escaped from the dungeon. I wanted him to know my favorite shows, my favorite color, and what I wanted to be when I was old enough to marry him.

"Tillie. I mean it."

He continued to write words on the blackboard, while something as red as the apple burned in my chest. And rather than returning to my seat, I slumped under his desk, where— throughout the entire lesson and up until the class got in line for recess—he ignored me. Only then, my back hurting by that time, did he poke his head under the desk and say I could join everyone, or I could stay under there all day long. It was my choice.

I chose a third option. When he left me and Shirl behind to escort the class to the playground, I snuck the apple off his desk. I took it to the bathroom and (thanks to Shirl, who stood guard at the door) I peed on it, letting it soak into the smile on the bottom. After I dried the apple with a paper towel, I put it back on his desk, and Shirl returned to her seat, giggling. I stared straight ahead, dead serious.

I stomped all the way home, past my mother, asleep on the couch with the same books open to the same pages, and continued upstairs to my room. There, I unpinned Mr. Woodson's note from the wall—not letting myself read it or smell the painted paper or touch the thick red dots to my lips.

Everything ached. It was the feeling I had at my last birthday party, dressed in Momma's high heels with napkins shoved into the toes to make them fit, and listening to the phone ring with one cancellation after another. Everyone had a good excuse, but I knew the reason they weren't coming was because I might bite.

Before I could change my mind, I dropped the note with the painted ladybugs behind my bookshelf, where I couldn't reach it or look at it. I couldn't be comforted by it, and I couldn't tear it up to bits.

And after that, I brought my spelling book downstairs and turned on the TV to see if Momma would wake up. The kinds of shows on TV in the afternoon were the awful, slow kind, where the conversation that was happening two days ago was somehow still happening. The characters on TV droned on, and I turned the pages of my book, but nothing went in. Momma, however, had opened her eyes.

"A friend invited me to her house," I told her. "Momma? I'll need a note to ride on her bus after school."

"Okay." She rubbed her forehead, like my voice had given her a headache. She searched within arm's reach for something to write on. "What does it need to say?"

"That I can ride Bus 14. Her name is Shirl."

Momma wrote on the back of an envelope, tore off the portion she'd written on, and handed it to me.

"I think you need to sign it," I said.

Hardly concentrating, she took the note back.

While she signed it, I thought about Mr. Woodson behind his desk. He said he'd eat the apple after school, and maybe he was holding it right then, cupping it gently in his hands, even though it was not as good an apple as he'd believed. Nothing perfect about it at all.

28

⤙❧⤚

Riding Bus 14

THE DAY SHIRL AND I stood in line for Bus 14, I could feel the stares, not just from the brown children waiting to board, but from the kids who lived in my neighborhood crowding the sidewalk. Knee-deep in exhaust, I locked my eyes on the glass door, suddenly feeling aware of the expression on my face. Was this how my face normally looked when I stood in a line? And did I normally whistle, or just now? The door opened and the line pushed toward the steps until I was standing in front of the brown bus driver.

"Young lady, are you sure you're on the right bus?"

As laughter crackled through the line, I handed him my note, and he wrote my name on a clipboard.

"Go ahead, then," he said, and I moved through the aisle behind Shirl.

I'd never ridden a school bus before, and once in my seat, I sat at the edge and stared at the words "bus ride to hell" carved into the vinyl with a paper clip. The paper clip was still attached to the seat, and I wondered if we were heading away from hell, or toward it.

The kids all faced me, like I was an animal at the zoo, and as we rumbled there, stuck behind the other buses, I thought of making a run for home. I could spend another afternoon with the side of the couch digging into the backs of my legs. Momma would stare at the TV whether it was on or not, with books sitting between us, always turned to the same pages. The driver revved the engine, and I sunk back in my seat.

It was a long way from the school to the other end of Montgomery County. I faced the window, studying every detail and landmark on the way to Shirl's neighborhood. And all the while, she named toys we could play with. "There's Hula-Hoops, Twister, Creepy Crawlers, Monopoly."

Hers was the last stop. I held the back of each seat as I moved through the aisle and off the bus. Once on the sidewalk, she stopped to remove the bells from her shoelaces, wrapped them in a cloth so they wouldn't jingle, and put them in her book bag. This made perfect sense to me. Who you want to be out in the world is hardly ever the same as who you need to be at home.

"Maybe you'll meet my momma," Shirl said, as we walked down the uneven sidewalk. "But she usually works late at the bank. Sometimes she brings home lollipops."

I recognized her street from the day Dad drove her home. We walked up the hot, unshaded steps and into a blast of air-conditioning. Her house smelled of floor cleaner, and we dropped our book bags in the tiled entryway and walked up the white-carpeted stairs past a white-carpeted living room. Other than a wraparound couch, the living room was all electronics—a large TV and a stereo with loads of knobs.

"Hello?" An older woman's voice came from the kitchen.

"You girls ready for your snack?" The short and wrinkled brown woman greeted us from the stairs, wearing a housedress and slippers.

Shirl answered, "Yes, ma'am."

We sat on stools at a spotless counter as the old woman moved from the refrigerator to the sink to one cupboard or another, always taking her pocketbook with her. I wondered if she thought I'd steal it if she left it unattended.

"I just finished doing the dishes, so you're going to use paper plates," she said, and set before us two cans of Dr. Pepper and plates of rolled-up bologna stuck with toothpicks.

We said, "Thank you," each of us calling her ma'am.

Every appliance in the room was on. Steam came from the dishwasher, coffee dripped into a pot, *The Guiding Light* played on a small television, and the tap was on in the sink where she washed her hands.

"So you know each other from school?"

"Yes," I said. "Yes, ma'am."

"And we're in the play together," Shirl said.

"I see. And tell me, what does your father do?"

"I'm not really sure what he does," I said. "Something to do with missiles. He's tried to explain, but I don't get it."

"Her daddy's a general," Shirl said.

"A colonel," I corrected. Dad would be upset if I allowed someone to call him a higher rank than he really was, but the old woman raised her eyebrows as if I'd been bragging.

"I've seen him at the school," Shirl cut in. "You should see all the pins on his uniform."

"And your mother?" the old woman asked, as if to quiet Shirl.

"She stays home."

"You're lucky," Shirl said. "My momma would love to be a homemaker but she needs to make money."

The old woman slapped her hand on the counter in front of Shirl's plate. "Shirley Chisholm, shut your mouth. You are lucky to have a mother who works so hard for you."

I kept my eye on the bologna after that, thrilled with the idea that my home life was so desirable. When we finished our snack, we dashed off to Shirl's room, where we emptied her closet of every toy and game, trying each for only a minute or two before claiming we were bored, hopelessly bored.

"Are you girls having fun?" the old woman asked, peeking into the room.

We shook our heads and told her there was nothing to do.

Her lips puckered, and lines like stitches formed all around her mouth in a show of pure disapproval that Shirl had chosen me as a friend.

"Follow me," she said, leading us to the bathroom, where she handed Shirl a toilet scrub brush and pointed to the bowl. "There's always something to do. I wish *I* could be so bored."

"Your maid's a little cranky," I said when we were safe in Shirl's room again.

"My *grandmother*."

"That's what I meant."

"When was she cranky?"

Shirl pulled a suitcase from the closet and we dug through the miniature clothes inside it until we found the Barbies. Each tanned and skinny doll walked on her toes and had glossy hair that went past her butt.

Shirl explained how she had named all the dolls after colors you get by mixing various amounts of cream into coffee. "This is Cappuccino. This is Espresso. And this one's Mocha. That's what color my grandmother is."

All the dolls had the same color skin, more like a cashew nut, but perfectly smooth. We dressed their long, thin bodies in ball gowns, and when we grabbed a doll in each fist and ran through the house, we were like ugly trolls kidnapping them.

"This way!" Shirl said, running out the back door to her mowed back lot, where we taught the dolls how to dance the Bump and the Bus Stop. We cartwheeled and played tag and sat Indian style beside a honeysuckle bush, sucking the one sweet drop from each flower, when a small brown face and then another peered over her fence.

The first asked, "When's your mom coming with her lollipops?" And the second, more curiously, asked, "Who's *she?*"

"Quit spying," Shirl yelled, running toward the house, and I followed behind her, squealing, through the back door and into the kitchen.

Her grandmother, who cooked spaghetti sauce at the stove while staring at the small television set, turned at once. "No more running in and out with your muddy shoes."

"I don't have mud on my shoes," Shirl said.

"You don't *now* because it's already tracked across the floor."

"My shoes are clean. I didn't track anything."

"Don't sass me," she said and swatted Shirl's behind. "Must be your little friend has muddy feet."

We got out of there fast, slipping into her mother's room, which smelled of wet towels and laundry detergent. Lingerie hung on doorknobs, and drawers were stuffed so full they didn't close. Shirl opened the cupboard under the sink in the master bathroom and pulled out a bottle of blood-colored wine. We filled two Dixie cups and snuck back to her room, sitting with our backs against her closed door so her grandmother couldn't sneak up on us.

"I wanted to show you something," Shirl said. She dug through her book bag, pulling out wrinkled homework papers and a collection of animal-shaped erasers she bought at the school store. Finally she found what she was after.

"Here," she said. "I found it at my dad's house. He keeps it in the drawer by his bed."

She passed me a photograph of a naked lady.

"It's my mother," she said. "I think they're getting back together. Why else would he keep it?"

She'd told me enough about her father's nagging and the fights her parents had when they dropped her off from one house to another for me to doubt anyone wanted to make up.

I'd never seen a naked woman's body except for cartoon drawings on bathroom stalls. And I was shocked to think that a body could just bulge out like that, or a bottom could get so big, or something that looked like a second bottom could grow right out of those flat, pink nipples on the chest. I wanted to look away but couldn't make myself.

"She looks weird," I said. "Is she drunk?"

The photo had all her attention. "He still thinks about her," she said.

"I guess."

Both of her parents seemed so unlikable that I could see why she'd want them back together: Then there would only be one home to avoid.

She swiveled the wine in her cup for some time before she said, "I wish I had your life."

Until then, I'd been debating whether to tell her what it

would be like if she came to *my* house. But as I held the Dixie cup under my chin, I thought about what telling those secrets did to my friendship with Hope. Maybe the best way to keep a friend was to not let them know a lot about you. I took a large sip and tasted something familiar and comforting in the bitterness and the way my head spun when I swallowed.

"Girls? Girls, are you in there?"

"It's my grandma," Shirl said, taking the cup from me and burying it at the bottom of her trash can.

"Girls, I'm starting the car right now."

I lay my head on the carpet, looking sideways at Shirl, and started to giggle. "Your teeth are purple."

"Come on," she said, pulling on my hands until I stood up and followed her to the garage. The engine was already running.

"Your teeth match the car," I laughed, trying to whisper.

Shirl punched my arm as we filed into the backseat of her grandmother's Buick. During the ride to my house, her grandmother hummed along to the radio, turned down so low, all you could hear was the tinny drumbeat. Each time she turned a corner, her pocketbook slid left and right across the dashboard. I thought of them eating spaghetti and lollipops after her mother came home and wished they'd invited me to stay longer.

We winded up the short streets and hills, past the big houses and well-tended front lawns, neighbors looking long into the window of our car.

"It's that one," I said.

Shirl's grandmother stopped humming when she pulled in front of the house.

"And just one family lives in there!" Shirl said and then whistled. When no one responded to her comment, she whistled again.

"Stop that," her grandmother snapped, and then to me, "All right, child. Time for you to go."

I closed the car door, and Shirl's grandmother backed down our cul-de-sac rather than turning around at the end. As I went up the walkway, I tried to see my life the way Shirl did. I was the daughter of a homemaker and a colonel with a silver eagle on his shoulder. For a moment, I pretended there wasn't even a hint of the constant worry I'd feel when I went inside. I threw my book bag down on the porch, wrapped my hand around a column, and walked in circles.

꧁꧂

29

The Mall

THOUGH IT WAS A Saturday and the weather was sunny, I didn't feel like going outside. I sat on the floor of my room, my back against the bed, and let an hour go by. When I finally began to move, it was only to alphabetize my books by the authors' first names, as Momma liked to do. I quit partway through.

Dragging my hand down the banister, I wandered past the unfinished puzzle, past Dad coming around the corner with a stepladder and a package of light bulbs, and found Momma on the living room couch, a pillow in her lap, picking at the seam.

"I don't feel good," I said, wrapping my arms around my middle as if the pain were only there.

"Do you think you have a stomachache?"

"It kind of hurts all over. It doesn't actually hurt anywhere. I can't really explain it."

There was the squeak of Dad twisting light bulbs in and out of a socket.

"I know the feeling," she said with a heavy sigh. "Sorrow is a stubborn thing."

It seemed sorrow was doing cartwheels and tasting honey-suckles one day and then returning to your own kind of normal the next.

When the doorbell rang, we both flinched. It was rare for anyone to ring our bell—and always an appointment we were expecting—a Sears delivery, the exterminator. Dad hurried down the ladder.

There was the bell again, and then we heard Anne's voice through the mail slot. "Knock knock?"

"Don't answer it," Momma whispered, but Dad turned the knob.

"Oh, good, you're home!" Anne said, walking into the foyer. "I was so excited about this, I had to drive right over. He loves the proposal you wrote, just loves it."

When she saw me enter the room, she turned to explain, "The congressman who wants to get the missile project funded." Then, giggling, she corrected herself, "The *navigation* project."

"He called?" Dad asked.

She nodded energetically. "Yes. He was planning to leave a message, but there I was, getting some extra work done. He just went on and on about how he's looking forward to meeting you."

She stepped deeper into our house, two wrapped presents in her arms, and her purse slipping down to her elbow. "One for you," she said, sticking the gift in my hands. "And I hope Phil's around." She turned her head toward our practically bare living room with Momma's things cluttered in the corner.

"He isn't," I said as Momma joined me, food crusted on her bathrobe, her hair uncombed and loosely twirled on the top of her head.

"Sleeping in?" Anne said. "Oh, I could never do that. I get too antsy about all I could get done."

Anne's tidy new hairstyle, parted on the side and curling outward around her face, her pressed white slacks, carefully tucked-in pink blouse, and matching purse reminded me of the officers' wives at the air force base—how, when Momma stood beside them, she looked shy and messy.

"I have to tell you about our phone call," Anne said, turning back to Dad. "We had such an enthusiastic talk about Block 1 satellites, NAVSTAR, and attitude control systems."

"She's just saying all of this to be a show-off," Momma whispered, watching with astonishment as Anne, who had not let anyone else talk since she came over, uninvited, walked farther into our house. "I'll set Phil's gift over here," she called from the dining room. And when she was standing over the puzzle, she reached down and put a piece in its place.

"Sorry. Couldn't help myself," she laughed. "My mind has always loved numbers and shapes; I can't help seeing where the pieces go."

"It's not a good time," Momma said, crossing her arms. "Roy?"

"Thank you for stopping by," he told Anne. "It really isn't the best time."

"Oh," she said with exaggerated concern. "Anything I can help with?"

"He means *leave*," my mother said, but the tone of her voice didn't match her words. She sounded weak and unsure of herself.

"Mara," Dad whispered. "She's only trying to help."

"We don't need her help."

"It's all right," Anne said, calmly slipping her purse strap to her shoulder, and grinning at my mother with the kind of glee I saw in the kids who teased Phil. "Maybe we'll see each other another time. If you're feeling well enough."

"Get out!" Momma yelled.

"But Roy," Anne said, placing her hand on his arm. "Roy, I'm sorry, but he wants to meet with us right now. That's why I'm here, to give you a ride."

"I don't believe this," Momma said.

"Mara," he said, "it's my job."

Anne walked tall and triumphant out of our house, Momma holding her hands on her hips, and the hair that had been swirled on her head flopping down over her eye. Dad let Anne get a few paces ahead before he said, "This meeting could change everything."

"Go, then," she said, slamming the door behind him. But the moment it latched, she bent over sobbing. "She was throwing around all those scientific words just to make fun of me. Did you see that?" She leaned against the door.

I was glad all of Anne's talking and Momma's yelling had stopped.

"I wonder what she got you," Momma said, frowning at Anne's present in my hands. "Aren't you just dying to know?"

My finger had already ripped a tiny opening in one end, but now I tucked it closed. "Whatever it is, I don't want it," I said.

"Well, then, you have my permission to throw that thing away," and she waited until she heard the *thunk* it made in the trash can. "We'll get you something much better than that. I know the kinds of presents you'd really like."

She opened the hallway closet and dug through the deep pile until she found a skirt and a top. And believing she was hidden by the door, removed her robe and stood there perfectly naked except for her baggy pink underwear. Her shoulders were sharp, her breasts like thin, hanging sacks, and one whole side of her body was marked by seams from the couch and her robe.

She pulled on an emerald green tube top, and then a slightly sheer, very wrinkled white skirt, took the bobby pins out of her hair, squirted herself with perfume, and used the television screen to apply her makeup. She outlined her eyes in thick black, the way Rhoda, our favorite character on TV did hers, and asked, "Are you ready to go?"

"Go?"

"We're going shopping," she called out as she went to my father's bedroom. "We're getting presents we actually like."

Shocked, I stood up tall. "Shopping?"

She came back dangling the spare car key. She had Dad's credit card in her other hand, along with a blob of toothpaste on one of her fingers, which she spread on her tongue and swallowed. "We could both use some cheering up, don't you think?"

She opened the front door, and heart beating fast, I found my sneakers under the table and stepped my bare feet into them, mashing down the heels.

She breathed heavily as we walked to Dad's car. Her tube top was on inside out, showing the tag, and a bobby pin was tangled in the bottom of her hair, but I didn't tell her. I didn't want to be one more person in our family to criticize her, or remind her how she was different.

"I can't believe her nerve," she said, unlocking the car. We both sat up front where I had never been allowed before. I extended my legs and enjoyed looking through the windows in every direction. It felt dangerous being up front. I'd never shopped anywhere but the commissary or the PX, but here I was, doing what my classmates did with *their* mothers: walking out the front door together, buckling into a car, heading to the mall.

Momma showed me how to move the seats back. She blasted music and the a/c, and it didn't feel like Dad's car anymore. We backed out of the driveway and drove through our neighborhood roads lined with green lawns and perfectly trimmed azalea bushes. No one stopped us.

"First, I need to find out where the mall is," she said, and crossed to the other side of the road, honking at a woman walking down the sidewalk. "I'm trying to get to the mall," she called out as she rolled down her window.

"The mall?" the woman said, her forehead suddenly showing three horizontal strips. "You've got a long ways to go." And there was a lot of back and forth, trying to explain how to get to the highway, and which exit to take.

I sank in my seat, and when Momma started driving again, I asked, "Do you think we should just go home?"

"No, I've got it." She rolled up the window. "Are you having a good time?"

I wasn't sure, couldn't actually move my head yes or no.

She turned the music so loud I felt it in my legs. Kris Kristofferson, Roberta Flack, Donny Hathaway. Momma sang along to the choruses, humming when she didn't know the words. Sometimes she made the car go fast or slow to the music, and sometimes she made it go *bump bump bump* with the drums. I would have rolled down the window to get a break from Momma's perfume, but I liked the distance the glass provided me from the other drivers, some who glared at my mother. One flipped her the bird.

As we got near enough to the mall to see the signs and the massive building in the distance, Momma made a series of

U-turns until we finally reached the underground parking lot. She drove up several cement ramps, then followed the arrows through the shady rows, until we found a space.

It wasn't until she took the key out of the ignition, that I noticed the mood I'd felt that morning was still there. I was slow to get out of the car, but the strong smell of exhaust and the bustle of women carrying shopping bags and calling children out of traffic soon put that feeling out of my mind again.

"Want to know how we can remember where we parked?" Momma asked as we got out of the car, walking under the low ceilings and dim fluorescent lights.

"F5?" I said, reading a sign on the wall.

"But how will we remember F5? Think of an author whose name begins with F."

That was easy because of the way Momma organized her books. "Franz!" I said.

"Good! And now let's think of something he's written with five syllables in it." In no time, she answered her own question, "Metamorphosis! We've got it. And now how will we remember all of this?"

"F5?" I guessed, pausing as a car with its blinker on turned into an empty space.

"No, no. How about *bug*?"

"We just have to remember bug?"

We had now walked through the parking lot and entered the automatic glass doors that parted for us. Until that moment "the mall" meant the Smithsonian museums, but now it meant a giant indoor city decorated in tiny white lights. As we rode up the glass elevator, Momma pointed to one store after another, and it seemed the bright and colorful items inside might fill something that had been empty.

Our first stop was at a variety store, where Momma found a ballpoint pen so decorated with feathers and glitter I thought it was a toy. She used it to draw a small bug on my hand to help us remember where we parked, then, smiling, said, "We'll buy this, for starters."

30

What's Lost Is Found

STORE AFTER STORE, WE bought t-shirts with iron-on decals, compact mirrors, beaded bracelets, Love's Baby Soft perfume, Certs breath mints, blush we knew even at the counter was too orange to look good against Momma's pale skin. Anything I pointed to, she simply said yes and handed over the MasterCharge card with Dad's name on it, then signed Roy Harris.

At the clothing checkout, where we collected armfuls of clothes we hadn't tried on, Momma spun the earring tree, finding handfuls of hoops and studs and gave them to the clerk.

"You'll look great in these," she told me.

"But I don't have pierced ears."

"Do you want to?"

"Yes! Yes, I do!" I was terrified, but I'd be the only one in my class to have pierced ears, and that in itself was worth someone holding a staple gun to my ear.

"Ma'am." The clerk held up an earring. "This one doesn't have a match to it."

Momma placed her hand on my back. "We'll mix and match, won't we?"

My face felt hot as the clerk waited for my response.

Momma's fingers drummed against my skin as she whispered, "You want that beautiful earring, don't you?" And not looking at the clerk, I nodded my head.

After sitting on a stool in the center of the mall and hearing the terrifying bang of a gold stud going into each earlobe, we took a breather at the Magic Pan restaurant. I set the bags down on an empty chair, and the handles left a deep pink stripe on the insides of my fingers.

"I'm going to the bathroom to look in the mirror," I told her.

"Here," she said, tossing me a t-shirt we'd just bought— stretchy and yellow with a drawing of Gloria Steinem's face on it. "You can change into it while you're there."

Dressed in my new shirt and examining my sore earlobes in the mirror, I was surprised how much I didn't look like myself. And I wondered, *Where was I? Where was I anymore?*

When I returned to the table, Momma had ordered us spinach crêpes and coffees. I'd never had either before, and we unwrapped sugar cubes, then dropped them in our cups. I unwrapped another cube and put it directly into my mouth.

"How's this for presents?" she asked, showing me how difficult it was to find space under the table and around our chairs for all the shopping bags. "Are you feeling better now?"

"I think so." I couldn't tell. I'd been too busy to notice, though, now, it seemed the sugar did help a little.

"I wonder if your father's enjoying his little meeting," she said, and we both opened plastic containers full of cream and poured them into our coffees.

It felt as if I wasn't supposed to answer. I held my hands around the cup, as Momma did, sorry I'd added so much cream. I had wanted to see the color of Mr. Woodson in my cup; instead, I saw Shirl's grandmother.

"Have I ever told you the story of when we first moved to the air force base in Albuquerque?"

I straightened in my seat, surprised she wanted to talk about the old house. I had been so careful not to mention it, afraid to bring up anything that might remind her of the days she lay crying on the floor.

"The house," she said, "smelled like dogs and cigarettes. We opened all the windows to let in the breeze. It was a hot day, and your father and I went down the street in search of an ice cream shop that sold root beer floats. This was when Phil was in diapers, and we strolled him down the sidewalk. Everyone thought he was such a cute, fat baby.

"When we came back to the house, the smell had aired out, but inside was completely coated in red sand."

"I remember it," I said, my voice so quiet I hardly recognized it as my own. "That red dust got on everything."

Something about her story made me nervous. Why tell it now? Why on a day he'd been so cruel to her?

"I started to cry," she said, continuing her story, "because our new house was ruined and it was too much to clean. Roy told me to go wash my face, and I felt ashamed of my tears, hurrying to the bathroom to see if my mascara had run. But this was all a ploy to get me to see that he'd written 'Cootie' on the mirror with his finger."

"Why Cootie?"

"On our first date, he tried to call me Cutie but was nervous and it came out wrong."

"It's a nice story," I said, though it was also a terrible story, because the man in her memory, this nervous man who would go out of his way to please her, no longer existed.

"Those are the kinds of things that keep you going," she said. "Otherwise, life is just an awful rowing toward God."

"That's one of your books," I said, remembering the title.

"Yes," she said. Normally when we talked about books, she was pleased with me, but this time her eyes were distant.

We both turned our attention to the spinach crêpes, though I mostly cut mine into smaller and smaller pieces because my stomach hurt again. We hardly looked up until the waiter cleared our dishes.

"It's been such a pleasure to serve you today," he said, a kindness in his voice that seemed to break through her mood, however slightly.

When she pulled out the credit card, I couldn't help but imagine this man as a replacement for Dad. *Maybe he'd be nicer*, I thought. *Maybe he'd dance with her.*

"How about the bookstore next?" she asked after signing the bill, though she seemed as tired as I felt.

"Okay. And then maybe we're done for the day," I said, cringing at how much I sounded like Dad. When we got up from the table, I brushed some spinach from her hair.

"Did you like your coffee?" she asked as we weaved through the restaurant's tables, our hands full, once again, with shopping bags, and I realized I hadn't even tasted it.

At Waldenbooks, Momma found a copy of *The Feminine Mystique* and handed it to me. "Here," she said. "One of your very own."

The cover was crisp, shiny, and not as nice to hold. "Are you sure?" I asked. "I could just borrow yours when I need it," not that I was ever expecting to need it.

"I'm absolutely sure," she said. "Would you like anything else while we're here?"

As I panned the store, my eye stopped on a sandy-haired girl who had paused at the entrance to turn one of the book racks. It was not until I saw the one-handed lady move her along to the next store that I was sure who it was.

"Anything else?" Momma asked again.

I pointed to the stacks of *Ribsy* and *Ramona the Pest* in the children's section. "Hope likes these," I said.

"Hope?"

I was so curious about the books with girls my age on the covers and the ones Phil used to tell me about, with words like "dumb" and "snot" in them, but no one expected me to read those anymore.

In the checkout line, I turned to my mother's favorite chapter in my new book.

"Oh, is that a sight," a woman in line said, approving.

My jaw hurt from what had been a long day of pretend smiles, and I worried, as we stepped back into the glass elevator, that when the door opened we might continue shopping.

"Do you think maybe we can go home now?" I asked.

"Oh. Well, I guess we could."

The bags were heavy in my hands and I did a quick count. "Aren't we missing one?"

She gave a hurried look at what we carried and sighed, "What can you do?" We'd shopped so mindlessly that we couldn't remember what was in the missing bag or be bothered to retrace our steps.

. . .

The air in the mall was icy, and I wished my hands were free to rub my shoulders and warm them. As we headed through the exit, I heard someone shout behind us. Momma kept going, but I turned to find Hope.

"I *thought* that was you," she said.

We stood on either side of an automatic door, which buzzed and clicked, trying to shut itself. The cold air blew against my kneecaps while the humidity hit the backs of my legs.

"What are you doing here?" I asked.

"Shopping."

"Me too."

The doors buzzed again as my foot swept back and forth on the pavement, pushing a rock of tar with one side of my sneaker and then the other.

"That's my mother," I said, pointing across the parking lot, remembering they'd never met. Momma adjusted the bags in her hands, continuing toward the car. I worried if I took too long, she might leave for home without me.

When Hope didn't say anything else, I said, "You should come over some time." But even as I said it, it was clear too much time had passed and we would not play at each other's houses again. The friendship was lost forever, maybe lost long ago, but I'd only just become aware of it. I pushed my thumbs through my belt loops, feeling hot behind the knees and itchy from bugs.

Hope leaned slightly to one side, holding her hands behind her back, then placing them on her hips. We stood there saying nothing at all to each other, though I tried desperately to think of something because I didn't want to leave just yet.

Finally, the one-handed lady emerged from around a corner and called, "Time to go, Hope."

I had never gotten a good look at the stump before. It was only the slightest hint of a hand—a wrist, and three bumps where fingers might have formed. Seeing it straight on took away my fascination of it, and my eyes soon wandered to the denim purse she carried on that arm, and the strawberry blonde hair at her shoulder, until, for the first time, I noticed her face, and that she had freckles.

"Okay," Hope told her. And then turning back to me, she said, "I have to go."

I thought to shake hands with her, wanting to stall or to have some last contact, but it seemed silly, something only boys would do. "Well, see ya," I said, and slowly turned from her to find my mother. I had to jog to catch up to her.

"Who was that?" she asked, keeping up her pace.

"Hope."

"Hmmm." She was focused on reading the row numbers to find where we'd parked.

"Bug," I reminded her.

When we got to the car, we stuffed the bags into the back-seat. Then I got in front, cooling my head on the window.

"Here," she said, handing me the most enormous bag of potato chips I'd ever seen. "Snack on these if you get hungry."

I was still full from the Magic Pan, but I opened the bag and ate anyway, trying to imagine Hope's room at her new house: lavender walls, dust ruffles around the bed, a portable record player on a small table, and her collection of trolls all around. I thought of us singing and dancing in front of the mirror, and how it might feel to laugh like that again.

As we made our way through the parking lot, I thought of silly jingles we used to sing: "Mr. Bubble in the tubble . . ." "My bologna has a first name . . ." "Two all-beef patties, special sauce, lettuce, cheese . . ."

Momma pulled on to the road, while I ate potato chips until the roof and the corners of my mouth started to burn. "I can't believe Hope was there," I said.

Momma hadn't heard me. She'd turned on the radio, and sang a little to Debby Boone before switching the station to a Stevie Wonder song. I brought my knees to my chest and squeezed them hard. "Hope was so short," I said, turning to the window. "I don't remember her being short."

My reflection in the glass—a lost look in the eyes, a greasy mouth that turned downward on one side—showed that the feeling I'd had that morning had traveled with me. It was a stubborn sorrow that would go home with me as well.

Momma and I climbed out of the car with shopping bags on our arms. I didn't remember buying so much, but between the two of us, we could hardly carry it all.

In the dining room, I noticed the table was set, and there were plates of cold dinner at my seat and at Momma's. I felt sick from eating so many chips and wished I'd waited for Dad's cooking.

"We'll hide these under the table," Momma said.

"Who are we hiding them from?"

"It's just for fun. Like a game." She nodded for me to go first into the living room, and I did, with the bags behind my back, though they were still completely visible. It didn't matter, though. No one was there.

"The closet," she whispered, taking a few items from the bags first. "Hide them in the closet. There's more room."

Momma took her regular seat, and using one of the items we bought at the mall—our new Ronco Rhinestone & Stud Setter machine—pressed rhinestones and metal studs onto a new stiff jean jacket for me.

I opened the door to the closet, stuffed so full of Momma's things I didn't know if I could close it again. To make room for our shopping bags, I had to push piles of clothes and random objects to one side, and while I was doing this, I heard a clank. Fearing I'd broken something, I began to sift to the bottom of the pile. I lifted a towel and then a scarf, and underneath, my heart beginning to pound, I found a small, white mug with a broken handle and rubies glued all around the sides.

31

Rubies

I HELD THE CUP, BREATHLESS, and slowly fingered the ridges where the handle had once been. I touched the rim and brought it to my mouth. Everything came rushing back—lying warm in my old bed, Momma coming to sit beside me, talking and reading as if she had all the time in the world.

I walked back to the couch, the cup in my hands, and sat beside Momma. I sat closer than I normally did and let myself feel small next to her. "I've been looking everywhere for this. Momma, do you remember how you'd sit by my bed and tell me stories and I'd have my drink in this cup? It used to have more rubies on it. Remember? And how I used to save them in my pillowcase?"

She tried to laugh but it came out weary. Put on. "That little drink you liked had a way of calming you down. You'd talk and talk and talk, and then you'd talk yourself right to sleep."

"It had such a strange taste."

"Mostly," she said, distracted and looking toward the couch, "it was Tang and hot water."

"But it was bitter, too."

"Well, that was the *magic* ingredient." She smiled a bit, but her eyelids drooped, and I could feel our day coming to an end.

"I know! Let's make it tonight." I blew the dust out of my cup and wiped the inside clean with my shirt.

"Oh, I don't think this is a good time. Aren't you tired from all the shopping?" Then, meeting my eyes, she sighed. "I suppose I can make you Tang with hot water."

"No. Make it just like you used to. I like the bitter. Oh, I know! . . ." I jumped up with a thought so thrilling I thought I'd burst. "I'll wait under my covers. You've never seen my room before. It's up these stairs."

I handed her the ruby cup, and her hands sank lower as if it were something heavy.

"Momma, please." I didn't know how badly I wanted this until I said it out loud. I wanted her to see my room. I wanted her to tuck me in. I wanted to have back what had been taken from me.

"Tillie, really, I . . ." Finally, sighing again, she took the cup. "All right. I'll make it for you."

I laughed with a joy I couldn't hold in. "I'll wait for you in my room."

I leapt up the stairs, but when I got to the doorway and imagined Momma seeing my room for the first time, I worried she'd be disappointed. If we were so alike, my room didn't show it, except for the mess. There were no literary classics or choice pins. Instead, she'd find tacked to my wall a picture of Peter Frampton (with his girlfriend Penny cropped out), along with pages of my favorite song lyrics, written in bubble letters. I heard the kettle go off downstairs and knew I only had time to pull the books she'd given me forward on the shelf.

When I heard her clump up the stairs, I got into bed with my sneakers still on. She slowly rounded the corner, holding my ruby cup. I felt wonderful, excited. My legs were restless under the covers, and I patted the mattress to show her where to sit. She sat near the edge and placed the cup in my hands. I held it just below my chin to feel the steam and listen to the ice cube squeal and pop. The warmth and its sharp smell gave me a strange flash of memory from the old house—Momma with her face close to mine, crying.

I'm sorry, Bear. I never meant to hurt you.

I took a sip, then another, hoping for a different memory. The drink burned as it went down, and the bitter taste was strong. It was a drink that forced you to slow down.

I rubbed my fingers over the remaining rubies. "I was so afraid someone had thrown it away."

"You'll have to ask your brother how it turned up in there."

I took another sip, hardly surprised that he was to blame, but I didn't want to ruin our time with thoughts of Phil. "Do you remember how you used to tell me stories at bedtime?" I asked.

Her shoulders raised the tiniest bit, then dropped again. "I just can't think of one," she said, when Phil burst into the room with something bundled under his arm.

"Dad's been pretty berserk looking for you."

"He's always berserk," I said. "That's *his* problem."

"Well, he's been searching the neighborhood for hours and then coming back home to check."

Momma stood, arms wrapped about herself, and Phil paused, as if just now taking in the idea that she'd come upstairs.

Slowly, she unfolded her arms and extended them toward Phil as if he were still that boy beside the crashed sled, calling for his mother. He shook his head, but barely, and stepped backward.

"Well," he said, his voice breaking, "that's the message, if anyone cares."

"We were shopping," I said. "Why does he think he has to check on us?"

"I'm just passing along the message."

When he turned to leave the room, Momma said, "Phil, I can come tuck you in as soon as we're done here."

Phil, who was so confident when he was rolling his eyes or making one of his rude comments, froze. His face, without its usual sneer, made him look more like the little boy who wore a lucky rabbit's foot on his belt and picked up pennies on the sidewalk.

Momma was only a few steps away from his room. All he had to do was say yes, or just nod his head.

Instead, he took another slow step backward.

"Okay then," she said softly. "I'm sure you're much too big to be tucked in."

I almost felt sad for him, the way he had to be the one who didn't need anything, who could do it himself. But I also wanted him out of my room. This was *my* time with Momma.

"I thought you said you had other things to get to," I told him, gulping down my drink.

"I did," he said. "I do." And then he took the bundle from under his arm and threw it on my floor. "Oh, and I found this ugly thing downstairs. I figure it's yours."

My sneaker caught on the sheet when I sprang out of bed, which just made me all the madder. Never letting go of my cup, I grabbed my new jean jacket. I knew he'd meant to hurt me, thinking *I* was the one who punched the metal studs onto the back of it, but that didn't keep the tears from streaming down Momma's face.

"Don't mind him," I said, picking it off the floor. With my finger, I traced the crooked star she'd begun, then slid my arm into the sleeve. Just the weight of the jacket, as I pulled it around me, gave me an immediate sense of importance, though it also hurt to wear it. The metal prongs that weren't clamped all the way down scraped my skin. "I love it," I said, turning in a circle to show her until I came to a dead stop.

In the doorway, Dad stood breathless, the veins out in his neck and forehead.

"I've been looking everywhere!" he shouted, his voice hoarse. He turned to me and put his hand on my shoulder. "Where have you been?"

I jerked away from him as Momma whimpered behind me.

"We were shopping," I told him. "We were having fun until now. And we've already eaten," I added, my way of telling him we knew how to feed ourselves. We weren't idiots or pets. We weren't his prisoners.

"We decided to have a little fun while you were visiting with the congressman," she said, her voice chilly, but weak. "Did you enjoy your meeting?"

Annoyed at the change of subject, he said, "It was a fine meeting. It was a *very* fine meeting, if you want to know. We talked about some civilian uses for the technology—navigation for commercial airplanes or even ambulances—and he says we'll get the funding we need."

"Isn't that wonderful," she said, sniffling. "I'm glad you enjoy your work so much."

"Do you know what I like about my job?" he shouted. "When I work hard, I actually see progress."

While my father had been saying this, Momma slowly moved closer to me and reached out with shaking hands to take the empty cup.

"What is that?" he asked. "What's going on here?"

Without answering, she began to walk toward the door when he lunged forward, grabbing the cup. She shrieked in surprise while he dipped his finger inside to take a taste. Everything about his face tightened.

"I can explain," she cried.

He squeezed the cup tight and drew back his arm.

"Dad, what are you doing?" I screamed, as Momma whimpered and covered her face with both of her hands.

His arm shot forward and my cup slammed against the wall, smashing to pieces. I turned toward the orange stain it left, and felt a fury building inside. "Dad! What's wrong with you?"

"Tillie, get into bed," he said. "Right now."

He put his hand on my shoulder, guiding me, but I flailed my arms and bolted from my room. I passed Phil in the hallway, turned down the stairs, and kept going out the front door.

"Tillie!"

My father had taken away everything important to me. Momma. The decorations in our home. Now my ruby cup.

I ran hard, pumping my arms and legs faster than I knew I could go. I cut through one yard and then another by the time I heard my father yelling from our porch. I knew he'd head to the school, so I took a different street and followed the route of Bus 14.

· · ·

I could hear myself breathing and panting. My chest burned. It felt good to run, to hear the soles of my tennis shoes slapping against the street, to feel my legs on fire, to run faster than the cars that waited at each traffic light. I took shortcuts and ran places I'd never run before. Someone shouted from his car, "Run, girl, run!"

Finally, I stopped to catch my breath, proud of how far I'd gone so fast, like I'd shown him something—that he could measure my anger by how far I'd run from him.

It was chilly, surprisingly so for how warm it had been during the day. I found myself on a street with no people—all the buildings dark, except for a bar on the corner with steamy windows and a light that blinked on and off. I turned in each direction, hoping to see the YMCA building that was so big and well lit I shouldn't have missed it. I felt unsteady and reached out to grab a signpost. I could see cars blurred in the distance, and closer, small animals with glowing eyes, scurrying around the dumpsters, but there was no sound at all, as if my ears were clogged with cotton. The buildings and streetlamps began to sway, and I held tighter to the pole. I knew this feeling.

I turned round and round, taking in the pawn shop, the bar, the small grocery store, and wondering how far Shirl's house was, and in what direction. It was getting dark so fast, and each street seemed to lead somewhere even darker.

"I'm afraid. I'm afraid." I spoke out loud, but the words didn't sound right because my tongue was heavy. Someone, however, heard me. A man walked toward me, not saying a word.

"I'm trying to find . . ." I couldn't remember what I was trying to find. My brain wasn't working right. I didn't remember the name of the building near Shirl's, and I couldn't remember her last name. Finally I said, "I'm lost."

"I'll say you're lost."

Soon, there were many people gathered around me, all brown, and moving closer. I felt dizzy. Confused. A metal prong from inside my new jacket snagged my shirt, pulling it down in back so my collar tightened against my neck. Someone reached for me and I realized I was on the ground.

"I know this girl. She goes to the school I work at." A man stepped through the crowd. It was the janitor, and he knelt beside me, trying to lift my head off the sidewalk.

"I'm trying to find Shirl," I said, but my words were slurred. Several voices asked, "What did she say?" And then there were many voices talking at once. "She's looking for someone." "What's wrong with her?" "Is she sick?"

It was harder and harder to stay awake. I felt myself cradled in the janitor's arms, both of us on the sidewalk. And I heard him tell someone Shirl's last name.

The beauty of sleep is the way the world around you disappears. You forget you're cold, forget there is something poking into your back. The problems you had, the worries, the dark, all of that fades away. You forget to care if your face is mashed against a near stranger's shirt buttons, or if your feet hurt from blisters. For a moment, there is a perfect peace. And even as voices interrupt that sleep, the sound is far away, like a dream.

"Tillie!"

"Tillie!"

I heard my name and that, alone, soothed me. I nestled back against the janitor and let myself fall into a deep sleep again.

"Tillie!" It was my father. And the shaky, high-pitched voice that came after it was Momma's.

The janitor continued to hold me but he sat up straighter, and the cold rushed in where my cheek was no longer pressed against him. I tried to call back or wave my hand to let them know where I was, but I was too tired, and the janitor was warm and sturdy. I shut my eyes again.

"Tillie!"

"That's my mom and dad," I mumbled into his shoulder.

"Over here, sir," the janitor said, his voice vibrating in his chest and against my face. "Over here," he called again, and this time, the noise jolted me awake.

There was a whole crowd of people surrounding us—until they parted and my father pushed through. Momma stood farther back, near the car. The janitor helped me stand, and when I was steady, he let go. I felt a second wind, enough strength to make it to either parent—Momma, with her hands to her mouth and the car door open for me, or Dad, who made me so angry.

Every step felt like effort, and I steadied myself on strangers as I walked faster until I was running. I ran toward my father, who stood soldierlike until the very last moment when he caught me in his arms.

"You're fine now," he said. My earrings hurt when he pulled me close.

"I'm so tired, Dad."

"I'll carry you."

I kept my face pressed against his cheek, which was stubbly and wet with tears. I didn't even hold on, but put all of my weight onto him and trusted he wouldn't drop me.

≈≈≈

32

Locked Doors

O VER DAD'S SHOULDER, THE blinking sign above the bar lit up the crowd at intervals, as he carried me to our Volvo. The windows of the car were steamed, and even through the glass you could hear Momma sobbing. When Dad set me down, I reached for the handle, but the door was locked. The same thing happened when Dad tried his door. He knocked on the window. Momma shook her head, and Dad reached into his pocket for the key. Even more hysterical, she placed her hands over the lock so it wouldn't open.

"Mara!" he shouted. "Mara, for crying out loud!"

I held to the side of the car, tired of the commotion, and not quite certain whether I was hearing my name or not. I stood up straighter. "Shirl?"

She made her way down the street, and I called out louder, "Shirl!"

"Ernie called our house," she said, jogging closer. "He said, 'Come get your little friend. Get here right away.' "

"Who's Ernie?" I asked, my lips and tongue moving too slow.

"How can you not know Ernie? He cleans up your trash every day at school."

The man who'd let me sleep in his arms. I started to speak but was just too tired.

"My mom didn't want me to come. She called your house so someone could pick you up, but she said it's too late for me to be out, and I have no business being on a street with a bar on it."

I was certain the woman glaring at me farther down the sidewalk was her mother. But she soon took her eyes off of me and turned, along with the rest of the crowd, to watch my mother move from lock to lock as Dad tried his key in the different doors.

Shirl put her hands on her hips and shook her head in disbelief. "You better go before someone calls the cops," she said.

"Cops?"

"Yeah, that's what I said. If some black folks had gone to *your* neighborhood and acted like this, they would have been arrested. Or worse."

"Not funny," I said.

"Who says I'm being funny?"

"Tillie, get in."

Momma had finally given up her control of the locks, and Dad opened the door for me. He did not remind me to buckle, so I didn't. As soon as I got inside the car, I felt how cold I'd been, how much my legs ached from running.

Shirl stood beside our car, her mother now holding her hand and staring at me with the same expression of deep disappointment on her face that Shirl's grandmother had shown. Dad slammed his door and started the engine.

"Unbelievable!" he said, choking the steering wheel.

Normally, in a neighborhood like this, we would lock our doors, even in the afternoon. That night Dad didn't bother. As we drove past Shirl, I raised my hand to the window and she raised hers in reply.

We moved down the short, dark streets, Dad gripping and ungripping the wheel while Momma wailed almost silently, her mouth open and drool running down to her chin. I used to work so hard to stop Dad from fighting with her, but I was exhausted and wanted to return to that feeling of sleeping against the janitor while everyone around me rushed to figure things out. I lay down in the backseat and watched the streetlamps fly by.

"Do you even understand what you did?" he finally asked, practically spitting. He turned to the backseat to see if I was awake. I quickly closed my eyes. "You *drugged* her."

"I didn't *drug* her," she said, hysterical. "You've given her the same medicine before."

"Was she swelling from a bee sting? Did she have hay fever?"

"Not so loud."

"You can't give someone medicine when they're not sick," he said, not remembering to keep his voice down. "It's wrong. Do you have any idea what could have happened tonight?"

She answered with her face to the window. "I didn't know she'd leave the house. I wasn't the one who upset her so much that she ran off!"

I couldn't concentrate on the words, just let them float through my ears and back out.

"Didn't you even *consider* what happened before?" he said.

"Of course I did!" Her voice was high-pitched, desperate. "I never meant to hurt her."

I'm sorry, Bear. I never meant to hurt you.

He looked behind again to see if I was asleep, and once more

I shut my eyes. "Don't you remember how cold she felt? She hardly moved."

"Of course I remember. What do you think I am, a monster?"

"Then what on earth was going through your head?"

"Do you think I'm the only mother who gave her child something to help her rest? We had a little girl who wouldn't sleep through the night. She always had more to say. More questions and requests. They taught me to add a little Sudafed to her drink at bedtime. The other wives. It was just to relax her." She spoke too fast, squeezing her hair in her fists like she might pull it out in handfuls.

"I can't believe you're defending yourself." He lifted his hand off the wheel and she backed away. "It was to relax *you*. And it's wrong!"

"I know that!" She leaned against the door so hard I thought she'd fall out. "Don't you think I know? Don't you think I've suffered for that mistake every day?"

"Then how could you do it again?"

"Because"—she started to cry fiercely—"because she begged me. Because sometimes you just want to know that you can still make your child smile. You want to say yes to something." Her voice cracked, and it was some time before she spoke again. "You wouldn't understand what it's like to have to win your children back."

33

Tumbling

WHEN WE PULLED INTO our driveway, I kept my eyes closed and let Dad carry me to my room because I didn't want to see Momma. He grunted as we went up the stairs, and held me too tight, like the anger had to grab hold of something. When we were halfway, I pretended to wake up. "I can go the rest myself," I said, and he set me down, winded, and not in the mood to say anything comforting.

Phil waited at the top of the stairs. "Dad?"

"Not now, Phil," he answered, already at the bottom again.

I walked into Phil's room, only so far as the cans lying on his floor. I felt groggy but not as tired as I wanted to feel now that I could actually crawl into bed and forget about everything.

"Do you hear them fighting?" I said.

"Sure, I hear them." He unplugged his rock tumbler. Now I heard the quiet buzz of his electric clock.

"I think this is it," I said, my legs starting to shake.

"Good riddance." He took the tumbler out of its frame, unscrewing the lid.

And now my teeth began to chatter. "Don't you care if they break up?"

"Not particularly." He kicked through the beer cans on his way to the bathroom sink, where he rinsed the polishing solution off the rocks.

He was good at this. He'd get calmer the more I got worked up. And then he could call me hysterical and needy, but I wasn't going to let him trap me. *Swallow*, I told myself. *Just swallow!*

I let myself imagine the end of their marriage as a relief. A chance to be free from Dad's rules, to have a house of our own with bright colors and pictures on the wall again. We could drink soda whenever we wanted and spend evenings watching *Rhoda*.

When he came back into the room I said, "I guess we'll live with Momma," trying for a calm expression on my face.

"As her babysitters?"

"Stop being mean." My body wouldn't quit trembling.

"What? Do you think she's going to get a job?"

"Of course she is!"

"And what job can she do from the couch?"

"Why do you always have to hurt her? She does so much, and you don't appreciate any of it."

"Does she cook or clean? Does she buy groceries?"

I tried to push him but missed, falling into the cans. "That's not the only thing women can do."

"Does she know the names of our teachers? Do you think she's going to go to your stupid play?"

"Shut up!"

"All I'm saying is, she doesn't do any of the things mothers do."

My breathing got faster, my legs knocking beneath me as I tried to get up. I grabbed a pair of jeans out of his hamper, ready to strike.

And now he folded his arms and looked at me—hysterical, needy. I hated my brother for being so cruel. For being right. The lives we'd led outside the house—riding bikes, drinking Slurpees, and going to Pentagon picnics—never intersected with Momma's world, even in conversation. You could not, no matter how hard you tried, imagine Momma buying groceries or cooking. You couldn't imagine her getting dressed each day, or even answering the telephone.

I felt the sensation I used to feel before I cried—though I didn't, *couldn't* cry anymore—a tightness in my throat, my face scrunching and stretching against my will. She would never be like other moms. We both knew it.

"Jerk!" I yelled and swung the jeans at him, feeling, mid-movement, that I was too tired, too terribly tired to take another swing.

He grabbed a handful of polished rocks out of the tumbler and threw them at me. I ducked on his floor, covering my head. The rocks smacked against me and against the cans, and I let myself feel the only kind of pain I was certain would come to an end.

It was the drink Momma had given me that made me feel as if I was spinning. In the old house, when my hands were too weak to hold on to the cup, she would smile because I'd finally settled down. These were the thoughts I woke with, thoughts that seemed as unreal as a bad dream. I lifted my head, finding that I was still on my brother's floor with a sweater over my shoulders. It was my father's—the itchy one.

Nothing but Phil's electric clock could have told me it was morning. His room was always dark because of the flag covering his window, and there was no smell of eggs or toast cooking, no sound of rummaging in the kitchen. In the corner of the room, Phil tossed a can opener back and forth between his hands.

"Dad wants us to get our own breakfast this morning," he said. "Here, have a fork."

He opened two tins of ravioli, and we sat still between the beer cans, listening to the fight continue downstairs.

"It's over, isn't it?"

He shrugged like it was a stupid question to ask. There was such an ache in my gut, I couldn't even think of eating.

"What's going to happen to us?" I asked.

"We'll live with one of them or the other." He shoved two raviolis in his mouth at a time. Then, before he swallowed, he asked, "What was that thing Dad threw last night?"

"The cup Momma made me. Remember? With the rubies?"

"Yeah, I know the one."

"Momma said you knew where it was all the time I'd been looking for it."

"I didn't know anyone considered it missing. I just packed it when I packed the rest of the stuff back at the old house."

"You were the one who packed it?"

"It was one of the last things I found. It was under your bed, and I'd run out of newspaper to wrap things. There was only the cup and my model airplanes to go, so I packed the cup. It was already broken, so there wasn't as much pressure to be careful with it."

"You packed my cup instead of your models?"

"It's okay. I don't play with that kid stuff anymore."

I thought to tell him that Dad broke the cup, and then I decided not to. I didn't tell him about the bitter drink, either. He didn't need to know everything.

"Here," I said. "You can have my ravioli, if you want it."

As he took it, our parents raised their voices again. I wrapped my arms around my legs. "If they split," I said, "I'll go where you go."

He didn't look up from his ravioli, but he stopped eating and nodded.

We tried to keep quiet and out of the way, but we were too distracted for books or music or the partly finished puzzle sitting downstairs on the dining room table. In the end, without either of us saying anything to the other, we started to pick up the cans.

At first, I put them neatly back on the shelf. Behind me, however, Phil dropped one can after another into the metal wastepaper basket, and when it began to overflow, he got a Hefty bag. We threw out every can—his Black Label, Genesee, Fyfe & Drum Extra Lyte, Schlitz "Tall Boy," and even his Iron City Beer with the 1975 Super Bowl Championship Steelers on it. The sound was like shouting a secret we'd been warned not to tell, like we were agreeing about what that secret was, for once.

After we were done cleaning up the cans, Phil kept going. He threw away cards, dice, framed pictures, trophies, and his notebook filled with newspaper clippings, until his room had nothing in it but a bed, stereo, stack of library books, and a rock tumbler turning a new batch of rocks in wet sand.

Downstairs, Momma still wore the outfit from our shopping

trip. Dad had changed clothes but hadn't shaved and didn't look like he'd slept, either. They no longer bothered to lower their voices. And when I stood in the doorway to Dad's bedroom, he seemed irritated to see me there.

"Tillie, this doesn't involve you."

But it *did* involve me. I had spent the last year, if not more, trying to help Momma get better, trying to protect her from harm, trying to keep her in my life. Every bit of this fight concerned me, though I no longer rooted for anyone or anything.

"Tillie, out," Dad said.

"But I'm hungry."

Briefly, I caught my mother's eyes, full of disgrace, before she looked away.

"I said, 'Out.'"

I went only so far as the puzzle around the corner and tried to find pieces that would fit together. They waited till they thought I was gone, then, exhausted, Momma said, "I can't take any more of your lectures. You only want to point out what you think is wrong with me."

"How can you even say that?" He threw or kicked something that landed with a thud on the carpet. "I'm trying to *help* you! Do you have any idea how much I've cooked and cleaned and looked after the kids so you can get better?"

She started bawling.

"Get up. Don't lay on the floor when we're talking!"

"Just say it," she sobbed. "You were happier when I was locked away."

"Fine. So tell me, what, if anything, will make you happy?"

"Well, it's not living with a man who has always wanted me to be someone I'm not. You seem to want some officer's wife in a nice suit, who can't wait to spend the day cleaning house!"

"Sometimes, there are things you have to get done whether you like them or not."

"I was spending every day doing only the things I hated. Instead of washing dishes and trying to make cakes shaped like wreaths, maybe I wanted to travel from town to town, wearing a gold sequined gown!"

"You're impossible!"

"Why? Because I dream of doing something I love? Because I want to spend my days doing something I find important?"

"Do any of us count on your list of what's important?"

I walked closer, listening for the answer. She didn't have one.

"If you could just make some effort for us," Dad said. "Just make us a priority. Make us more important than the television or a nap."

I had to back into the dining room to avoid Momma as she hurried from the room. She cried out like a wounded animal and turned into the bathroom, slamming the door, though it didn't latch the first time and she had to slam it again. I heard the lock slide into place.

Dad charged after her, shouting at the closed door. "That's the question I want you to answer, Mara! Do we count? Does your being happy have anything to do with us?"

Water exploded from the faucet and let him know she wasn't listening to him. With his face red and veins sticking out on his neck, he seemed to sense me there behind him. Without turning, he said, "Why don't you make yourself some lunch?"

I could hear him swallowing hard as he came over to the table and pushed the chairs under it. Then he swept the puzzle pieces into the box.

"But Dad," I said, "we were almost able to see the whole picture."

"The picture's on the lid," he said, closing the top and handing it to me.

He went to another part of the house, looking for something to scrub clean, while I sat outside the bathroom door with the box in my lap, thinking I should say something. Feel something. After she turned off the water, there was no sound of splashing, no sound that she was moving at all. I sat there long enough to know that the water had turned cold, knowing she wanted someone to comfort her, but I couldn't do it this time.

34

❧

Coin Trick

DURING THE DAYS AND nights of fighting, I didn't seek out my mother. There were times I had to be in the same room with her, during painfully silent dinners or to retrieve a paper I needed for school, and if she made any move toward me I turned away. She seemed to accept this as her punishment.

I wandered our huge house the way I did on my first day here, desperately searching for everything I had lost. I wandered in and out of the rooms where I never played because they were cold and empty. I wandered up and down the stairs—close to and away from their battle.

I saw little of my brother, except for the evidence of where he'd been: a toilet seat left up, a carton of milk on the kitchen counter, and when I opened our front door to a blast of our neighbors' power mowers and transistor radios, I found a bucket filled with river water on the porch.

Phil surprised me by catching the door behind me. He'd

been right on my heels. "I found these in your room," he said, holding out a handful of the silver dollars I'd stolen from him.

"What were you doing in my room?" That was as close to an apology as he was going to get—the fact that I didn't deny taking them. I hopped off the porch onto a thick tuft of crab grass.

"Did you really think you could run away with her?" he asked, pocketing the coins. "On less than twenty dollars?"

"I don't know." I could feel my face scrunching up and I turned away from him. "I just wanted to be able to see her every day."

"Well, you got your wish," he said, walking out onto our lawn.

"Why would you care? Maybe you knew she was locked in that room the whole time and just kept it to yourself."

The toe of his shoe pushed the backs of my knees, and when my legs buckled, instead of trying to catch my balance, I went ahead and collapsed in the tall grass.

"I *didn't* know she was in that room," he said. "At first, I thought she went to the hospital. But it didn't add up because we never visited. Eventually, I just figured she left us."

"I don't understand why you never missed her."

He sat down beside me, pulling up handfuls of grass. "When we left the old house in the station wagon with a U-Haul attached to it," he said, "Mom kept threatening to open her door and jump out while we were on the highway. Dad couldn't calm her down."

There was his story again, the one he tried to tell over and over. I didn't interrupt him this time, just curled on to my side.

"We stopped at a motel, and she wouldn't get out of the car. She just stayed there right outside our room, staring out the window. I was afraid she was going crazy. But mostly I thought, *I'm not enough. I'm not important enough to make her come inside.*"

This was something we shared. This sense that whatever our mother felt that made her so sad was stronger than her love for us, was stronger than her desire to be there when we needed her.

"I kept waking up in the motel room and looking out the window at her," my brother said as I stretched out on my back, clouds rolling over me. "She was still awake, but she hadn't moved, so I finally went out to the car and waved my hand in front of her eyes. They were blank, like a doll's. I wish I didn't remember how she looked. I ran back to the motel room, but I'd forgotten the door would lock when it closed. I knew Dad would be really upset with me if I knocked on the door."

He didn't tell any more of the story than that, just pulled up more handfuls of grass until we noticed the total absence of noise. The lawn mowers, hoses, and radios had stopped all at once, leaving only the faint sound of bells.

"Um. There's a black girl on our lawn," Phil said, standing up.

I propped myself up on my elbows, and with the rest of the neighborhood, stared at Shirl, panting and holding her hands on her hips.

"You're missing play practice," she said. "*Again.* Mrs. Newkirk tried calling and no one answered, so she sent me to get you."

I had vague memories of my brother nudging me down the hill toward the school, placing lunch money in my fist, but how often this happened, I wasn't sure. I hadn't even thought about the play.

"I didn't hear the phone ring," I said, brushing grass off my legs as I got to my feet.

"I thought maybe you were swimming in your pool," she said. The bells jingled impatiently. "Come on, already. We have to go."

"I can't."

I could see an expression settling in her eyes and in her mouth that I had seen from her mother and grandmother. She turned her head sharply toward Phil, who'd been trying to see where the sound of the bells was coming from, and asked him, "Do you have a problem?"

Something inside of me tensed up. We seemed to be fighting, and I wasn't even sure who started it.

"Hey," she said, still talking to Phil. "Aren't you the one with the metal tooth?"

"My brother doesn't have a metal tooth," I said.

"I guess he has a look-alike, then." She stuck her hip out to one side.

"You should probably go," I said, taking off my sneaker and emptying a rock out of it. "I'm busy today. Sorry."

"I don't care," she said. "It wasn't my idea to come here, anyway."

She set off toward the school, not turning to wave good-bye, and I figured our friendship would go the same way it did with Hope. After a while, we'd be strangers.

I parked myself on the front steps, feeling the brief stab of her leaving. But after another moment, it didn't hurt anymore. I found I could do this—could put my emotions in little boxes and close them up tight. I imagined there were rows of boxes, like the shelves at a shoe store. It was how I could be friends with Shirl and still laugh along to jokes that used the word I was never allowed to say. Everything fit inside of me at one time, in different spaces.

Phil balanced on the bottom step with just his toes. "She's kind of bratty," he said.

"I guess."

Once Shirl had disappeared around the corner, the mowers and radios and hoses started again, but Phil continued to stare down the road with a smirk on his face. Then suddenly his shoulders hunched and he brought his hands over his nose. "It's all the lawn mowing," he said. And with a phony sneeze, a silver dollar fell from his hand.

I smiled but couldn't hold it for long. We could both hear Momma crying again.

"Hey, I tried," he said, picking up the coin and putting it in his pocket. "I'm going to take off. You want to come?"

"I'm going to stay," I told him, opening the screen door.

"Suit yourself." And in a little while I heard the wheels of the skateboard rumble down the road.

"Maybe I tried all the wrong things," Dad said from behind the door, "but I tried my hardest."

I opened the mail slot. The end was near. You could hear it in their drained voices. And I wondered which single word would bring the fighting and their marriage to its finish.

I pressed my face closer. "You told me things would be better if I could just keep everyone from disturbing you and let you rest, but that was a terrible solution," he said. "We needed you."

"I didn't know you wanted me back."

"Of course. We all did. But sometimes, Mara, you're barely here. I don't understand why being with us takes so much out of you."

Momma cried so hard she couldn't catch her breath. "I wanted to be like those mothers who loved baking cookies," she said, heaving. "Playing board games and sitting all day long at the playground. I'm so ashamed they got me as a mother. I stayed away because it was the best thing I could give them."

She broke down sobbing again, and Dad said, "I don't know what to do, Mara. I really don't."

I chewed on the inside of my cheek until I tasted blood. When I closed my eyes, the image I couldn't shake was the one of Momma slamming her hands over the locks. Something troubled me as I stood there, a question Hope had asked me long ago: "Who would lock your mom in the closet?" I knew the answer now. My father hadn't locked her in. Momma had chosen that room and could have unlocked and opened the door whenever she wanted. She wasn't held prisoner; she was hiding from us.

I had taken so many risks to be with her, and I'd let myself out of her room night after night and walked the black stairwell all alone. Now I understood why she had never walked up that same staircase to find me.

My face had been pressed to the mail slot—who knew for how long?—when I realized the fighting had stopped, and all that was left was an indention on my forehead and an eerie silence. I quietly opened the door and crept closer to the bedroom. With a sense of dread, I peeked inside and found my father holding her.

"I can't be the only one trying. That's not going to work anymore," he said. "You have to want to be here."

I didn't know if this meant he would try harder, but only if she did, or if he was betting that this was more than she could give. One thing was sure. He wasn't going to accept more of the same.

35

The Skipping Brick

LIFE WAS EASIER WHEN there were villains and heroes. My brain didn't feel so squeezed. I'd grown too close to my mother to hate her, and yet she wasn't the person I had defended. Not the prisoner who needed to be saved. To love her now—and I did—was to love someone who could hurt me, someone who could hear me searching for her and not tell me where she was hiding.

I had grown too distant from my father to thank him for trying so hard to keep Momma with us. Instead, all of this made me feel worn out. I walked around in a fog, feeling as if time had warped so that in one instant, a single minute might feel as long as a day, and in another instant, an entire day might disappear as fast as a minute.

I missed the final rehearsal for my play, simply forgot it, along with the costume I was meant to have ready. The painted yellow box was complete and stored at school, but I needed makeup, a yellow t-shirt, and yellow tights by seven that evening, when the cast was to meet at school. I told this to Dad around five, when I remembered. The muscles twitched in his jaw and he breathed in loudly through his nose, before he got his car key and drove to JC Penney.

Phil was out of the house, and that left me alone with Momma. Something hurt in my chest whenever I saw her now, a sensation of being crushed that might always be there.

"Why don't I do your hair and makeup for the play?" she offered in a quiet voice.

I didn't answer, but sat down on the couch while she pulled a crimping iron from one of the shopping bags in the closet and plugged it into an outlet. "It needs to heat up," she said. "I'll just put some rouge on your cheeks and maybe a little lipstick, okay?"

I shrugged.

"Is it okay?" she asked again.

"If you want to."

She rubbed her fingers on my cheeks, and all the while I looked straight ahead. I tried not to move or even blink.

While the iron heated up, she combed through the tangles in my hair. My shoulders jerked to my ears with her touch. How long, I wondered, would she have been down there in the secret room if I hadn't found her? How long would it have taken for her to miss me? She squeezed a handful of hair in the iron, and a shiver moved through me.

"Am I pulling?" she asked. "I hope I'm not pulling."

"Not much."

"I'm sorry," she said. "I'm so sorry."

She kept working through small sections of hair at a time, as I sat stiff and silent. There were things I could not tell her. I could not tell her how it hurt. How I had needed her. I could not tell her that during those days I didn't speak to her, as much as I didn't want to, I missed her. I could not tell her that, even then, while I was still so mad, I was glad for her touch.

"Mirror?"

I shook my head.

Dad had searched in three stores for yellow tights and came back, furious, with white ones. Phil, at Dad's insistence, lent me a yellow t-shirt, which Momma turned inside out to hide the picture of Mayor McCheese. She cut off the tag and said no one would notice. The shirt came down to my knees.

"Must have been a great audition for them to cast you as a yellow brick," Phil said. He pulled the crust off a slice of Wonder bread and dropped the crust in the trash.

"Are you coming?" I asked him. I knew the answer, but wondered which excuse he'd use.

"I'm not going to go to school when I don't have to," he said, rolling the rest of the bread into a ball and putting it in his mouth.

"Can you hurry?" Dad pressed.

"But Dad, I'm *ready*." And then I noticed he wasn't speaking to me.

"This is important," Momma said. "And I'm nervous. Don't rush me."

"You're *going*?" I asked her.

"If she can get ready in time," Dad said.

Momma's lips trembled, and she kept her head toward her lap. "I'd like to be there for Tillie."

She didn't look at all ready to leave the house again. The trip to the mall, the fighting, had left her looking worn out.

"Well, you can't go like this," he said, then made a frustrated grunt and took the comb out of his pocket. She lowered her head, crying.

"I think we should go," I said.

"Go on and get started, Tillie." Dad shooed me with his hands. "You better head down to the school without us."

In my costume, minus the box, I looked very much like someone who hadn't finished getting dressed. It was muggy outside, and the stage makeup Momma had applied made me even hotter. I scraped my tennis shoes along the edge of the sidewalk on the way to school. Halfway there, I wished I'd thrown on a pair of jeans, but I kept going, my mind churning.

When I reached the school, my parents still not in sight, I sat outside the entrance of the auditorium, feeling stunned and lost. *Was I the reason she went away?* I squeezed myself to the side of the steps as families filed into the building, only now willing to consider all I'd learned.

I was the girl who talked too much, bounced too much, the kind who tired people. Whenever my mother believed she had a moment to herself, I was there, needing and pestering her. Maybe she only meant to do it once, to prepare the warm, bitter drink on a day that seemed to go on and on. She could use the trick all mothers knew to help quiet me down and bring the day to an end.

I couldn't say there was anything cruel about that time. I looked forward to the drink as much as she did. I still liked bitter tastes: dark chocolate, swiss cheese, the bloodred wine Shirl snuck into Dixie cups that stained our teeth. I loved how falling asleep felt like spinning on a merry-go-round—my mother's voice becoming a part of my dreams.

But now it was impossible to look back at that time and feel the same way about it. Instead of remembering her watching over me, I thought of her waiting for me to settle down, hoping for the break she so desperately wanted. What I understood more than anything else was that Dad didn't take her from us. All along, Momma was the one who wanted to flee. She walked down the stairs on her own, then closed and locked the door herself. It was being our mother that made her so tired, that made her unable to reach her dreams.

⇢⥼⇠

"THERE YOU ARE, TILLIE. Come inside. We need to find our places."

I stood slowly, dazed because I hadn't remembered that I was at school. And something inside—a force stuffed down for too long—stood, as well. I followed Mrs. Newkirk to a crowd of other girls with no speaking roles. Shirl was in the very back, and I headed her way until I remembered we were fighting.

"You'll need to get into your costume," the teacher said, pointing to the yellow cardboard box against the wall.

I passed the group of stars. The lead looked ridiculous in her short haircut with fake braids attached. I knew Shirl thought the same thing because she stared at Dorothy with a wicked grin on her face. And before you knew it, both of us were bent over, belly laughing.

Mrs. Newkirk marched right over to Shirl, held her by the chin, and told her to quiet down. She said nothing to me, just frowned a little and pointed again to my costume.

I stepped into the yellow box and put my arms through the holes in the sides. Then Mrs. Newkirk gently herded me across the backstage wing, where I was to wait until it was time to skip down the aisle, leading Dorothy, Scarecrow, Tin Woodsman, and the Cowardly Lion, to see the Wizard.

Shirl waited with the other poppies in her green leotard and giant crêpe paper flower pinned to her head. She was the chubby one with the pointy starter breasts poking out. As she tried to straighten the flower, she caught my eye. I quickly turned away so she couldn't turn away from me first. Then, to demonstrate just how unconcerned I was with her being mad at me, I peeked into the auditorium filling with parents and siblings. This was what I did best these days. I had become a performer: the little academic, the soldier's soldier, the girl who never cried, the girl who could not even be hurt by losing her only friend.

Scanning the auditorium again, something stirred in me—nerves, maybe—as I searched for Momma. She had never come to my school before. What if they were still arguing and wouldn't get here on time? But there she was, stepping sideways between the chairs with my father, and wearing the outfit she'd worn to the mall—her skirt wrinkled and her hair greasy. She looked out of place beside my father, beside the other parents, and I wondered if this effort to be a part of our family again would last.

When she noticed my head sticking out of the curtain, she waved, and I slowly raised my hand only so high, not moving my wrist or fingers. Who knew what the first lie was—a nod of the head, a failure to speak up? A lie that led them to believe I was kinder, smarter, more obedient than I really was. But truth is stubborn. Our nature, our secret hearts can only hide for so long.

When the house lights dimmed and Mrs. Newkirk walked to the microphone, the feeling came over me again—not nerves, I was wrong before—but the feeling I had feared for so long. The one that was hard to push down and seemed stronger than my will. I would not stop it this time, even if I wanted to.

"Welcome, families and friends," she said. "Welcome to our production of *The Wizard of Oz*."

The door at the back of the auditorium was propped open by a metal chair, but the breeze didn't reach to the stage area. I felt hot in my costume, could hardly stand to hear the music start. It was such a dull play when you practiced for so many months.

"So sit back," Mrs. Newkirk finished, "and let our kids show you what they've got!"

The curtain opened to the dreary Kansas set. I knew all the lines that were coming, despite how desperately I tried not to pay attention during practice. And as the opening music began with the sixth grade orchestra playing, I knew it would be a very long time before we got to Oz, where I would finally stand on stage to skip in front of Dorothy whenever she sang about the yellow brick road.

It was building, something buried deep—restless and not wanting to stay down any longer. My legs couldn't wait, and I skipped toward the audience in my yellow box. One yellow brick, the surprise star of the show.

The box was difficult to manage, the corners banging into chairs and shoulders. And because my arms couldn't hang straight by my side, they, too, slapped into the audience as I raced down the aisle.

When I reached the back wall of the auditorium, when there was an obvious place to stop and let the play continue as planned, I took off again and made another run down the aisle.

The applause was wild. Even the poppies stuck their flowered heads out from the sides of the stage. The orchestra had stopped playing and there was such a commotion in the audience, believing I'd made a mistake. I had not made a mistake. I wanted to be ridiculous and disobedient, out of control.

There were plenty of boos, and Mrs. Newkirk was waiting for me at the end of my run for a certain scolding. But above all the other voices, I heard Shirl cheering. She had walked out in front of the Kansas set, where poppies did not grow, and raised her hands. I turned toward her and shot my arms out to the sides like I was flying. She cheered louder.

After the play, Phil, with the skateboard tucked under his arm, was the first to reach me. He'd come after all. "I was really embarrassed for you," he said.

"It was nerves," Dad said. "You'll do better next time."

My face was streaked in makeup from the tears I didn't understand. I couldn't stop smiling.

"I liked it just fine, Bear," Momma said, smoothing my hair. "And here we are, all dressed up. You'd think we were going on an outing."

The strangeness of this idea hung there before us until Dad said, "I suppose we could have a stroll around the neighborhood."

My parents seemed both pleased and nervous with this thought as they shuttled me through the crowd of whispering parents and students. Phil stayed far enough behind that he could pretend we weren't related.

When I passed Mr. Woodson, he bent close to my ear and said, "I was wrong. You haven't lost *that thing*." I giggled all the way out the door.

It had taken a year for us to walk through the neighborhood together. As we got farther from the school, the sky blackened and trees pulsed with cicadas. The houses were lit up inside like little viewing boxes, and Momma felt she knew something of the people who lived in them by what we observed: a rocking chair, rocking itself on a porch; a house with pastel balloons tied to the door handle and the muffled sounds of laughter and dogs barking inside. Perhaps people did this with our home, taking a peek as they walked to and from their cars, and believing our lives were successful or trouble-free compared to their own.

It was humid, but not uncomfortable as night cooled us just enough. I struggled to climb onto a low wall and balanced along it. My arms out the sides of the yellow box, I felt how unnatural it was for me to walk in a straight line and pay such close attention to every step.

Momma walked slowly, not used to the exercise or the impractical shoes. And Dad, who could not walk at her pace, raced ahead and then waited at each corner, urging her to catch up. At one of those corners, he called her Cootie, though the moment he said it, he tensed his shoulders, like he hadn't meant to offer so much hope.

I thought about how we might look from a distance. You could not tell that these adults were trying to decide if they should stay together, or that the boy would never be as close to anyone in his family as he was to the river. You could not tell that the girl in the cardboard box had just ruined her school play.

Whenever I thought of myself bursting through the aisle, and the crowd in an uproar, I buzzed with satisfaction, barely holding in the giggles. Sometimes what you fear, what you spend all your energy avoiding or pushing down, is not as terrifying as you thought.

I banged along in my box, my brother beside me, pushing

up the hill with one foot, the wheels going *shuk shuk shuk* against the road.

When we reached the hill where the crossing guard usually stood, Momma questioned whether she could continue. Her skin moist between the shoulder blades and her back bent forward with exhaustion, she turned for home. Dad, still out front with his quick but unathletic walk, reunited with her at each corner. His hands swung at his sides and I knew, if I only bothered to catch up, he'd take hold.

I hopped off the wall, arms out, flying again, the giggles building. This time I laughed out loud.

Phil picked up his skateboard and turned to me, asking, "What's wrong with you?"

And there was so much that was wrong. This was what had been bubbling up, a desire for them to see me when I wasn't pretending—to see me flawed and impulsive—and have that be good enough.

MAY 29, 1991, 7:03 PM

I SEE MY BABY, ONLY *a glimpse, coated in white grease, silent. I try to sit up as Dr. Young, in bloody gloves, cuts and ties the umbilical cord, his face tense, deep lines between his eyebrows.*

"Is something wrong?" I only have the strength to sit up well enough to see them hurry my baby out of the room. "Where are they taking? . . ." It occurs to me I might be alone in the room, and the shrillness of my voice frightens me so much that I stop speaking. It's so terribly quiet.

"It's all right." I hear the voice of the nurse who's been so rude to me, and her kind words and sudden smoothing of my hair troubles me. "They're just making sure everything's all right."

"Oh, God, is something wrong?"

"They've taken the baby in the other room, just making sure everything's okay, giving her a good evaluation."

"Her?"

She nods with a close-lipped smile.

"But I didn't hear her cry."

"It's very common for a preemie to need some help breathing," she says, moving back between my legs. "You'll just have to trust that they know what they're doing."

I grip the side of the bed as my stomach tightens again. "I think I'm having another contraction."

"That's right. Here it comes."

"A twin?"

"No, no. The placenta. Just give it one gentle push." It slips out with barely any effort. I want my feet out of these stirrups. I want to curl up and cry. I want them to hurry up and tell me if my baby's okay.

"Do you want to see the placenta?"

"Do I want to what?"

"Sorry," she says. "I'm supposed to ask."

My belly feels like a squashed soufflé, no little kicks and turns. She's gone and I don't know if they'll ever bring her to me. The nurse rinses off instruments, washes her hands, opens and closes cupboards. And my arms—all of me—has never felt so empty.

"Here, take a sip," she says, holding a plastic cup filled with apple juice below my chin.

I start sobbing.

"It's all right. It's all right," she says, rubbing my arm. "Is there someone here for you?"

I fold my arms over my breasts, hard like stones, and shake my head.

"Well, how about your mother? I'd be glad to give her a call."

"Not possible." I cry harder, inconsolable.

"I'm sorry to hear that," she says. As she quietly washes things and puts them away, I turn my head to the wall, feeling that familiar knot in my chest.

In the end we couldn't save my mother. Our family walk and what looked like the beginning of something new, was actually quite close to the end.

Our shopping trip, her attending my school play, they were a sort of last gasp, something too hard to sustain.

It was my brother who found her as I was still trudging up our street after school. I heard him yell in a thin voice that still haunts me: "Goddamn you!" I remember my book bag going light as the feeling in my hands disappeared, then my shoulders—a sense of being erased. For some time, I stayed right where I was, my feet planted in the center of the lawn where the sash to Momma's pink and tattered bathrobe lay.

My book bag fell from my fingers. The ground swayed beneath my feet. And when I began to walk—my legs wobbly, like they'd never tried walking before—I felt completely disconnected from the sneakers that followed the stone steps down the side of the house. White noise pumped through my ears—shh shh shh—a radio turned between stations, my brother's voice far away, as if from another world, one I would wait to enter. I concentrated, instead, on the ivy vines grabbing for my sneakers, holding my face toward the ground, not daring to look up. Some part of me knew what I would find when I got to the backyard.

My brother's desperate cries sounded as if they came through a cardboard tube. "Oh God, oh God, oh God." We had never said the word "God" in our home until that day. There were no other words for seeing our mother facedown at the bottom of the swimming pool, her hair like seaweed, rising and swaying.

Phil jumped into the plant-stained water filled with branches and ivy vines, and Momma's body shifted left and right with the waves, as if she might swim.

"Call Dad at work!" he yelled, but it was like a squeak, and after he yelled, he started panting and gagging, trying to make himself touch the body that was our mother and not our mother. She was weighed down by her bathrobe, arms out to the side; her orange hair seemed alive, reaching toward Phil.

"Oh, God," Phil cried, drool coming from both sides of his mouth. And suddenly the sound came back strong like someone had turned up the volume of the world, my brother's voice too loud, too high, "Oh, God. Oh, God."

I took panicked steps toward the pool, where Phil had grabbed the neck of the bathrobe, shrieking when Momma's hair tangled around his wrist. He pulled hard, but her pockets were weighted, stuffed full with Dad's medals, and fighting to keep her under the water.

After what seemed like impossible effort, the top of our mother broke through the surface, her bathrobe sliding off one shoulder and exposing her thin, floating breast.

Phil, with wide, terrified eyes, told me, "Don't look."

The last protective act my brother took over me was telling me this, not to come closer, not to see what he had seen. But I never listen.

I climbed down the metal ladder. I, too, got in the water, warm like a puddle, and waded out through the sticks and leaves.

"Oh, my God. Call an ambulance," he said, his voice high-pitched and cracking. "Call them right now!"

But I continued toward her, my feet scraping against the peeling blue paint and the crack along the bottom. Some part of me believed, as I had all year, that my mother could be saved. The loose skin of her fingers rippled in the wave I was creating. And I had not expected, when I reached out to touch her arm, that it would be stiff like one of the branches, or that touching that stiff arm would rock her entire body the way a boat rocks when you touch one side of it.

It was the sight of her face that told me she was never coming back— froth coming from her nose and her blue lips, her eyes glassy and wide open.

I stayed in the water, not sure when Phil left to call the ambulance. The sirens, the sounds of walkie-talkies all sounded so faraway. I was hardly aware of the police in our backyard until someone put her arms around me under the water, saying, "I've got you."

I wonder what her name is, this woman who wrapped me in a blanket, this woman who cupped the back of my head and rocked me against her breast so I wouldn't see them pull Momma from the water. "There, there," she said, smoothing my hair and ever so gently covering my ears to quiet the sound as they zipped the body bag.

I wonder if Momma had considered what it might do to us to find her like that. What it might do to leave a twelve-year-old boy in charge of calling for help and answering the police officers' questions.

My brother. The soldier betrayed by his commander. The soldier who, in the middle of the war, stopped believing in its cause. He's a geologist now, which makes sense to me. Rocks can't stop loving you, and they can't die. Once a year, he sends a carton of them with no return address to Dad's house. Each rock is marked with its scientific name and where it was found, so we know where Phil's been but not where to find him. I haven't looked for him, and don't expect I will. We survived that year by believing different stories, by deciding on our heroes and villains. He blamed Momma, and I can't. She was never strong enough for my anger.

There was no question her death was a suicide. She'd left a note my father gave to the authorities—her fear that she was a burden, that she was destroying us.

I've often wondered where she went after she died. I imagine someplace in-between, where people with heavy pockets drag close to the earth, close enough to see the mess they've handed to others, but unable to help fix it.

I've felt my mother in the room with me. She comes close like warm breath, and makes the hair stand up on the back of my neck. I've only told this to Simon, who doesn't doubt me, how I've heard the faint sound of her weeping, as if she's there, surveying the damage.

. . .

"You're starting to wake up, I see." The nurse checks my blood pressure, and I'm shocked to find I could have fallen asleep, and that I've been moved into a new room—this one like a pastel bedroom with a dresser, rocking chair, telephone, and a vase full of daisies.

"The flowers are from your husband," she says. "He's going to try calling again in an hour or so."

I reach for my stomach, used to the reassurance of my baby's size and her kicks, but find it's flat, still.

"I have good news for you," the nurse says. "Your baby's getting a little oxygen and nourishment. A real thorough check." She hands me a clear plastic cup filled with juice. "You'll be able to hold her soon."

I turn to the wall and cry until I'm trembling all over. I feel so un-prepared for all of this, for being here with strangers who irritate me, for failing to keep my baby safe, for already messing up as a mother.

"Is that your father in the waiting room?"

I nod.

"You look alike," she says. "You know, he's been out there for hours and seems pretty anxious to visit with you. Should I invite him in?"

I don't answer or turn around. But in a little while, I know he's here because he's someone who always has to clear his throat, even if he's only thinking of talking.

Still facing the wall, I hope he'll think I'm asleep. When the room becomes so quiet I wonder if he's left, I slowly turn my body—sore like I've been beaten—and there he is, standing just out of reach from my bed and holding a bouquet of flowers.

It's true—despite growing my hair long like Momma's and having none of Dad's orderliness—we share the same boyish faces and full cheeks, though his now sag like a bloodhound's, and I suppose mine will, too.

He approaches the bed cautiously, stands there in his button-up with two pens in his shirt pocket—one black, one red—his shoulders rounded from decades of bending over papers at a desk. He clears his throat again and hands me the bouquet, a ridiculous assortment of too many colors, still wrapped in plastic. "How are you feeling?"

"I don't know." The bouquet lays stiff across my arms.

"I'm concerned about you," he says, pulling a chair beside the bed.

"What kind of concerned?" The flowers drip a continuous stream of water into my lap.

"Well, to be honest" he says, pausing, then taking the flowers back, and cupping his hand under the point where the stems join, "I'm concerned about your emotional state."

I don't like his face without the mustache—the too-small upper lip, the expressions I'd rather not see. I sit up taller, the anger building fast. "Oh, that! How silly of me to be upset about going into labor a month and a half early and having no one here for me!" And seeing the disapproval he can never hide, and the way he keeps staring at my hair, I reach up to find it's completely knotted around the rubber band.

"Tillie," he says, lowering his voice as if I might copy his example. "You can't let yourself get so overwhelmed that you aren't able to take care of this baby."

"That's what you're sitting there thinking? Seriously?" I try to unwind the rubber band from my hair until it becomes clear it will take hours of work, if not a haircut, to remove it. I growl out loud.

"Don't get worked up, now."

"Excuse me for getting worked up! I'm stuck here in this bed. They've told me almost nothing about what's going on. My dad, who I should have never called, is lecturing me like I'm still a child. You tell me how I'm supposed to act right now. I mean, what exactly are you expecting me to do?"

He presses his bald lips together as if counting to ten. "Well," he finally says, "you haven't asked to see the baby. You haven't asked to hold her."

Squeezing my fists so tight that the nails cut into my palms, I begin to understand what it must have been like for my mother to have him constantly judging her. No wonder she preferred to stay locked in a room by herself.

"Dad," I say, wanting to stand up, "I thought I had another month or two to prepare. I didn't think I'd be doing this alone."

Silence.

A strange squeak escapes from the back of my throat where the fear is hiding. "Why can't you understand? I just don't feel ready. Is that so crazy?"

I want from him things he can't give. I want him to be a man who understands and says something to comfort me. I want him to be as powerful a father as he is a scientist. Instead, he crinkles the plastic wrap on the bouquet of flowers.

"What went wrong with her, Dad?"

He shakes his head.

"Please," I say. "It's my story, too."

"I'm not sure what you want to know."

"Tell me what she did that night before Anne took me away."

He sets the bouquet on the floor beside his chair, then, slowly, he says, "She went to tuck you in to bed, though it was still quite early. The whole evening was upsetting to her and she wasn't in a good state of mind." He stops again as if that's enough.

"What did she do?"

He takes a deep breath. "She was in your room for some time when she became hysterical."

"What do you mean?"

"She started wailing and calling for me to save you. I ran to your room, and when I got there, she was shaking you. I didn't understand why she wanted to wake you up, but when I put my face near yours, you were colder than I expected."

I remember this—the feel of his mustache against my forehead before he covered my shoulders with the blanket.

"Your mother began to rock back and forth, and wouldn't answer me when I asked what had happened. But she mumbled over and over that she was sorry."

I remember this, too. Her face was hot and wet against mine, whispering, "I'm sorry, Bear."

"At first I thought this was your mother's problem—what we'd been dealing with for some months—and I was just trying to quiet her down. But what she said worried me. And when I noticed a cup beside your bed, I decided to taste what was in it."

The bitter drink.

"That's when I knew our problems were bigger than I'd thought."

I find the story strangely comforting because I've heard something I needed to know. That we are different. That my mother could do things I could never do.

"Did I go to the hospital?"

He shakes his head, and here is where he made the calculation I'd always suspected. The kinds of problems our family had were the kinds he couldn't get help for, not without risking everything.

"I checked your pulse and your breathing," he says, massaging his upper lip as if there's still a mustache there. "You were a fighter, like we could have guessed. And we stayed beside you all night, touching your skin and feeling for breath under your nose."

"But you didn't get help."

He looks right at me. "That was a decision we were unsure of all night. We were unsure of many of the decisions we made that year."

· · ·

Someone knocks gently on the door before coming inside. "I've got some-one here who wants to meet you." It's the nurse who cut me free from the bathroom door. She walks into the room, carrying a small bundle in her arms. "Are you ready?"

"I'm not sure."

"I think you'll change your mind when you see this face."

It's a shock to see how small she is, her face thin with blue veins running across her forehead. She looks too fragile to hold, but without thinking I've extended my arms. And now that I am thinking, I'm not exactly sure if my arms should be turned this way, as if I'm accepting a bag of groceries.

"I've never held a baby before."

"Really? Never held a friend's baby? Never did any babysitting?"

I shake my head, but that doesn't stop the nurse, who lays my tightly bundled daughter in my arms.

At first, I hold her like I did the flowers: She's just stretched across my stiff arms. Then I cradle her closer, and the nurse, who has not yet let go of the baby, moves my hand under her head before she steps away.

"See?" she says. "You've got it."

She's unbelievably light, and, right now, I can't imagine being re-sponsible for anything so small. Dad leans forward on his knees as if he doesn't believe I can do it, either.

"Baby Girl Harris-Williams. Four pounds, six ounces. Perfectly healthy. She just needed a little oxygen and an ounce of formula to get the hang of swallowing and breathing."

I can't relax with my dad watching my every move.

"It's okay to unwrap this blanket and have a peek at her hands," the nurse says, exposing delicate arms and tiny, perfect fingers. "Have you thought of a name for her?"

"I'm not sure yet," I say. "Maybe Mara."

It's spite that makes me say this, a chance to remind Dad that my mother is more to me than just her mistakes. Sometimes I think of her twirling, singing, telling her story of the woman in the golden gown, and I wonder who she might have become if we'd gotten her help.

The nurse squeezes my arm and whispers, "I'm going now. I just wanted to say congratulations on your beautiful baby."

She's still leaning over me when the phone rings. I shake my head as she answers it, letting her know I don't want to talk.

"She's not taking phone calls just yet," she says. "M-hmm. M-hmm. Yes, I see. Hold on a minute."

Covering the bottom of the receiver, she asks, "Would it be all right if your husband speaks with your father?"

Surprised, I slowly nod.

I've often wondered if they'd get along. I worked hard not to marry a man like my father. I avoided men in the sciences and found Simon in the music section of a bookstore. Dad seems to be enjoying their conversation, asking about the museums in Paris, and stunning me by mentioning the painter Paul Cézanne. Maybe they would have always gotten along like this, but I've kept them separate. My life has been easier that way: past in the past.

The baby wriggles in my arms, roots around, suckling my shoulder. When I stroke the side of her face, she turns, trying to suckle my hand.

I put my lips to the top of her fuzzy head and whisper, "I don't know what I'm doing." My lips stay there against her skin, which smells of sweet rice.

"I think she's thinking of the name Mara," I hear my dad say before the long pause. He holds the phone out to me. "He wants to talk to you."

I've never tried holding a baby and a telephone at the same time. I don't want the cord to touch her face, so I switch ears, and fumble the phone until Dad has to position it above my shoulder.

"Hello, Momma," Simon says.

The tears come easily. "I wish you could see her right now."

"Tell me what she looks like."

"She looks like a little old man," I say, cracking a smile. "Little droopy cheeks. Wrinkly forehead. A big tuft of sweaty black hair that sticks straight up like a troll doll. She's amazing."

"Tell me about her hands and her toes."

I'm annoyed that Dad is still right here, listening to us, but I tell Simon, "She has her hand on the side of her face right now. The tiniest fingers you've ever seen. And her other hand is squeezed into a fist the size of a Super Ball. I haven't seen her feet yet. She's all wrapped up tight."

"And she's healthy?"

"She's small." I try to swallow the lump in my throat. "She had some trouble breathing and needed oxygen."

"But she's okay now?"

"I think so. I've been afraid to ask." My father doesn't seem the slightest bit bothered by his eavesdropping. I turn my shoulders a little toward the wall and ask, "When will you be back?"

"I just booked a flight," he said. "I'll be there soon, and then we'll find out when we can take her home."

"But nothing's ready. The house is in boxes. We don't even have a crib."

"Can you imagine having her sleep that far away from us, anyway?"

I can't. I can't even stand to have this phone between us when I could take my other arm and curl it around her. I'm captivated with her eyelids, her little lopsided mouth, the way her nostrils flare with each breath.

"Are you ready to talk about names?" he asks, but my father is driving me crazy the way he just stands there, hovering over the bed, as if he's waiting his turn.

"You know what—can you call me back?" I ask. "I'd rather talk when it's a little more private."

My father helps me hang up the phone, moves it close by so I can reach it on my own. "I'm going to have to go home for a while," he says. "I have a cat to feed, and I need to take a shower and get some work done."

"It's okay," I say, because the word "thanks" won't come out.

He kisses me on the cheek, something he's never done, and says, "Isaac Newton was born early, too," the word "too" coming out of his mouth like a choke.

I can't speak.

"I'll call you," he says, and walks to the door.

When he turns back for one last look, without even thinking, I salute him.

A part of me will always be eight years old, living that last year we had Momma with us. And my story of that year always ends with our walk because that's when there was hope. That's when we could still choose any ending.

The power of suicide, the thing that makes it particularly poisonous, is that it lets one person have the last say without giving others a chance to respond. My mother left us with her fear that she'd pass down the parts about herself she hated. And I know, in many ways, I look like the very mess she worried she'd create with my knotted hair, quick temper, and easy tears. Some nights I'm startled awake with the ways we are similar—how, on certain days, I, too, could sit and stare at nothing, could fill my pockets with something heavy and sink underwater. But what I desperately want to tell my mother, if she'd given me a chance to respond, is this: It wasn't perfect, but I never needed perfect.

The baby cries and I pull her close. Then, because no one else is in the room, I open my gown and hold her against my breast. It's a clumsy movement—not at all like women who nurse easily and discreetly in parks and museums—as I flash the room and forget to support her head. Sensing the nipple against her cheek, she quickly turns her head, mouth open wide, and takes it, just the tip at first. The pain is so sharp, my eyes water. We try again, this little one mad now—mad the milk is trapped on the other side of her tightly clamped lips, and mad I'm tugging that nipple away. This time when she opens wide, I shove a mouthful of breast in, wince in pain, but soon forget the hurt. I'm too caught up in her little face, one side mashed against me, and eyes that are gray-green—not like anyone else's I know.

Wherever my mother is, I hope I can offer her this mercy, that she might know she didn't destroy me. That she might see me here, falling in love.

My husband calls again and I tell him about the baby's toes and the teeny little diaper and crusty piece of umbilical cord still attached to her navel. Simon relishes every detail, and then tells me he's just gone from store to store in search of a book of baby names written in English, which he's now holding in his hands and will stay on the phone with me until we've found her a name.

"Look up my mother's name," I say, brushing the baby's hair back from her forehead. "Tell me what it means."

I hear the pages flip, and Simon quietly saying M names: "Marion. May. Maggie." He pauses. "Mara. Bitter sorrow."

"Bitter sorrow? Are you serious?"

"I'm afraid so."

"But that's awful. We can't name her that."

"Then we'll start at the beginning," he says.

He reads out names, beginning with A, pausing to know our baby's cry and to hear the funny squeak she makes whenever she swallows. He reads until his voice is hoarse, and when he gets to the end of the R's, her name, the one that so clearly belongs to her, is right there: Ruby. Small and lovely. Shining after so much has broken.

I feel the hair stand up on the back of my neck. I close my eyes, holding Ruby close, tears spilling into the corners of my mouth, and I see my mother, in sleeves like angel wings——twirling. Lifting.

ACKNOWLEDGMENTS

Absolute gratitude to my agent, Dan Conaway, for his wicked genius and, more important, for his friendship, which was what allowed me to finish this book; to my editor, Brittany Hamblin, for giving me such creative freedom and for the suggestion that made the story pop; to Stephen Barr for being a consistently positive force; to Carrie Kania for being my kind of badass; to Emin Mancheril for the perfect cover; and to the smart and supportive team from HarperCollins——Paula Cooper, Jennifer Hart, Alberto Rojas, Vanessa Schneider, Brenda Segel, Stephanie Selah, Juliette Shapland, Carolyn Bodkin, and Amy Vreeland——for making things happen.

My deepest thanks to those who read and edited early drafts, encouraged and pushed me, made me a better writer, made me a better friend, kept me in this game, opened doors, hugged all of my important packages before mailing them, shared Thai food during an ice storm, helped me finish off bottles of scotch, drew pictures that cheered me, lent my character bells for her shoes, came up with the beautiful title, restored my spirits over a glorious weekend in

Canada, gave me much needed pep talks, and believed in me when I didn't believe in myself: Zett Aguado, Bob Arter, Terry Bain, Lauren Baratz-Logsted, Bruce Bauman, Laura Benedict, Ritchie Blackmore, Melvin Brooks, Terri Brown-Davidson, Kim Chinquee, Tish Cohen, Elizabeth Crane, Keith Cronin, Jim Daniels, Juliet DeWal, Karen Dionne, Frank DiPalermo, Kevin Dolgin, Xujun Eberlein, Richard Edghill, Pia Ehrhardt, Janet Fitch, Patry Francis, Neil Gaiman, Sands Hall, Tom Jackson, Tommy Kane, Jessica Keener, Roy Kesey, Josh Kilmer-Purcell, Dylan Landis, John Leary, Brad Listi, Kathy and Kenny Machin, Brian McEntee, Ellen Meister, Darlin' Neal, Lance Reynald, Jordan Rosenfeld, Gail Siegel, Robin Slick, James Spring, Tracy Tekverk, Jim Tomlinson, Amy Wallen, John Warner, Kimberly Wetherell, and Tom Williams.

Thank you to some very important communities in my life: the candid Zoetrope Virtual Workshop, where I learned to edit fearlessly; the nourishing community of writers at Squaw Valley, where I realized I could dream bigger; Nile Rodgers's inspiring We Are Family Foundation, where I volunteer; and my beloved LitPark, where I'm constantly renewed.

Finally, thank you to my mom, who read the first terrible poem I ever wrote and told me I had talent; and to my brilliant, artistic, funny, big-hearted boys, for being so understanding of this long process. Now we celebrate!